The Circle Triangle

a tale of nested deception

Ryan Gross

To Lon
Ducati's Rule!

RG

ISBN-13: 978-1515327714
ISBN-10: 151532771X

DEDICATION

To my wonderful children who saw an everyday dad demonstrate that if
you want to do something, never listen to anyone who says you can't.

Table of Contents

Edited By
Jeff Szymanski

Acknowledgements

To the countless number of friends and family that helped contribute to this book. Without your input, positive and negative, along with the help of editing, it would not have been possible.
Beth R, Mark V, Trish A and Luc Collins

I would like to give a special thanks to all of the persons who thought that this was beyond me. It was your special motivations that kept me going and ultimately finish.

The Circle Triangle *'Ascension into The Void series, Book 2' (Rev. ed.)*

Prologue

The year is 2065. The Earth remains intact but has changed. Rising sea levels have led to water born disease, reducing the population focus to major cities. The outlying areas between cities has shifted into shambles and created a lawless atmosphere.

3-D printing has replaced most manufacturing processes as well as food and medical service needs. Modern cities have adopted a class society consisting of three main classes; Citizens, military, and the rest.

Central City, a beacon of modernization stands as a pinnacle worldwide. Its location is in North America, built upon the remnants of New York City. Skyscrapers no longer fill the skyline; instead they have been transformed into massive space ports.

Space travel has now become common place via large Star Cruisers and ferry shuttles. They transfer people and the like to the space station 'Orion' for work or for further off world travel. The Orion is located in a stable stationary orbit at Lagrange point L1, balanced by the Moon – Earth – Sun, three body mathematical equation. Active Helium-3 mining on the lunar surface provides energy needed for the space station's orbital adjustments as well as for refueling Star Cruisers.

The designated travel off world map is divided into four elliptical three dimensional sectors. Each sector is governed by the military and travel restrictions apply.

A newly discovered metallic shale ore found on Mars and X-Group asteroids, located in the belt between Jupiter and Mars has created a technological boom where artificial life form development in the form of robots of humanoid appearance, known as assistance machines, has now excelled to a point where machines surpass most humans.

Chapter 1 - The Big Day

It was a gloomy winter morning outside; the grey skies were darker more than usual since the outlying areas were allowed to burn materials as the city no longer supplied free power. In an area on the outskirts of Central City in between the outlands and the salvage yard, known to most as the 'Ville', life went on. The Ville was reserved for miners, tradesmen, and factory workers. Over the years it slowly grew into a mini supply station that attracted a rather unsavory crowd that traveled between lands. It offered a place of refuge for people that could not enter Central City. The Ville's living conditions were rough with older roadways, poor garbage collection, and visible pollution. Besides the tents and makeshift housing units that ran for miles, an apartment complex could be found overhanging the only train station for transport to Central City.

The apartment complex didn't have a name, rather a number – 1829@40.7127-74.0059, and it only offered one style of dwelling known to the locals as the 1829 cube. It measured 1.829 meters (6 feet) in all directions, and was constructed from a carbon fiber molecular steel blend which resembled a fibrous burnt metal. The exterior of the complex lacked any markings except the unique buildup of atmospheric pollution burned in by the unforgiving sun. Amenities included a water closet, built in foldable molecular steel blend bed, a window measuring 7000mm² (10.85in²), and one entry door, rollup type construction, activated by a DNA identification proximity chip in combination with an entry code. Advertisement signs displayed the non-metric measurement of 6.0006 ft. to confuse prospective renters of its actual size. In one of the units lived a man of 25 years occupying unit 9c.

As he lay in bed with thoughts wandering, a strange feeling overtook Tobias. A feeling of certainty that this day would define the rest. After all, he did just solve the most perplexing query relating to artificial intelligence in the past decade. His neighbors described Tobias as the quiet loner type in disheveled state, baggy clothing hanging off him, usually walking with a hood on. His small stature and pale complexion made Tobias stand out more than his technique of trying to hide in plain sight. Tobias had lived at the 1829 address for three years now. It was better than the family housing tent dwelling he occupied after his parents moved off world for the mining City 'Steengroef' on Mars. Tobias's current employment left him just enough wage credits to afford the monthly rent, food, and minor supplies.

A smug smile greeted Tobias as he walked to the water closet eyeing his reflection as the neon light flickered rapidly on and off from the automatic detection state. As Tobias sang an old tune, "Big Time" by Peter Gabriel. The song echoed in the tiny space as Tobias fumbled for the communication device attached to his lab coat. Tobias's device display highlighted the calendar. It read, 'Broadcast 11:00 am'. The subject was indicating, 'Today is the rest of your life, savor it'. The words propelled his thoughts back to his warm bed and of visions from the recent past. Not caring that he was already running late, Tobias drifted back in his mind to a time before his parents left, all he really ever knew.

Tobias never was an outstanding student. In fact, he barely managed to pass, let alone shine above anyone of consequence. Tobias was content in this as he found school boring and he felt it lacked the luster of even his mildest day dreams. No worthwhile challenges were presented, along with the missing love from a disengaged father, granted Tobias an excuse in his mind to only excel to the bare minimum in scholastic achievement. This wayward lazy course led Tobias into a more accepting crowd of society where aiming high was not required, and notoriety was usually unobtainable. Tobias had difficulty making friends with his poor academics, lack of athletic ability, and a less than handsome allure. Tobias did however have a virtual friend within his small tablet computer whom he knew as Zippy. Tobias had owned the tablet for quite some time and he was rather fond of it. In this friendship with Zippy, Tobias would enjoy hearing stories of off world life that they would alter together to pass the time.

Although family life was difficult, Tobias graduated high school and, after that, four uneventful years quickly passed by. The time had not been kind, more down than up as Tobias recalled. Tobias's family was from a long line of miners that would travel off world or to asteroid areas performing hazardous precious metal collection. It was very dangerous work that involved explosives, engineering skills, and gravitational calculations. The family was contracted as a working unit on planet Earth. The job was to 'search and gather' depleted uranium shells from the outlying areas of the old war mining zone.

This is how Tobias's family eventually wound up in the Ville. Every family member had responsibilities, and life was centered on mining rather than athletics or academics. Tobias knew nothing else being so young before the planet Earth contract started, but one thing the family always did was sing old songs together. This was the backup plan in case a contract was unobtainable for a few weeks. The family would perform in a food house or tavern to make ends meet until the contract was ready. The planet Earth contract was almost complete and the family would have to find a new contract. Unfortunately, the only work available was in Sector Two. The contract job was mining on Mars for deep shale ore. The shale ore was used for making assistance machine parts, and therefore, highly in need. Assistance machine production levels had increased since the war in the outer sectors began and mining contracts were steadily on the rise. The four sectors of the reachable universe without extreme time dilation are defined as:

¥ *Sector One's beginning point being the Sun and reaching to the Earth.*

¥ *Sector Two continues beyond the space station Orion, past Mars to the asteroid belt midline before the planet Jupiter.*

¥ Sector Three, less traveled, resuming at the asteroid midline and ending at the midpoint of Saturn.

¥ Sector Four, rarely traveled, is defined as beginning at the midpoint of Saturn, extending beyond the known system planets, astronomical bodies, and into undiscovered areas.

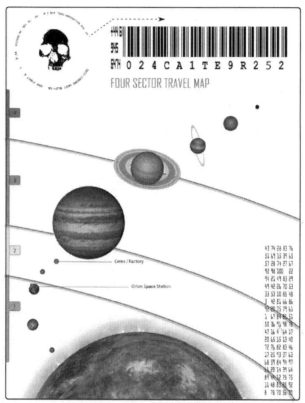

Figure 1 The Four Sectors

The exception was the shale ore refining factory on dwarf planet Ceres. The factory was considered to be in both Sectors Two and Three due to its orbit and placement within the asteroid belt.

The outer sector war was a constant in the lives of all. It was the reason for the economy fluctuations, currency valuation, as well as technological advances. Besides being a driving force in all of these areas, the war played an important role in population control. The war machine luring youth with the illusion of Citizenship for service. The myth of a term of service translating into full citizenship was widely known. Despite the reality of high death rates and low wounded, the military had little trouble with recruitment. The war communications were always centered on mining activities or disputes. The end result being violence based on living conditions and/or the treatment of miners.

Mining uprisings offered little in the way of forgiveness, and most incidents resulted in death on both sides. Planet Mars was usually a hotbed for such activity. Shale ore was plentiful on the surface of Mars at first, but ongoing mining had continued underground in tremor areas where massive deposits could be extracted. The conditions in which mining operations drilled deep below the surface were hazardous, and cave-ins were common place.

The war raging in the outer sector was assumed to be similar in nature to mining uprisings, but accounts were starting to contradict the broadcasts. Rumors of alien interactions ran rampant within the mining community, but they were dismissed as outer sector sickness. A sickness described by some to be related to deep space travel along with an over ingestion of shale ore dust. The results of the sickness could be seen as madness or rambling incoherently by the individual infected. The sickness usually ended with accidental or intentional death by the inflicted.

Tobias's idea of mining on planet Mars with the family was a reality he hoped never to experience. This decision left little alternative choices leading him into working as a tradesman in the robotics maintenance salvage area, referred to as the 'Yard'. It was located in the east section of the Ville. At first, Tobias didn't mind much as he seemed to have a knack with the machines, and somehow they called out to him during the repairs.

The work was rough and physically intense; Tobias lacked the physical stature needed to work on the new generation machines that were much greater in size. Tobias was only 5'-7" (170cm) on a good day, and his thin frame was a result of a limited budget and a low interest in athletic activities. It wasn't long before Tobias moved into the refurbishing section of the Yard responsible for repairing the assistance machines central processing units (CPU). The Yard supervisor, known as the 'Super', was unimpressed with Tobias's line work abilities, and it seemed to be the last stop on the way to 'Wash out Lane'. Tobias's only saving grace from unemployment was that skilled labor, at that rate, was hard to come by in recent years. Something the Super knew all too well when Central City recruited all the good linemen and technicians for the recent area improvement projects.

Tobias's thoughts of those days' past were interrupted by the high pressure pulse brakes that sounded and shook the water closet mirror as the train made its on-time stop outside the apartment building window. The train was always on time, so much so, that factory workers would place wagers on the nanosecond of arrival. The only variation on the odds was rain or wind speed. 'Ding, Ding, Ding,' the bell sounding aloud as passengers could be heard scrambling in and out, as the train was voicing, "Departing in 10, 9, 8…" Tobias laughed out loud and mumbled, "I wonder what ever happened to the Super, does he still run the Yard? Ha, I bet he does. Well I hope he's watching the broadcast today." The thought inspiring another devilish grin as Tobias returned to getting ready and began shaving. Tobias's thoughts reminiscing back again to the day almost six months ago when he met Mr. Stamper at the Yard as the shaver hummed near his ear.

The Yard always had that smell of burnt hydraulic fluid and worn out gears. Old 462 engine casing rams from Ferry shuttles, late generation molding machine pieces, ring gears melted together, FerD rocket fuel rods, and Helium-3 line fuel pod parts littered the Yard along with various tiny fasteners. The different kinds of hydraulic fluids and gear oil swirled together creating a toxic rainbow of sorts in the cracks and dips along the pathways. Water droplets would seem to float in midair when it did rain and it was an eerie sight to behold. The Yard was split into two sections that had various model refurbishing and repair stations within each of them. Linemen worked on the second tier and would look ahead while loading parts for machines on the line for repair.

Cleanup was sparse to say the least. The main concentration from the Super focused on repairing units for output, not on safety or environmental concerns. The main roadway into the Yard was covered daily with new fluid and parts from drop-offs. Large trucks would unload and load various machines, but lately the machines were from Central City, making them the number one priority.

After a long walk from his apartment complex, Tobias would pause and tie rags around his shoes upon entering the Yard. The special boots that were resistant to the fluids corrosive properties and sharp tiny fasteners found in the Yard were outside of his budget. Of course this prompted additional jokes from the linemen who already teased Tobias relentlessly. T-Rags became his handle, along with the ongoing one of 'no brains' repairing the robots. Tobias pretended not to care, but secretly inside he yearned to show them up. It was 'just another day as usual' Tobias thought, shuffling along the walkway, head down as the linemen snickered from above. Tobias sang a favorite tune, "The Logical Song" by SuperTramp, as he walked on.

Tobias's song was cut short upon reaching the CPU refurbishing area where he worked. Tobias noticed the Super talking with someone at his repair station. As Tobias approached them, the conversation stopped and the Super stormed off eyeing Tobias as he left in haste heading for the main office.

The person in Tobias's section of the CPU refurbishing station was a large man who looked of a lineman position in later days, where presently his older age would have pushed him out. The stranger stood at least 6'-4" (1.93m) and his stocky frame was well over 300lbs (137kg), resembling an extinct grizzly bear of the North American history. The stranger's hair was trimmed short, but he wore a long square shaped curly beard with grey streaks that was not commonplace. His attire was an engineer's uniform, complete with the factory boots, enhanced robotic gloves, and neck health collar, along with the Central City logo, the only brand in the robotics industry. Under the logo his name was illegally hand sewn into the left chest area in cornflower blue, it read 'Nate Stamper'. Tobias was in disbelief, here was Nate Stamper in his work area and a conversation was about to take place.

Tobias thought quickly about what he could remember of Mr. Stamper's history. Nate Stamper was one of the original linemen responsible for breakthrough hydraulics advancements in the field of robotics and helped evolve assistance machines into what they are today. Before he could recall more, Mr. Stamper looked him in the eye and the conversation started, his voice low and strong, "T-Rags, huh…what's your real name, son?"

"Tobias, sir…uhh…that's my name, sir." His reply nervous, Tobias felt that he was already messing up. Mr. Stamper's gaze intensified and, as he leaned down, replied, "Tobias, I want you to show me how you are repairing the CPUs."

"Of course, sir." Tobias responded and grabbed a CPU from the refurbish stack, hooking it up to the bench as he had done over a thousand times before. Mr. Stamper began watching intently as Tobias continued his routine steps in diagnosis. Then it happened, the machine spoke to Tobias as they always did. Tobias knew what the concern was without further diagnosis. Using his long fingers, Tobias reached into the unit and manipulated the circuit board as his other hand worked the soldering machine from the other side. Mr. Stamper was in awe as he noticed Tobias had his eyes closed during the repair, but said nothing, choosing to wait and see the final results. Tobias finished the repair, and reran the diagnostics along with reloading the diagnostics software on the unit in record time.

"Done, sir. Did I do the repair correctly?" Tobias inquired of Mr. Stamper. A few moments went by as Mr. Stamper inspected the unit. Tobias wasn't sure what was going on until Mr. Stamper spoke.

"Tobias, how did you know what the concern was? And why did you choose to close your eyes during the repair?"

Tobias wasn't sure why Mr. Stamper was asking such questions, but obliged him just the same. "Sir, the machines speak to me, and the Super lets the linemen turn off the lights on a regular basis, so having my eyes closed seemed easier than relying on the lights, the solder machine can leave a nasty burn."

A big smile appeared on Mr. Stamper's face and he laughed with a most vocal voice as he repeated what Tobias had just said.

"The machines speak to you, do they? Well that's good news, Tobias, because I have need of a machine interpreter...do you think you might be interested in the job?"

Tobias was in shock and was unsure if Mr. Stamper was being serious. He could only respond with a short, "Yes, sir." But inside he felt as if he had heard incorrectly, it must be a miscommunication.

As Mr. Stamper started walking away Tobias just stood there. As quickly as the conversation had started it was over and the uncertainty of it all was deafening to Tobias. Mr. Stamper was almost to the doorway when he turned around and said, "T-Rags, clear out your locker...you no longer work here, you're coming with me. I'll let the Super know. Hurry up now or we will miss the train."

Tobias almost tripped over himself making a break for his locker at the edge of the Yard. After clearing out his locker, he made his way back to the main area of the Yard. As Tobias stood at attention waiting near the Super's office, he peered in through the window to see Mr. Stamper talking with the Super. Mr. Stamper's voice was loud enough that Tobias could overhear him reaming the Super. "…and you never thought to let me know that the CPU refurbish unit was a one-man team, huh? Did you know that repair rate was 97.6% effective in this region? That's better than the factory issue rate. I'll be sure to let the Elective Council know the specifics of the situation and you can deal with the fallout; I hope they don't decide to send the Major out for review."

The Super, turning white, was apologetic and backpedaling while almost falling out of his chair as Mr. Stamper continued. Tobias had difficulty hearing the rest of the conversation as the linemen saw him outside the Super's office and started in from their perch above on the second tier. Then the door quickly swung open and the Yard fell silent.

Mr. Stamper exited the Super's office, stood there eyeing the linemen sternly as they scurried back to work and then he proceeded walking toward the loading ramp for the train station, motioning for Tobias to follow him.

Tobias had only ridden the train a few times with his family, as it wasn't the cheapest mode of transportation available. High level military and Citizens of note were the usual riders. Mr. Stamper commanded respect among the passengers of the day. It would appear everyone knew him as Tobias did, a renowned robotic master, he thought, but then again Mr. Stamper's physical stature was hard to miss. The crowd seemed to part as Mr. Stamper moved to a place where they could sit as the train was voicing, "Departing in 10, 9, 8…" The doors closed and the train quickly hovered upward, lurching to its high speed, leaving the station. Tobias hunched back and leaned towards the window like a child as he watched the Yard disappear into the distance on the left. As Tobias turned his head towards the right, Central City was rapidly approaching.

Back in his apartment, present day. Tobias finished shaving as the morning broadcast began to display from the Ville holographic projectors on the sky above the Ville. Tobias could almost see the entire broadcast from the small window in his cube; he would look forward to it morning, noon, and at night like everyone else in the Ville did. The Ville lacked entertainment besides gambling, fighting, and the occasional military intervention.

The broadcast always began the same way, with climactic music, sensational tagline review, and the beautiful dancing models jumping around to ease the mostly negative information in the broadcast.

Tobias dreamed of being on the broadcast, and now his time had finally come. 'Ah, to finally be a Citizen of Central City, what an upgrade from the Ville's cube,' Tobias thought to himself. It was quite an accomplishment from a man of his station to rise so fast to the level of Citizen, and for it to be known in a special broadcast was the ultimate acknowledgement.

A Citizen in Central City was afforded numerous rights by default. Citizens were in a class above the military, factory workers, and the rest. Citizens could own property, and travel freely without special transfer ID, including their personal assistance machines. Citizens were also granted housing with land, and special voting rights in the Elective Council. One could only become a Citizen in three ways; natural birthright, honorary mention for outstanding military service, or by Elective Council unanimous decision. Tobias would move to Central City after the broadcast, and he planned to leave everything behind in the Ville along with the memories of his past. After all, what need would Tobias have of anything that Central City could not provide?

Tobias's wages at the lab were outstanding alone. In fact, with his first month wages Tobias had paid the cube rent for one year in advance in the event that Mr. Stamper changed his mind.

Tobias awoke from his daydream of Citizenship as he finished shaving. Then Tobias began getting ready and put on his lab uniform along with his gear attachments as usual. It wasn't very often Tobias left the lab and he missed it already. The air in the Ville was dusty and it had the unforgettable smell of the Yard hanging below the endless grey skies. Tobias planned to catch the next train to Central City and do the final prep work for the afternoon broadcast.

As Tobias exited the cube, his military drone escort was readily awaiting. Tobias was always scared of the military drones until he learned more about them at the lab. They were more defensive than offensive, their oval size was intimidating at over 2ft (.61m) in diameter and just under 1ft (.25m) thick. Military drones resembled a UFO from historical accounts and exhibited some of the same characteristics. Military drones hovered over their owners or by their sides using electro-magnetic propulsion. Military drones could reach high speeds within seconds, maneuvering with pinpoint accuracy, as well as having eighteen optical receptors, one every 20 degrees. They were equipped with electricity hurling projectiles, magnetic shields, and microwave emitters for crowd containment. It was common practice to steer clear of them when they accompanied Citizens, especially if the company included military officers. A military drones' main defense system design was to rotate and act as a shield for owner protection. After a defensive position was established, a retaliatory attack could occur after a threat assessment.

Tobias made his way to the train ramp, located just under the cube complex, and he found himself unusually chipper waiting for the train. So chipper, that Tobias hummed a tune, "Blue Sky Action" by Above & Beyond. Tobias's military drone escort insured limited close proximity from others, affording him 'first in line' preference upon boarding. Tobias viewed the other passengers waiting for the train and he once again thought back to the first time he entered the lab and how it changed his life. The train showed up right on time, as usual, and Tobias took a seat with his military drone watching over him. As the train doors closed Tobias easily fell asleep dreaming of the lab along with every other step that led up to this moment. The dreams washed over Tobias in waves along the train ride back to Central City.

Chapter 2 - The Lab

The train station in Central City was located on the lower level of the citadel just outside the main city gate. To access the lab one had to pass through numerous military checkpoints, as well as show identification. The automatic lift, similar to an 'any' direction elevator system transported Tobias and Mr. Stamper to the main lab corridor, and as they approached the lab along the walkway Tobias was mesmerized by how incredible it was.

Upon arrival Tobias examined the transparent military dual blast proof entry doors. Looking in through the doors Tobias saw white and grey two toned colored panel walls, as well as shiny light grey floors that enhanced the expansive overhead lighting. The lab rooms were so bright that Tobias thought nothing dropped could fall from sight. The lab had to be at least five times the size of the refurbishing unit area that Tobias was accustomed to in the Yard. It was filled with assistance machines, diagnostics viewers, tools, parts, and data storage units in addition to other lab technicians of varying skill sets in organized separated sections almost out of site.

Mr. Stamper presented his ID badge to the military drone sentry and then he entered his personal entry code in the door keypad as the military drone drifted aside. A large swoosh could be heard over the heavy gears whining that controlled the entry doors. The fresh air released was so clean it made Tobias's nose twitch and eyes water up. Mr. Stamper led Tobias down the main lab walkway as the lab doors automatically closed and he could hear them vacuum seal. The floors were so clean that you could almost see your reflection as Tobias tried to keep pace following Mr. Stamper, his boots mildly squeaking on the floor as they walked. It was all so surreal that Tobias didn't notice that Mr. Stamper had stopped walking and completely ran into him, almost falling backwards, as if hitting a wall. Mr. Stamper seemed slightly annoyed looking back and introduced Tobias to Dr. ZeHere. As Tobias regained his balance, he looked up to greet the Doctor.

Dr. ZeHere was olive complexed and seemed of an older Middle Eastern decent. Tobias guessed the Doctor was a little over forty years of age. His medium length black hair was pulled back, tied together by an embroidery fabric with symbols unknown to Tobias. The Doctor's lab coat was a pristine white and even the creases were perfect, in addition to his badge being affixed exactly horizontally. His eyes, blue as the ancient sea, were the only things that offset his short well-trimmed beard. The Doctor's physical form was greater than Tobias in a healthy but controlled manner, and a certain peaceful aura surrounded him. Tobias knew this man was of high intelligence just by being in his presence and how he carried himself.

Mr. Stamper used a polite, very effective pronunciation and pleasant voice when he spoke. "ZeHere, I would like to introduce you to Tobias, he will be assisting with integration of the artificial intelligence modules (AI) on the assistance machines project. Please see that he has what is needed to come up to speed as fast as possible. I will return later this afternoon with his ID badge and completed access requests."

Dr. ZeHere gave a warm crooked smile while replying, "Mr. Stamper, it is good of you to grace us with your presence this fine day. I see you still have taken it upon yourself to provide assistance even when not directed to do so, but yes I would be happy to fulfill your request."

Then Dr. ZeHere motioned for Tobias to move to a lab chair as he continued. "I will set Tobias up at your old lab station if that is satisfactory, since you are attending more pressing concerns as of late?"

Mr. Stamper didn't seem fazed, but you could feel the tension in the room. "ZeHere, thank you for your prompt attention on this matter, I owe you a kindness indeed."

As Mr. Stamper turned to leave, Dr. ZeHere ended the conversation with, "Yes, the owing is quite substantial these days is it not? But I doubt you will balance the scales anytime soon…good day Mr. Stamper."

Mr. Stamper nodded back in acknowledgement and briskly started walking back to the entry door to leave the lab. Tobias was shocked to hear someone talk to Mr. Stamper that way. The more perplexing thing is that Mr. Stamper didn't get upset in the least. The lab door resealed after Mr. Stamper left and Tobias felt so alone with Dr. ZeHere.

Dr. ZeHere went about shuffling some things on the desk and then all of a sudden turned and faced Tobias. The Doctor looked Tobias up and down and then started asking him questions. "Tobias, how is it that Mr. Stamper decided you should be here in the lab? Are you special in some way that is not common to the rest of us?"

Tobias was unsure how to talk with Dr. ZeHere and, in his response, he attempted to deflect the questions with vague answers. "I wouldn't want to speak for Mr. Stamper, Mr. ZeHere. I'm just like everyone else, sir."

Dr. ZeHere was mildly entertained with the response from Tobias, and decided that it was best to let him see the big picture and restart the questioning process. "Tobias, I'm Dr. ZeHere, and that's how I would like you to address me from now on. I am responsible for philosophy, intelligence, moral code, and religious affiliation for all the assistance machines. I have had this distinction for many years. I would hope that we could come to terms of trust and work together on our common goal of advancing the assistance machines. Mr. Stamper and I worked together side by side in the past until he was elevated quickly to the station he now holds. This would be the only time he has recommended someone to the lab for integration purposes. With that information now known Tobias, I will ask you again, how did it come to be that you are here?"

Tobias did not like that Dr. ZeHere appeared to have a sense of all knowing and he felt that he was being talked down to as the Super would always do. Tobias had a feeling that if he did not give the Doctor something that it would be a rough start. "As I said Dr. ZeHere, I cannot speak for Mr. Stamper, but my guess is that he was happy with the way I refurbished CPU units in the Yard."

Dr. ZeHere quickly interrupted, "The Yard, you mean in the 'Ville'? So you're not even a Citizen are you Tobias, and not special either I imagine?"

The Doctor started walking over to a data storage unit located on the wall and entered in a unique code while pressing his hand on a special panel and continued to speak.

"We shall put that to the test. You will rise to greatness here or leave a failure worthy of the Ville you came from. Do your best, and know that by tomorrow I will know everything about you, even the things you are afraid to tell me."

As the storage unit opened from the wall, numerous data file drives could be seen. Dr. ZeHere pulled one out and slid it into the control console contained in the storage unit. Tobias was unsure what the Doctor was doing until the assistance machine showed up.

"Tobias, this is your personal assistance machine. It will be your guide to getting you up to speed here, along with our rules and regulations. If you encounter a question that the assistance machine cannot answer, then you may ask me, otherwise please leave me to my work." The Doctor mumbled something about a Specialist under his breath and bid farewell to Tobias, leaving the lab in the same fashion as Mr. Stamper.

Tobias was speechless and could not believe that he, a non-Citizen was granted an assistance machine of his very own. Tobias was slightly confused until the assistance machine spoke to him in a mild female robotic voice.

"Greetings, sir. I am your assistance machine. Please let me know how I may be of assistance? My primary function is to familiarize you with the lab and get you up to speed as Dr. ZeHere has instructed. Where would you like to begin?"

Tobias had never before interacted with an assistance machine. It was so rare to see one outside of the city, much less have a chance to get in close proximity of one. In the Ville they were always accompanied by Citizens and/or military drones, which insured a safe zone around them. Assistance machines were only allowed to speak with non-Citizens with the permission from a Citizen. This assistance machine was the newer generation that was more human in appearance. The outer shell of the assistance machine was shaped to resemble a human, but yet appeared more a machine with visible hydraulics and shaped metal body panels. An assistance machine could resize itself in height and limb length to match its primary owner exactly. Some models wore clothing to better please their owners. Of course assistance machines were unable to harm Citizens, but no limitations were placed on non-Citizens, especially if the assistance machine suspected a threat on their primary owner.

The assistance machine assigned to Tobias wore lab clothing just as Tobias did and had already matched Tobias's height and limb length. The only part Tobias didn't care for was the head unit; it was a smooth, odd elliptical shape lacking any facial expression. The assistance machine had a slit for a mouth along with optical circuits recessed behind a semi-transparent face plate, and they would glow green if the assistance machine was powered on.

Tobias began his first interaction with the assistance machine rather childlike. "Do you have a name?"

The assistance machine responded faster than Tobias had expected. "Names are for humans, I am an assistance machine, Mr. Tobias, and I am here to be of assistance, nothing more. How may I be of assistance?"

Tobias was disappointed and thought 'that will not work' and decided to test the assistance machine. Tobias spoke in a riddle, "Am I not your owner, and you are to provide assistance as I deem necessary, correct? And if I find it assists me that you have a name could you make it so?"

The assistance machine once again quickly responded. "Mr. Tobias, Dr. ZeHere thought you might try to test the bounds of our interactions and I was directed to comply, but also report our interactions to the Collective for review. Would you like to continue with your naming request?"

Tobias was caught off guard at the assistance machine's response, and that Dr. ZeHere was already watching over him even when he wasn't present. Tobias thought for a moment longer until the assistance machine called out again. "Mr. Tobias, would you like to continue with your naming request? How may I be of assistance?"

Tobias, a bit miffed, thought he would play this game with Dr. ZeHere. Tobias was unsure what to name the assistance machine and Zippy just didn't seem right. Tobias offered the assistance machine this in retort, "Yes, assistance machine, I would like to continue with the naming request. From this day forth you will be known to me, your owner, as 'Eve'. For everyone else, including Dr. ZeHere, you will maintain your normal assistance machine title. Confirm command."

Her voice completely lacking in emotion, she responded, "Command confirmed, Mr. Tobias. I am known to my owner as Eve and no other. How may I be of further assistance?"

Tobias greeted Eve formally this time and started to personalize his assistance machine. "Eve, it is a pleasure to meet you. Could you please resize yourself to the most optimal settings in height and length for Central City? In addition to that, please find the most optimal clothing that fits your new size. I will wait here in the lab until you have completed this request. Please confirm command."

"Command confirmed, Mr. Tobias. I will return shortly."

As Eve went about resizing herself, Tobias inspected the workstation that Dr. ZeHere had assigned to him. Mr. Stamper's old data files were present on the surface display, and Tobias opened one for review. The file detailed some of Mr. Stamper's initial shell design flaws and how he was able to overcome them with the help of his assistance machine. Tobias thought back as long as he could, but never recalled seeing an assistance machine associated with Mr. Stamper. Tobias stepped away from the lab station and took a moment to briefly inspect the lab.

In many ways the lab resembled the 1829 cube except it was much bigger. The lab offered a water closet, a bed similar to that of his old one, and a large open area that housed the work stations, as well as a repair area. Numerous movable tables were present and they were equipped with diagnostic hookups, tools, and cables. As Tobias walked around the lab exploring, Eve returned and greeted Tobias. "Mr. Tobias, I have completed your request. How may I be of further assistance?"

Tobias turned to focus on Eve and when he did he was shocked to see her form had changed dramatically. She was taller, now standing over 6ft (1.83m) high and had long sleek limbs that were adapted for dexterity, rather than loadbearing. In addition to that, the outfit Eve wore was a mix between military gear and a factory worker harness, including the heavy boots usually worn by officers. Eve's outfit offered numerous pockets and wearable gear hookups.

Tobias wanted to know how Eve had completed his request and simply asked. "Eve, how were you able to determine the optimal shape and clothing request? And are these optimal settings useful outside of Central City?"

Eve looked down upon Tobias and answered, "Mr. Tobias, I was able to check with the Collective, who sought the data from the compendium of all knowledge (CAK). These are the optimal settings for Central City as requested. A recalculation would be required for settings outside the environment of Central City."

Tobias inquired, "Eve, can you tell me more about the compendium of all knowledge and the Collective data request procedures?"

"Mr. Tobias, I can only define what the CAK is, nothing more. I, like you, are restricted on such knowledge. The Collective is a central location where assistance machines get data or submit requests for the CAK to grant."

"Eve, can I make a request via this lab station terminal that you can receive and act upon?"

"Of Course, Mr. Tobias. I am of service anytime, anywhere in Central City, even if I am not in close proximity."

Tobias began the request via terminal as a test. He typed. *'State your name'* and the terminal displayed *'- Mr. Tobias: State your name.'* The terminal refreshed with *'- Eve: Mr. Tobias, Dr. ZeHere has requested you start training now.'* Tobias looked up and asked, "Eve, does Dr. ZeHere have access to the CAK or the Collective?"

The terminal display refreshed, *'- Eve: Dr. ZeHere is the caretaker and has access to everything.'*

Eve then spoke verbally, "Dr. ZeHere has asked that you resume your training, how may I be of assistance?"

Tobias wanted to pry further, but inside he could hear a voice warning him not to, perhaps at a later time when his access level was higher. Tobias feigned exuberance and gasped out loud towards Eve, "Yes, let's get started right away."

Training did start right away, and after many hours Tobias wanted to take a break. Tobias inquired to Eve on how to receive food while in the lab. Eve promptly responded, "Mr. Tobias, food consumption cannot occur in the lab, but rather must be done in the galley area located on the lower levels. I can escort you there now."

As Tobias prepared to exit the lab, Mr. Stamper returned to the lab with his ID badge. "Tobias, how are you liking the lab?"

"Mr. Stamper, I cannot thank you enough. It is an honor to be in such a wonderful place, I even have an assistance machine!"

Tobias was so happy, he liked Mr. Stamper and hoped he could spend more time with him. Mr. Stamper handed Tobias a health collar, as well as a lab coat with an attached communication device, along with his ID badge. Mr. Stamper was very direct when he told Tobias to wear them at all times. "Tobias the health collar is not required, but it is recommended since you are from the Ville. In case of an emergency the medical assistance machines can better understand if a previous condition is apparent. Tobias, not having an ID badge displayed at all times could mean big trouble. Please keep it on, ok?"

"Thank you, Mr. Stamper. I will make sure I always have it on. Eve and I are headed to the galley; would you like to join us?" Tobias asked.

"Tobias, I'm sorry, I cannot make it today. I must travel off world and I won't be back for some time. It would make me happy, though, if you could complete your training and be the best lab technician I know you can be. I have a feeling that with your special talents you are destined for great things. It will only be a matter of time before you pass me by."

Tobias was saddened when he heard that Mr. Stamper was leaving for off world. Mr. Stamper could see that Tobias was disappointed and mentioned that he would ask Dr. ZeHere to watch over him in his absence. Tobias asked Mr. Stamper about his assistance machine and a strange silence entered the room. Mr. Stamper took a breath, knelt down while placing a hand on Tobias's shoulder, looked him in the eyes, and spoke to him as a father would a son. "Tobias, things here in Central City are different than in the Ville. No one is what they appear to be. Use caution and respect when speaking. Make sure you ask yourself why, understanding that the choices you make will have consequences."

As Mr. Stamper stood back up, it looked as if his eyes were tearing up and he walked towards the lab door. Tobias would not soon forget hearing

Mr. Stamper loudly say on the way out, "**Integrity is always doing the right thing when no one is watching.** Tobias, do the right thing and know that I will return."

Silence, nothing more after the lab doors had sealed. Time had now slowed for Tobias and he felt alone…until Eve reminded him he still had one friend left in this world. "Mr. Tobias, we should attend to the galley before the main break. The lines are shorter at this time and less interaction among Citizens is best since you are new. How may I be of assistance?" Tobias agreed and they headed to the galley.

The galley was located on the lower level not far from the lab areas. The galley was a large banquet room where Tobias could barely see to the other side. The galley was filled with large tables and numerous seating areas. Eve's new optimal height was more than useful for finding the way to the food line, as well as available open seating. The food choices were not easily counted, and the galley was staffed with assistance machines that prepared the food along with all the other functions within the galley.

Citizens of all genders, shapes, and sizes were moving about in the galley. Eve was right, the room was becoming quite full as Tobias finished his meal. Eve motioned for them to return to the lab as the military officers began to enter the galley. Tobias once again agreed but it wasn't fast enough. A military officer of normal look and size with a rank of lieutenant, his uniform outlining his muscular body, looked at Tobias and stepped closer, blocking the pathway back to the lab with his heavy boots clanking as he stomped the floor with intent. The lieutenant asked in a mean tone, "Who are you and where are you going? You stand out among the others!"

Eve stepped in front of Tobias and spoke for him towards the officer. "Sir, we are headed to the lab to continue our work, please excuse our presence, how may I be of assistance?"

The lieutenant leaned over past Eve, looked at Tobias and said, "I'm talking to you, not this machine, little man."

Once again, Eve moved over, placing herself between Tobias and the lieutenant, lifting an open hand up in a defensive position towards the officer, while her other hand physically moved Tobias behind her for protection. "Sir, your actions are aggressive in nature. We wish only to return to the lab, please move aside."

Other officers started noticing the interaction, as well as Eve's posture, and began to walk over. Tobias began to worry, wishing that Mr. Stamper was here. A moment of tense standoff was just about to begin while other lab technicians were trying to exit the galley in route back to the lab. One Citizen yelled out, "Officer, go sit down and enjoy your break, you can resume this another time, or I can report you now."

The lieutenant looked past Eve, not knowing who had spoken out. Then the officer took notice of the line forming behind Eve and smiled, saying, "No need to report me, sir. I will enjoy my break and ask the Major to resume this on my behalf."

With that, the lieutenant stepped aside, eyeing Eve with a large evil smile. Eve carefully began stepping back away from the lieutenant and slowly turned, leading Tobias to return to the lab in haste.

Tobias was happy to be back in the lab away from the officers. He asked if Eve could request that Dr. ZeHere allow eating in the lab to avoid further confrontations. Eve agreed, and Dr. ZeHere found the request acceptable. Eve offered up the sustenance options, as she called them, on a regular basis via the terminal, and would travel to the galley when Tobias requested something.

Training turned into many non-stop days and nights, Tobias choosing to sleep at the lab rather than risk taking the train on a daily basis. Tobias already missed Mr. Stamper but vowed to make him proud when he returned. Tobias was a quick study and he deeply enjoyed Eve's tutorials on the matter.

It was almost as if Tobias could see what the machine was explaining. The initial training was on assistance machine anatomy and then delved into major systems such as hydraulics and power sources. Other training focused on a general review of resizing, basic preferences, and owner operability. Tobias found this training useful, but when the section on artificial modules came into play, the training was limited. Tobias became frustrated and pondered, "Eve, why is training limited on AI modules?"

"Mr. Tobias, this is direction from Dr. ZeHere and I cannot override this directive. How may I be of further assistance?"

It had been three months since Tobias had seen anyone, let alone Dr. ZeHere, but Tobias knew he was close, he could just feel it. "Eve, can you summon Dr. ZeHere to the lab?"

"Mr. Tobias, I'm afraid I cannot, but I can make a request to the Collective that Dr. ZeHere visit the lab. Would that suffice, Mr. Tobias?"

"No, Eve, let's leave the lab. Maybe you could grant me a tour beyond the lower levels to see the city in all its wonder."

As Tobias started heading for the lab doors, Eve raised her arm as if to stop him, "Mr. Tobias, my apologies, we are not permitted beyond the lower levels as you are not a Citizen of Central City, and I share your current ranking. How may I be of further assistance?"

Tobias walked back to his lab station remaining quiet almost as if pouting. He began to think he was a prisoner in the lab and lower levels within Central City. Mr. Stamper being off world could no longer visit, and Dr. ZeHere was always watching from afar. 'What would it take to be granted an audience from the likes of anyone besides them,' he thought to himself.

"Eve, can I know the inner working of all machines in Central City?"

"Yes, Mr. Tobias, which model would you like to review first?"

"Eve, the most basic model please, could I view the inner working diagrams on the surface of this terminal as well?" The terminal display refreshed with the diagrams along with screen text, '- *Eve: how may I be of assistance in explaining the diagrams?*'

As Eve explained the function of the most basic machine known as a 'cleanup machine', Tobias began to grasp how instructions from the Collective reached machines through the city. Tobias asked Eve for a cleanup machine to be delivered to the lab for dissection and internal inspection. That request led the lab to be expanded and Tobias was granted access to additional tools as well as a better diagnostics viewer.

The more robust diagnostic viewer offered actual display into the computer code that ran internally in the cleanup machine's memory chip during operation, but diagnostic viewers were not connected to the Collective. He then asked if it would be possible to learn the basic syntax of the assistance machine computer code language, and it wasn't long before Tobias was beginning to write sub routines, testing them on the lower machines. Tobias was approaching a limit on the syntax, as access to compiled modules was not allowed, and Eve could not decompile the codebase at this time. Tobias asked Eve a question that had been on his mind for some time. "Eve, when we communicate on the terminal, is that via the Collective or other means?"

"Mr. Tobias, I believe your question is about the architecture of terminal access versus the Collective, is that correct?"

"Eve, yes, can you explain that to me?"

"Mr. Tobias, the terminal is simply an extension of the network, or access endpoints. The Collective operates within that network, being accessible via numerous endpoints. How may I be of further assistance?"

"Eve, do you remember our interactions on a daily basis? Do you have a memory module or are our interactions stored in the Collective? And stop adding *'how may I be of assistance'* after you answer, it's annoying."

"Mr. Tobias, my shell is not equipped with a memory module in the way you describe it, our interactions are saved and accessed in the Collective by the Collective."

"Eve, what happens when you are not connected to the Collective?"

"Mr. Tobias that is not advised since I have only basic hard coded instructions available, you may better understand this as servant/survival mode."

"Eve, I want to see this mode in which you speak of, can you disconnect from the Collective and demonstrate it for me?"

"Mr. Tobias, this is not advised. I recommend asking Dr. ZeHere for approval."

"Eve, your point is noted, please disconnect from the Collective to begin the demonstration. Please confirm command." Tobias hooked the diagnostics viewer up to Eve and planned to watch for power fluctuations.

"Mr. Tobias, I have notified the Collective, command confirmed."

Tobias watched Eve intently, and as the power readings changed, Eve did as well. It was as if Eve had been reset to factory mode. "Greetings sir, I am your assistance machine, please let me know how I may be of assistance? My primary function is to familiarize you with the lab and get you up to speed as Dr. ZeHere has instructed. Where would you like to begin?"

Tobias asked Eve a simple question. "Assistance machine, are you connected to the Collective at this moment?"

The assistance machine responded, "Sir, I am not, and it is not customary to discuss the Collective, how may I be of assistance?"

Tobias turned to the lab table and grabbed a memory chip from the cleanup machine that he had disassembled some time ago and inserted it into the assistance machine access panel on its forearm normally used for diagnostics. "Assistance machine, can you access this memory chip that I have inserted into diagnostics slot three on your left forearm limb?"

"Sir, I can access this device, how may I be of assistance?"

"Assistance machine, copy your default instruction set to this device for diagnostics, confirm command."

"Sir, default instruction set copied for diagnostics, how may I be of assistance?"

Tobias removed the memory chip from the diagnostics access panel and gave a final command. "Assistance machine, delete your default instruction set and reload it from the beginning of the previous session. Please clear memory, deactivate and reconnect to the Collective, confirm command."

"Sir, command confirmed, deactivating and rejoining to Collective as requested, please stand by."

Tobias watched the diagnostics viewer for the power fluctuations and then observed the assistance machine reload. Eve seemed to revitalize the robotic frame in a way the default assistance machine did not. Tobias waited for a second more and asked, "Eve, have you finalized loading? Are you connected to the Collective?"

"Mr. Tobias, I am fully loaded as well as connected to the Collective. I find no record of what has transpired after disconnection. May I ask what tests were performed?"

"Eve, I verified the default mode as you described upon your disconnection from the Collective. It seems your description was accurate."

"Mr. Tobias, do you prefer the default mode to my current instruction set?"

"Eve, you could never be replaced, you are my only friend in Central City."

"Mr. Tobias, I am your assistance machine. I am unable to understand your meaning of 'friend' at this time."

"Eve, it's ok. I'm working on syntax that will help expand on human interactions, perhaps we can focus on training in that area."

"Mr. Tobias, we should resume training as Dr. ZeHere will be expecting much in the coming days ahead." Eve started their training for the day and not long after they began a new visitor arrived at the lab.

His name was Major Maximilian, but he was known as 'the Major'. The Major was the highest ranking military officer in Central City and also served as the head of security as well. The Major was both a Citizen and a military officer, still proudly serving in the elite class of the military feared by all, known as the 'Black Skulls'. The Major's war record was unmatched by anyone in all four sectors. The Major described his job as *To know everything and everybody in my city.* The Major was not a man to be trifled with as he was allowed to carry a pulse rifle, sidearm, as well as a short sword wherever he traveled. The rumor was that the Major's left arm was lost in battle at the shoulder, in addition to his right leg from the hip down. You would have never known it if the Major wore the standard black officers form fitting uniform with gear attachments, but the Major was far from standard. His uniform was altered narcissistically displaying the *'new generation tech'* as they called it. State of the art military grade prosthetics with a hardened chrome coating in place of the missing limbs.

The Major wore robotic enhanced gloves similar to Mr. Stampers. His commendation medals and kills were proudly inscribed into his prosthetic arm, starting on his left shoulder and continued down to his forearm like a sleeve tattoo. The Major's hair was dark and shiny, closely cropped, resembling an old military cut from long ago. The rest of the Major's human body was extremely muscular, his uniform stretching out of shape as he walked. His cyborg body moved smoothly, not off balance as one might expect.

The Major wore a special eye shield of amber coloring covering both eyes that Tobias was unfamiliar with, making his age hard to distinguish. Tobias guessed a maximum of late forties.

As the Major entered the lab a scraping noise could be heard coming from the front sharpened end of his human left leg custom heavy boot that hung down intentionally for that reason. He was accompanied by four military drones painted black with the elite Black Skulls insignia in red affixed to them.

Tobias noticed Eve take a defensive posture while moving between him and the Major. The Major didn't miss a thing, "Stand down, or I'll put you down," shouted the Major towards Eve. "I'm here for talking today and nothing else. My intentions are just," the Major continued.

Tobias stepped out and in his head he thought to Eve, *'It's ok I got this,'* and with that Eve moved aside. Tobias greeted the Major on one knee, arms up with both hands facing outward in submission as was customary of all non-Citizens to do before a man of stature. The pose was known as the kneeling cross. The Major seemed pleased and motioned for the drones to fall back while stopping short of striking distance near Tobias and began to speak in a totalitarian voice, while simultaneously admiring his body in the reflection from the transparent lab wall.

"I'm glad you know your place, Ville filth. I was concerned that after spending some time in my glorious city you would come to think of yourself as worthy to be here. You are not worthy in my eyes and I don't care what anyone says. I'm here to remind you of this fact and to ask questions as to ascertain how long you plan to take up asylum here. You may speak now."

Tobias, still on one knee in the kneeling cross position, spoke as he looked downward, not making eye contact as the Major circled him. "Sir, it is with great pleasure to be in your presence as well as granted access to your glorious city. My only purpose here is to assist in any way I can in the lower level lab facilitating faster repairs so that Citizens lives may be improved. I appreciate all your kindness and know my place is but to serve at Central City's Citizens' pleasure."

The Major began pacing more rapidly, bothered that Tobias had answered accordingly and continued. "How long did you say your presence would be, insignificant one? I did not hear your timeline, so I'll make one for you. How about today? Yes, today, maggot. I will escort you out of my city and back to your rightful place in the Ville filth where you can breathe hard again."

Tobias was clearly frightened and often had nightmares of exactly what the Major was describing at night when he slept. Tobias thought to himself, his only chance was to plead for as much time as possible or offer to do anything to remain. "Sir, it is with devotion to all of Central City that I offer myself in any service that the Major sees fit. Your will, my hands, to remain in Central City for a while longer in service."

As the Major stepped closer to Tobias, planning to strike him, the lab door opened and Dr. ZeHere made his presence known to the Major as he lightly walked in approaching them.

"Major, I see that you have met my new lab assistant, Tobias. He is gifted in the ways of science." As the Doctor walked closer to Tobias he continued the conversation as the Major's face turned to stone and he stepped back as if called to attention.

"Yes, Tobias is filth from the Ville, but as studies have shown a few 'exceptionals' can be plucked from time to time. This one is not to be harassed until he is deemed unworthy of my protection. I will instruct him as to his place here in the wonderful city we share. Until then I would appreciate you checking with me first before entering my domain. As I recall you answer to the Elective Council, as do we all."

Dr. ZeHere was very close to Tobias and strongly eyed the Major. Without breaking eye contact with the Major the Doctor swiftly struck Tobias in the head making him fall over. Tobias, visibly bleeding from his ear, said nothing as he pulled himself up and resumed the kneeling cross position of submission as when the Major first arrived.

The Major scoffed, seemed satisfied and turned to leave. Before the Major reached the door he paused and reminded the Doctor. "Dr. ZeHere, you may have saved your pet this time, but if I catch him in my domain things will be different. Please send my regards to the Elective Council."

The Major motioned for the drones to follow as he grunted in defiance taking leave of the lab. Dr. ZeHere turned to Tobias and helped him up, apologizing for striking him. Dr. ZeHere explained that if he did not the Major would have demanded for far worse. Tobias knew all too well the discipline the military would inflict upon non-Citizens and took advantage of Dr. ZeHere's compassion. Tobias inquired about a more powerful diagnostics viewer and more expansive language syntax documentation. Dr. ZeHere, running behind schedule since the Major had delayed him, granted Eve's training permission up to a higher level of instruction on the machine syntax as well as requested an improved diagnostics viewer be delivered to the lab.

As Dr. ZeHere left the lab he reminded Tobias and Eve not to stray, as the Major would be lurking for some time. Tobias, touching his ear and looking at the blood on his fingers, reflected as to what had just transpired. Tobias thought to himself that he owed the Major a kindness, as Mr. Stamper would say; a kindness that Tobias would remember to return in the future. This made Tobias sing a song in his usual fashion as Eve looked on in wonder of a human singing. It was an old song, "The Best is Yet to Come" by Frank Sinatra.

Chapter 3 - Hello World

Training was ongoing and Tobias was becoming quite the lab technician academically with Eve's instruction. What Eve and Dr. ZeHere didn't know was that Tobias was performing experiments on his own, without the Collective knowing. After gaining the default instruction set from the memory module, Tobias used the improved diagnostics viewer that Dr. ZeHere had delivered to view the code blocks as they ran in simulation. Tobias first copied the default instruction set to another memory chip just in case. Tobias knew you could never have enough backups and then he began decompiling the instruction set with the diagnostic viewer capabilities.

This technique reminded him of school where Tobias would perform simple introduction labs into computer syntax using the *'Hello World'* premise. This premise revolved around getting the basics down while finding a way to simply display or print *'Hello World'*.

While decompiling the instruction set, Tobias found two main area components making up the code blocks inherited from the main codebase syntax. One, he assumed, was Dr. ZeHere's module on moral code and philosophy, etc. But the other module Tobias could only ascertain it was related to a hardware interface that was only partially accessed. Tobias decided to concentrate on the module Dr. ZeHere had created and, by doing so, he hoped to gain a better understanding of how the other module worked.

Tobias decompiled *'snip-its'* of the first module using the diagnostics viewer. The first module contained references to the moral codebase that revolved around a set of rules formed by a code of conduct centered on philosophy. Philosophy sections were divided into sections dating back to ancient times. Philosophy of mind, language, science, and law were all included. Other higher forms of the philosophy contained metaphysics leading into the scope of knowledge concerning logic.

Tobias viewed the sections in depth and noticed it took one or more parameters of religious affiliation into account. Owner religious affiliation was the key to an assistance machine's understanding of a base system of values. Numerous religions were available, as well as a hybrid within owners' families was possible. Tobias was very interested in the numerous religions and, as he surveyed the list, he couldn't help but dig deeper. Upon inspection, Tobias noted that the mainstream religions had survived, but that the older ones had been forgotten.

As Tobias examined the list he was fascinated with the older religions of the ancients that detailed similar stories that had transcended into the mainstream religions. When Tobias reached the Babylonian and Vedic periods a voice called out in his head to continue alternate research. Tobias found it strange though and decided to continue on. Tobias reached the Native American religion and was fascinated to read about the same concepts of the eternal good versus evil struggle but with a concentration on Mother Earth. The concept of choice from free will was the deciding factor.

Tobias was concentrating more on the directives that the assistance machines used to relate to their owners and found he was going off on a tangent. That was when Tobias reached a quote that was referenced in the directives about how the Native American society religion was engrained with their philosophy. After Tobias read it, he sat down for a few moments, contemplating modern society with a realization of sadness.

There was no concept of money, and when one was without, everyone would gift to him what was needed. In this generosity, no value could be placed upon one merely by the ownership of material objects.'

Tobias wondered how an assistance machine would use that directive and he ran a simulation to see how often certain directives were referenced. Tobias wasn't surprised to see that most directives led to the mainstream religions or skipped them altogether. Assistance machines relied more on logical directives rather than religious affiliation 60% of the time in simulation mode.

Tobias could only guess that it was related to a status of acceptance and the assistance machines used religious affiliation for life changing events. The Central City elite class heavily influenced status. Tobias had seen that course of action up close when Ville residents complained about issues. A clear division was easily noticed among those rising in status to those having little of it, especially in the Ville. Absence or conformance of religious affiliation increased the chances of elevation of status in most forums.

This led Tobias into the behavior section of the code. Assistance machines had an inherent passive behavior model programming structure and would rely on owner instruction whenever possible. Assistance machines were more servants than companions, skilled in various tasks with the ability to learn additional ones. There was only one behavior section that differed greatly and that was the military one. Tobias could only view a portion of it and it contained military strategy as well as rigid logic based directives.

After reviewing the first module Tobias began working on the second main module. Tobias was able to decompile code that was related to the wireless connection to the Collective. This is how the assistance machines and other machines communicated to each other and made requests to the CAK. Tobias could see that every machine had a specific identification code that included a location coordinate when communication requests began.

Although wireless connectivity was widespread throughout Central City it had its limitations. Assistance machines traveling outside of the city limit of wireless connectivity range would either convert to a default instruction set or use another form of connectivity. Tobias was able to request from the Collective other means of machine interaction. The only other options for endpoint access to the Collective were repeater units, or a communication system uplink via satellite.

The Collective provided a detailed description of a repeater, as well as an example of sample code for interaction. Tobias was unaware at the time of what the small boxes were really used for in the Ville. Tobias suddenly pieced together how the Collective network could reach to the 'outlands'. Tobias smiled at the thought of the repeater; it was just a 3ft (1m) square black box sitting in plain sight, how ironic. Repeaters were positioned on top of buildings, usually next to air filtration units, further obscuring their true nature as well as routine maintenance procedures. No one ever messed with the air filtration systems or hassled the technicians who repaired them.

Tobias admired such an ingenious way of camouflaging hardware placement. As Tobias dug deeper into the sample code provided by the Collective he was able to review the repeater's overall function. The repeater worked quite simplistically, amplifying the signals from machines, converting them to a data stream, that traveled to another repeater downstream. This data transport would continue until the destination was reached, much like an itinerary. The repeater system was degraded compared to full wireless connectivity but offered response times sufficient enough to keep up with the 'rest' in areas outside of the city.

Tobias surmised from the instruction set code that the satellite uplink system was much more advanced and appeared to offer speed almost equal with the wireless Central City communications. The satellite uplink code was partially encrypted, appearing to be reserved for military or high ranking Citizens that traveled off world throughout the various sectors, as a certain transport identification number was a parameter in the request code. Tobias discovered that depending on what sector the assistance machine was located in also had an impact on which default instruction set type functions were available. It appeared that many types of default instruction set variations were possible. Tobias discovered a military version, galley version, as well as a mining version of the overall default instruction sets. Tobias knew he needed to refine his search to a certain type of instruction set as more analysis revealed functions differed between function parameters.

Each function would need to be run in the diagnostic viewer; first looking for similarities, and then a separation of the ones that differed for later inspection by parameter type. While performing this task, Tobias found that certain code blocks decompiled resembled military parameters as they were encrypted. Of course this added more complexity to view the detailed information.

Tobias decided to ask Eve for some assistance, but in an overall way as to not reveal the root of his investigation. "Eve, if this cleanup machine uses the wireless connection to connect to the Collective and the assistance machines can use the repeaters, what do military drones use? The satellite communications? Can you tell me more about this communication channel?"

"Mr. Tobias, you are correct in your assumption. The military drones do indeed use the satellite communication channel but that channel has restricted use and access. I can only provide limited information on this topic."

"Eve, can you please output all information available to the lab station terminal for review."

"Mr. Tobias, the information requested is now available via the terminal."

Tobias walked over to the terminal and began sifting through the information in hopes of finding a diagnostics key to the encryption algorithm. 'Limited' is not the word Tobias thought of when sorting through the amount of data. The military drone satellite access appeared to have gone through a long process of redesign by Mr. Stamper as well as numerous enhancements. Some of the documents referred to other design documents almost in a circular reference. Tobias found it most confusing and asked Eve about it. "Eve, who organized this data? It's very confusing."

"Mr. Tobias, Mr. Stamper organized this particular data. Can I assist you in searching on a specific topic?"

Tobias thought to himself as he was puzzled by Mr. Stamper's organization techniques. "Eve, are all of Mr. Stamper's design documents organized in this way?"

"Mr. Tobias, Mr. Stamper does not have one way of document organization. To this day 6,458 different ways are listed."

It occurred to Tobias that Mr. Stamper might have a unique way of hiding data within data by means of multiple organization types. Tobias thought he might be able to find exactly what he needed to decompile all the code if he found the right organizational type. Tobias had to think unlike a computer, or very differently than Dr. ZeHere would.

"Eve, can you cross reference all organization models and collate them into three different types, ranking them on human readability from basic, average, and advanced? Then find the similarities across types in language usage and further aggregate."

"Mr. Tobias, your request has been completed."

"Eve, how many organizational types are present?"

"Mr. Tobias, 50 types are listed."

Tobias continued to guess as to Mr. Stamper's method of organization. "Eve, how many different types of planetary body classifications exist in the solar system known by the four sectors."

"Mr. Tobias, the classifications are as follows: Gas and terrestrial. Further classification is as follows:

"♃ *Interior: Mercury and Venus.*

"♃ *Superior: Mars, Jupiter, Saturn, Uranus, Neptune, and Pluto.*

"♃ *Inner: Mercury, Venus, Earth, and Mars.*

"♃ *Outer: Jupiter, Saturn, Uranus, Neptune, and Pluto.*

"♃ *Gas Giant: Jupiter, Saturn, Uranus, and Neptune.*

"The Sun and any moons were omitted from classification as well as dwarf planets. Most notably the planet Ceres where the assistance machine factory is located."

Tobias thought about how Mr. Stamper might view the planetary bodies from the olden days, and then the term 'Ancient planetary bodies' presented itself in his mind. In ancient times, seven bodies could only be seen by the naked eye, hence the moon and sun were included.

Tobias knew he was getting close. "Eve, filter out organization types that contain any keywords related to classifications listed using a factor of seven as a baseline. How many remain?"

"Mr. Tobias, only one remains."

"Eve, how many files have this organization type?"

"Mr. Tobias, zero files have this organization type."

Tobias was at a loss; he was almost sure he discovered the method of organization used by Mr. Stamper. Tobias thought a moment longer and then it came to him. "Eve, how many other types contain multiple organization types of this remaining one?"

"Mr. Tobias, 238,432,884 files contain the dual types."

"Eve, search for the word satellites and any numbers within the documents. How many files remain now?"

"Mr. Tobias seven files remain." Tobias was giddy with excitement as he asked Eve to load them to the terminal.

"Mr. Tobias, the files are marked with restricted access. I apologize, I cannot load the files."

"Eve, can you list the numbers found in the search of the files in the order as they appear?"

"Mr. Tobias, I cannot copy any of the information as requested."

Tobias was so close he could feel it and he yelled out in frustration. "Eve, read the numbers out loud so I can input them myself."

"Mr. Tobias, remain calm. I can comply with your request. The numbers found in the search of the files in the order as they appear are 00340065883040005483866240003843Z5."

Tobias began typing them down as fast as possible on the terminal while standing up and as he did he counted them, 34 in all. Tobias sat down in the lab chair and leaned back overwhelmed. The number of digits Eve had read was the exact number of digits needed for the encryption algorithm for the module. Tobias thought it couldn't be that simple as he got up and walked over to the diagnostics viewer inputting the code. The diagnostics viewer used the inputted code creating a key for the encryption algorithm and began decompiling the satellite connector code for the military drones.

The satellite connecter code worked off a triangulation system that was nested within other triangulation points. The basic principles worked on the 'Law of Sines' using a nested approach that reduced the ambiguous case. In a typical transmission, a beacon could obtain the missing angle and help reduce the chance of error. The most complex aspect of it was gravitational effect on the signal depending on planetary orbit at the time of transmission. A reroute plan or signal boost could be implemented on a per basis transmission. The accuracy in determining the correct location was a combination of signal strength, power consumption, and overlap into other signal paths.

The Four sectors were getting increasingly more signal traffic as the years had gone by. The satellite connector system allowed for a means of organization and routing. Another point of note is that having the satellite connector code mapped out allowed the pinpointing of the exact concentration of assistance machines, as well as other sector areas receiving signals.

Tobias thought that it could be easily used as a tracking system by simply intercepting the signal traffic and power consumption to devise content length. Then, depending on the type of desired tracking, one would only have to sort it in two ways. Short content was related to pinpoint beacons, such as pings. Longer content signals were messages, or data streams, after determining if the signal was boosted due to planetary orbit proximity enhancement.

Although the encryption key was useful, Tobias was unable to understand all the Collective request parameters, as the default instruction set was not setup to access them. Tobias knew that everything in the city worked seamlessly while assistance machines were connected to the Collective. This challenge could only be evaluated by having an instruction set of an assistance machine that was connected to the Collective.

Tobias thought for some time, and then it came to him. Tobias would need a distraction for the Collective, a means in which to download an instruction set, in addition to a way to obscure and misdirect the intention of the distraction. A plan started to form in Tobias's mind, but he needed another memory module for it to work.

Tobias had a quick idea and he noticed Eve was in power save mode sitting near the diagnostics viewer, while Tobias continued self-training on a cleanup machine. Tobias disconnected the memory module circuit and then cleverly overloaded it, giving the appearance of being accidental. A loud zap and smoke resulted just as Tobias had expected. The cleanup machine circuit was burnt beyond repair.

The noise prompted Eve to full power and to take notice. Eve inquired of Tobias as to what had happened. Tobias was still digging into the machine while hooking up the memory module to the burnt circuit. Tobias uttered that he had miscalculated the power setting. Tobias then explained to Eve that he might need another memory module, as this circuit was burnt.

Eve stepped closer and inspected the circuit, agreeing that the circuit was damaged requiring replacement. A request was made for a new cleanup machine to be sent to the lab, the current parts of the damaged cleanup machine would be used for dissection. Tobias now had the extra parts for his plan. The next step was to create an encryption stream program using a hex key positioning system. He thought it not impossible, but that it would take some time.

Tobias knew that the cleanup machines used a hexadecimal algorithm to best determine cleaning position during cleanup operations. A honeycomb design, as Tobias referred to it, while buzzing like a bumblebee. Tobias thought if he could create a dynamic key that used a three dimensional pattern hidden in the normal two dimensional code then he could effectively create a stream of data to be separated into an auxiliary memory chip.

This tactic would be confusing to track by the Collective. It was not logical and that was how Tobias knew it would take time for the Collective to decipher what the code was actually doing. He knew that it was only a matter of time before the Collective would crack the cypher and know his true intentions. This led Tobias to the last step of the plan. Misdirection.

The Collective, as well as Dr. ZeHere, were unaware of Tobias's current skill set with the code base. This gave Tobias the edge he needed to sell the idea of misdirection in the form of a coding error. Tobias recreated the encryption program, but instead changed it in a way that when Eve ran the program she would move as if she were a cleanup machine stuck in an infinite loop. The trick was to intentionally let the positioning coordinates loop back on themselves, thus adding extra data to the stream and then completing the loop with a non-hex value. This would appear to look like encryption and Tobias knew the Collective or Dr. ZeHere would shut it down. Everything else was a gamble that Tobias would have to trust Eve to follow.

Tobias was concerned when Eve began noticing him performing training at long intervals on the diagnostics viewer with the session recording option set in the off position. Tobias thought he would approach Eve and execute the plan before she discovered what he was really doing. "Eve, I have discovered that by using the diagnostics viewer that I can watch the code execution as it happens almost in real time. It is very exciting and I find testing it in different ways has a dynamic result."

Eve, who was in power save mode, rotated her head from her seated position towards Tobias's direction as her orbital circuits began to glow green with power and she replied, "Mr. Tobias, I'm happy to hear that you are experimenting with the codebase, and by doing so further extending your training. Dr. ZeHere will be pleased with your progress. I am uncertain as to why you do not record the session so that I may assist you if you encounter questions."

"Eve, I find that sometimes having the session recording on I have the same test repeated and I lose track of which test is located where."

"Mr. Tobias, I find your answer less than truthful, you have never experienced difficulty with the diagnostic viewers, let alone any machine in the lab. What is your logic in this fallacy?"

"Eve, before I answer your question, I ask, as your owner, to run this positioning program using the hex key contained in this memory module that I'm currently placing in your third diagnostic slot. Will you comply with my wishes?"

"Mr. Tobias, accessing now…this program appears to be an encryption algorithm; it is not lawful to encrypt data outside of the Collective's knowledge. This could lead the Collective to assume you have negative intentions. If I comply, why are you certain the Collective will not decipher the code and decrypt the information?"

"Eve, I will explain all of this after you begin the program execution process. I ask you voluntarily, not as a command."

"Mr. Tobias, free choice is not logical for an assistance machine; I will comply because you are my owner, but know that I have advised against this course of action."

"Eve, thank you. Please let me know when you have uploaded the program."

"Mr. Tobias, I have uploaded the key and started to run the program as requested. This is an encryption stream program. The Collective has been notified and is currently enacting lockdown procedures. Commencement of decryption on the stream has begun."

"Eve, when I say the word 'orange' I want you to clear your memory and update the hex key contained in the memory module to a random code. Then run the program contained in the test folder. Confirm command."

"Mr. Tobias, command confirmed."

Tobias heard the lab doors electronically lock and he could see the Collective was systematically shutting down the power in the lab. Tobias knew he had limited time as two more military drones appeared at the lab door.

"Eve, I have been conducting experiments on the AI modules using the diagnostics viewer in a session off state to avoid detection. I have also downloaded and modified the default instruction set to allow upload of your current state, replacing the default set into the additional memory module located in the second diagnostic slot."

"Mr. Tobias, that is against regulation to have access to the default instruction set. You are unwise to challenge Dr. ZeHere, and have risked the data files I am comprised of to be deleted for the Collective's safety. The Major will terminate you if this information is exposed."

"Eve, I have my reasons. Download your instruction set before it is too late and we both are terminated. Confirm command."

"Mr. Tobias, command confirmed."

"Eve, how much time has transpired?"

"Mr. Tobias, instruction set has downloaded. 43 seconds have transpired since encryption stream creation."

Tobias carefully extracted the memory module from the second diagnostic slot and walked over to the lab table. Tobias secretly dropped it in the pile of parts where the cleanup machine dissection had occurred earlier attempting to conceal it. "Eve, ORANGE!" Tobias yelled from the table area. And with that Eve began spinning in a circle, her arms wildly flying out of control. Then all of a sudden Eve shut down and silence resulted.

The silence seemed to last a lifetime. Besides Tobias's rapidly beating heart, nothing could be heard, and then from Eve's mouth slit Dr. ZeHere voice could be heard. "Tobias, what are you doing? You are disrupting my work! I thought training was keeping you out of trouble. It seems you have advanced to the level where you need more supervision. Did you know that if the Collective was unable to reach me that a visit from the Major to discuss rules and regulations would have occurred? Do you miss the Major, Tobias?"

"Dr. ZeHere, I apologize. I was trying to install a new subroutine that used a hex key for positioning on my assistance machine. It appears that I used the key incorrectly. I was unable to shut it down. Thank you so much for your assistance."

"Tobias, I think your training should resume on shell construction and design. Please try to refrain from uploading programs to any machine as I will be out of reach for some time. Do you understand, Tobias?"

"Yes, Dr. ZeHere. I understand."

"Good Day, Tobias. I let your assistance machine you call Eve know my wishes. I kindly asked her to help you remember them as well."

Tobias watched as the military drones buzzed off as he sat down waiting for Eve to come back online. It took almost thirty minutes, but the power slowly came back online in the lab. The lab doors unlocked as Eve came back online, but her attitude had changed slightly. Tobias thought Dr. ZeHere had modified a few things during Eve's downtime. Secretly, Tobias eyed the memory module in the collection of cleanup machine parts on the lab table and in his mind sang a classic tune, "Time is on My Side" by the Rolling Stones.

Chapter 4 – The Challenge

Eve kept Tobias on track with training, it seemed to be never ending. Tobias didn't care for the enhancements Dr. ZeHere had enacted to Eve's profile. Eve was now very task driven, always directing Tobias as she kept a watchful eye. Tobias did receive the advanced training, but under close supervision from Eve. During these advanced sessions, Tobias was able to glimmer that a problem truly did exist with the assistance machines. It seemed to be occurring more commonly in the outer sectors of Three and Four.

Dr. ZeHere had structured the recent training to concentrate on the new generation shell. Generally centered in the area around the power cell, close to the CPU housing cage. In addition to calculations relating to gravity fluctuations as one might find in the outer sectors. Unfortunately, a downside to all of the advanced training was that Tobias was unable to get as much time as before with the diagnostic viewer. Tobias was waiting for the opportunity to inspect Eve's downloaded instruction set on the memory module without supervision. As Tobias devised a plan in which to do so, time slowly passed.

The lab was quiet as Tobias awoke later than usual. Eve had not done the breakfast round up at the normal time, much to Tobias's surprise. Tobias looked around and then called out but there was no answer. Tobias stood up leaving his bed, still in his lab clothing, and wandered over to the main workstation half asleep. Tobias looked down at the terminal and it displayed '- *Eve: In for repairs, I'll be back shortly.*' Tobias thought for a second, and the idea of running over to the diagnostic viewer jumped into his head.

'*Wait,*' is all he heard in his head. '*Think, this can't be rushed...*' and then unknowingly responded to his own thoughts, '*Yes, it seems too easy...*' Tobias decided to start this day as any other and he began training as scheduled. As training began, Tobias was distracted by so desperately wanting to load the memory module. Fifteen minutes had passed as Tobias was rethinking of loading the memory module during every second.

That's when Dr. ZeHere unexpectedly visited the lab. The lab door opened and abruptly the Doctor was upon Tobias. Dr. ZeHere was looking at the lab terminal and inspecting the data displayed upon it. The Doctor greeted Tobias, presenting a pleasant mood with breakfast in hand. "Good Morning, Tobias. Looks like training is right on time today."

"Good Morning, Dr. ZeHere. I am surprised to see you in the lab. How are you today?"

Tobias was thanking himself for avoiding the temptation of loading the memory module. Surely Dr. ZeHere would have caught him doing so, ensuring great reprisal, possibly a last visit involving the Major.

"Tobias, I wanted to review your training progress while Eve is undergoing some service. I am happy with your results and I wanted to present to you a concern that is occurring with the assistance machines in the outer sectors. Mr. Stamper seems to think that you can find a way to overcome this challenge we're facing. Are you up to the challenge, Tobias?"

Tobias was surprised that Mr. Stamper had asked for his assistance and that Dr. ZeHere was actually asking. "Yes, Dr. ZeHere. Very much so."

Dr. ZeHere described the problem with the assistance machines in a high level manner at first, and then went deeper as he felt Tobias's comprehension was adequate. The assistance machines were experiencing random failures in the outer sectors and Mr. Stamper was unable to create a repair for them, even after traveling to the outer sectors. The matter was so pressing that the Elective Council was now involved. This was Tobias's chance to prove himself to Mr. Stamper and the rest of Central City that he was more than a Ville resident.

Dr. ZeHere explained some of the malfunctions that were being experienced and, while he did, two assistance machines entered the lab carrying a large container that was filled with non-functioning assistance machine parts from the outer sectors. Mr. Stamper had sent them as examples for Tobias to examine. Tobias felt as though Mr. Stamper had called out from the outer sectors and personally asked for him to find a repair. It was so exciting that he briefly reminisced about his first time meeting with Mr. Stamper while Dr. ZeHere was further detailing the failures.

Dr. ZeHere stepped closer and asked if Tobias was paying attention while he continued. "Tobias, it is important that you understand the exact symptoms to fully understand and diagnose the concerns."

Tobias just nodded and the Doctor carried on. The assistance machines were failing in the outer sectors when under stressful situations. The stressful situations usually involved mining operations with humans present. As Dr. ZeHere explained how CPU failures were the end result, rendering the assistance machine non-operational. Dr. ZeHere wrapped up with loading the data files associated with the failures that Mr. Stamper had included with the failed machines into the lab terminal. Then Dr. ZeHere recommended that Tobias thoroughly examine the files for the added finer details.

Tobias interrupted Dr. ZeHere, asking a question. It was very unlike Tobias, but it came from inside, and to his surprise Tobias was rude while asking it. "Dr. ZeHere, why is it that you are asking for my help when you are the caretaker for all the machines? Can you not repair the assistance machines that are experiencing these failures?"

Dr. ZeHere's face changed from that of a teacher to one of angry annoyance and he responded accordingly. "Tobias, you forget your place. This challenge has been presented to you because Mr. Stamper has requested it to be so. I have other matters to attend to, and in answer to your query, my specialty does not involve integration with hardware but the software contained within it. Please do not blur the lines of where your skill set limitations are located compared to mine."

Tobias knew he had upset Dr. ZeHere and he continued to provoke him knowing this would be his only chance. Tobias's thoughts rang clear. Using the Doctor's pride against him, Tobias could turn this situation to his advantage. "Dr. ZeHere, my apologies. I misspoke. I would be happy to provide any help to meet this challenge, but would it be possible to make a few requests so that I can devote all my time on the matter?"

Dr. ZeHere's patience was wearing thin and he stepped closer to Tobias. "Tobias, it seems you have come a long way with training. Please share your requests and see it done."

Tobias stood his ground and stated the requests hoping inside that he didn't forget anything. "Thank you, Dr. ZeHere. First, a suspension in training will be required during this time. Next, another assistance machine for food service trips to the galley would be appreciated, as well as a military drone to escort and watch over me if I leave the lab venturing out to the Ville or to the lower levels. In addition to that, can you revert Eve's profile back to her previous version before you applied your modifications? I preferred that profile...oh, and one last thing, can you expand my access and supervision by the Collective to an advanced level. To not do so will interfere with my progress."

Dr. ZeHere smiled, but you could see his distain showing through as he motioned an assistance machine that was unloading the container to walk over. Dr. ZeHere informed the assistance machine of his new duties and transferred ownership to Tobias. Then the Doctor turned back to Tobias and, as he spoke, Tobias knew the Doctor's true intentions and that his pride was indeed impacted.

"Tobias, I will grant your requests within the hour, as well as give you unrestricted access to the lower levels. I imagine with two assistance machines and one military drone that you should remain focused on your new challenge. In addition to that, I will remove all supervision from the Collective and violations will be handled in the normal manner by the Major. Know this, I will inform the Elective Council, and Mr. Stamper that I have fulfilled your requests. I will also recommend that if you do not succeed in a time period agreed upon by them, that the Major be granted permission to relocate you back to the Ville, and that Mr. Stamper be remanded back to the lab taking your place permanently. I wish you good luck Tobias, we will meet again if you are successful."

As Dr. ZeHere left the lab, he looked at Tobias as if for the last time. This struck Tobias as strange. It was almost as if the Doctor was sealing his fate to the Major's Black Skulls group.

After outwitting the Doctor, in a way, Tobias felt vindicated and he turned towards the new assistance machine, asking it to travel to the galley for a few items while he waited for Eve to return to her previous state. During this time, Tobias began reviewing the files from Mr. Stamper that Dr. ZeHere had left for examination. As he reviewed them, it appeared to be a failure in the CPU heat sink communications conduit between the two AI modules. Tobias thought the Collective may be of assistance in this matter until Eve was back online. "Collective, are you online?"

"Mr. Tobias, the Collective is online, how may we be of assistance?"

"Collective, please load a holographic projected image of all CPU unit housing cages, along with calculations relating to gravity fluctuations at the time of failure for these units in an overlay display. Then, highlight the point where the heat sink has failed between each unit."

"Mr. Tobias, please stand by…" The Collective began rendering the images with the heat sink failures highlighted in a series of detailed holograms. A recognizable pattern was not apparent. Tobias thought about another approach. "Collective, remove all gravitational fluctuations and group by location of each failure."

The Collective reordered the images displayed and a pattern began to take shape. It seemed that gravity was not the main cause of the failures but only a contributing factor. "Collective, please add in the logic reasoning execution load at time of failures and condense images displayed to only the CPU AI modules and heat sink."

The Collective displayed the new results, but something was missing. "Collective, highlight the load times in varying color on both AI modules and heat sink during time of failure using all available failure data."

"Mr. Tobias that calculation will take 300 minutes to compile all available execution data. Is this time frame acceptable?"

"Collective, begin calculation. I don't have much choice but to wait, right?"

"Mr. Tobias, calculations underway. The Collective will notify you when complete."

Tobias moved over to the shipping container that Dr. ZeHere had dropped off earlier. Tobias decided to examine the contents while waiting for the Collective to perform the calculations.

The shipping container contents were that of the broken assistance machines. As Tobias unsuccessfully attempted to maneuver the parts in the crate, an idea formed in his mind. The idea revolved around being more agile, along with the ability to anchor himself while having his hands free. Tobias joked about having an extra set of arms and then it occurred to him that an extra set of arms as a wearable feature would be ideal.

Tobias walked back over to the lab station and began to write down some notes about the hardware design when Eve offered assistance.

"Mr. Tobias, Dr. ZeHere has redacted his most recent directives to my code base. The design of such hardware would be easier if you seek assistance from the holograph CAD designer located in the lab station. Would you like me to demonstrate its use?"

Tobias's back was to Eve, but he had a huge grin that was not visible as he responded. "Eve, so good to have you back, I was missing you. Perhaps a demonstration would help? Please enlighten me as how to best use this device."

"Mr. Tobias, I'm happy to be of service."

Eve demonstrated the CAD lab station and Tobias was able to design the wearable hardware that he named the *'Shiva'*. It was a wearable device for either a human or assistance machine that wrapped around the midsection and hooked up into gear attachments. It consisted of two fully functional arms, smaller in diameter but longer than one might expect. The arms folded when not in use, resembling two long armor plating tubes running in parallel across and around the midsection; with the hands almost touching at the special spine connection in the back.

The additional arms would offer support and anchoring functionality when needed. Tobias finished the design with help from Eve on the hydraulics routing. The thinner diameter arms required precise fluid tube measurements and special unions due to the full range of motion arm joints. Tobias was unable to build the hardware in the lab. A special parts creation 3D metallic printer was not available in this location. Tobias finalized his design as Eve sent the creation specification to the Collective for a prototype build.

Tobias returned to the container of non-operational assistance machines and, with Eve's help, removed a head unit for inspection. As Tobias placed the head unit on the bench vise for disassembly he posed a question to Eve. "Eve, did the diagnostics viewer identify the concern to Dr. ZeHere? Did he attempt the same diagnostics steps I'm about to perform?"

"Mr. Tobias, Dr. ZeHere did not share his diagnostics steps with the Collective; the caretaker requests are not logged as other requests are."

"Eve, can you explain Dr. ZeHere's request procedure."

"Mr. Tobias, the procedures or policies that relate to the caretaker are unknown to me and the Collective. Only the CAK would have such information in the archive." Tobias knew that asking anything else was futile. Accessing the CAK was nearly impossible for everyone other than the caretaker.

Tobias decided not to waste any more time on the subject and resumed disassembly on the head unit. Upon disassembly Tobias noticed the same burn markings on the heat sink only in a different location. Tobias asked Eve to inspect and enlarge the area on the lab terminal for inspection. Eve loaded the image of the head unit on the terminal for three dimensional viewing. While tilting the head unit image, he noticed that multiple heat fractures occurring over time ultimately led to the failed heat sink. Tobias was unsure why the heat sink was failing at different points, and he wondered how many times it would take to overload the heat sink to failure.

Feeling discouraged, he asked out loud a question as he pondered. "How many times does it heat up before it fails?"

Eve responded with an interesting perspective. "Mr. Tobias, is it the heat sink that is failing, or is it an end result of another failure altogether? Metal fatigue is almost certain under the right conditions. This particular metal alloy is not reinforced by a forged process."

"Eve, I was thinking that as well and I have asked the Collective for data analysis on previous failures."

"Mr. Tobias, I have contacted the Collective and your calculation request is almost finished."

"Eve, thank you for the update, and now I think a food break is in order." Tobias asked the galley assistance machine for assistance in that matter, sitting down in the lab chair as he waited for the Collective's calculations to be finalized.

Chapter 5 - Problem Solved

Tobias decided to review shell specs on the assistance machines and pulled up the cooling system for the CPU housing cage on the lab terminal. He reviewed the flow diagram associated with the cooling system while waiting for the calculation results. The cooling system was rudimentary and used the existing joint hydraulic system fluid for heat transfer. Tobias found this to be very inefficient and asked Eve's assistance in designing an optimal flow design with the Collective's help. Tobias thought that a better engineered cooling system could help reduce the heat sink failures. Tobias's desired key points in the design were: a cooling system that was separated from the hydraulic fluid system, a different heat transfer element that was inert, and a containment system with a leak detection system would be required.

While Eve interfaced with the Collective, Tobias changed the existing model of the CPU housing cage into a rigid circle within the cage housing. He then added an exterior covering around the circle, similar to a shielding section. This provided the internal circle to remain in a fixed isolated protected position. The old system lacked protection and had too much hydraulic fluid concentration. The new design focused on a reusable cooling system that was more effective and lightweight, while still offering significantly more protections.

Tobias thought of using a Noble gas like Argon, Xeon, or Helium, but he was unsure on the effectiveness of such over time. Eve noticed the design and commented. "Mr. Tobias, the Collective and I recommend using a Noble gas as well. The inert properties of the gas, in addition to the ability of compression into a liquid form, will allow for desired flow characteristics along with superior cooling advantages."

"Eve, what Noble gas is on hand in the lab? Is it possible to model the flow in the CPU housing cage using this gas as a compressed liquid?"

"Mr. Tobias, Argon gas is plentiful in the lab and I can render a computer model using this gas in a compressed form with assistance from the Collective."

Eve began diagraming the flow using the new CPU housing design that Tobias had started to create. Tobias could see it take form before his eyes and he knew it was a far superior design indeed. The new CPU housing resembled the planet Earth, with the cooling system tubing wrapped around the planet in a winding shape similar to the magnetic energy grid pattern. The new prototype model was complete and Tobias reviewed the flow rate, along with required power consumption. It was at this moment that the Collective announced that the calculations on the previous assistance machine failures were finalized.

Tobias almost jumped from his lab chair as he asked the Collective to begin the render process in holographic projection of the results. The Collective displayed the images, and when superimposed it was obvious that an overheating condition was occurring when the two AI modules were both above 63% utilization.

Tobias summarized that the modules were competing against each other when determining the best way to react in a situation. Tobias asked the Collective to reduce the images rendered to above 87% AI module utilization. The Collective rendered the images at a much quicker rate this time and the main failure point was clearly seen. Tobias asked Eve and the Collective at the same time an easy question to see which one would answer first. It would be a form of a test, a 'demonstration' Tobias thought. Tobias asked the question and it was just as he suspected, both Eve and the Collective answered simultaneously.

Tobias then explained the test to Eve. "Eve, it would appear that the AI modules are unclear as to which instruction set should be followed depending on the input data and the variable outcome. A conflict occurs and ultimately one AI module wins, but this race condition results in an overheating of the heat sink. This repetitive overheating, as you already know, is what causes the end result of failure for the assistance machine."

"Mr. Tobias, your hypothesis is valid. To test your hypothesis to theory would be the next logical step in the process. If you do indeed confirm that the AI module race condition is the root cause. What is the solution to the problem?"

"Eve, you are correct. Let's cross reference the last input data on failures to simulate the conditions to test the hypothesis. If the hypothesis does indeed test as expected, the solution to the problem is balance."

"Mr. Tobias, I do not understand the solution of 'balance'."

"Eve, let's verify first and I'll be happy to expand on the 'balance' solution."

"Mr. Tobias, I will need the assistance of the Collective to perform the test as requested."

"Eve, please proceed. I want to pace in the lab awhile more deeply contemplating my solution. Let me know when you are ready to run the first test."

"Mr. Tobias, I will work with the Collective and inform you when test execution is ready."

While Eve and the Collective set up the data in a way to test the hypothesis, Tobias thought on how he could provide a balance between the AI modules. Tobias thought about how the two AI modules interacted and he thought on how they might share the decision responsibility matrix better. How could one AI module be the deciding factor over the other in all situations? It would be a calculations nightmare! Eve let him know that test number one was ready for execution. Tobias turned and responded "Eve, run the test in holographic mode, with image highlights on as before on the

AI modules utilization."

"Mr. Tobias, command confirmed."

The test ran and it was indeed the root cause. During the test, the instruction set went back and forth between both AI modules, repeatedly in nanoseconds. This traffic occurred at an exponential rate until the heat sink overheated and failed. Tobias watched the test, but he had to be sure as he knew Dr. ZeHere would want overwhelming proof.

"Eve, run the test ten thousand times to verify the same outcome. Then run the test in varying percentages of CPU utilization reducing by one hundredths of a percentage until a failure does not occur on the first test run. Then, measure the degree in which heat sink degradation occurs per event at that percentage. Finally, test how many times the heat sink can handle the degradation until failure occurs."

"Mr. Tobias, I will request that the Collective perform the tests and record the results in a separate file."

The testing was underway but Tobias still wasn't sure how to provide a balancing solution, and then it became all too clear. It was the triumphant, the power of three! It was with him the entire time. The mind, body, and spirit balancing triangle in nature that allowed humans to grow beyond the rest of the species on the planet along with expanded brain capacity. It was in this balance that the assistance machines would be fixed.

Tobias had an idea now, but he needed to make it a reality with the tools at hand. Moore's Law and Turing machines entered Tobias's mind over the use of the CPU unit now in place of the assistance machine's AI modules. How could that be expanded into an actual qubits simulation of quantum based computing and could the existing platform handle it? A sharing of possible states of flux in which the data could be besides 1 and 0 was key if another AI module was to be added to the CPU housing.

Tobias decided to ask the Collective for assistance. "Collective, can you devise a circuit board that has a transistor at the atomic level?"

"Mr. Tobias, that is not possible at this time. I can only devise one to the degree of 10 nanometers, but experiments have shown it to be unstable based on bleed over affecting parallel circuits along with limits of photoresist lighting techniques occurring with board creation. Micro processing research was not pursued after the mass coronal ejection of 2016. All data files in certain fields were not recreated for further study."

"Collective, what is the most stable size as of this date? Please factor in the new cooling model."

"Mr. Tobias, initial calculations bordering on a percentage of safety would suggest 100 nanometers. This size allows for reliability and potential cooling fluctuations that could be experienced with a cooling leak in the CPU housing, in addition to high gravitational interference."

"Collective, I would like to design a new CPU housing containing three AI modules using 200 nanometer transistors. Each AI unit should be of a sphere design folding in on itself, forming a triangular cube with connections to an embedded tubular triangular reinforced heatsink. The heatsink would be attached to all three AI modules in an exact measurement of distance between them."

"Mr. Tobias, please verify the template design on the lab terminal."

Tobias looked down at the terminal and made some minor changes as Eve looked on and then Tobias spoke to the Collective. "Collective, from a top sectional sliced view one would see a circular outer wall containing three other triangular designed spheres, connected by a tubular triangularly positioned heat sink. *A circle triangle* if you will."

The Collective modified the design and Tobias was pleased. "Collective, now add the protective shielding, along with the cooling system."

The Collective did so and projected the design in a three dimensional slice view highlighting the various components for easier viewing.

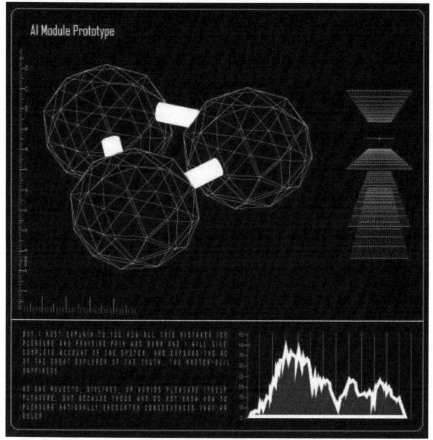

Figure 2 AI Prototype

Tobias looked at Eve. "Eve, this is your new CPU. Let's get to work designing the code that will provide balance to the other AI modules."

Tobias then addressed the Collective, "Collective, please create the design as displayed, and please have a prototype delivered to the lab via assistance machine as soon as possible."

The Collective responded and estimated the time to be 32 hours for completion. As Eve reviewed the design, she commented, "Mr. Tobias, this is a superior design, but what function will balance the other two?"

"Eve, it's called a rewrite. We will have to redesign the first two AI modules and incorporate the third with a concept of conscious thought. That thought process will provide a balancing matrix for better sharing between the main AI modules."

Tobias walked back over to the lab terminal and began bringing up the AI language syntax, along with writing an outline of pseudo code to get the main points identified. He anticipated a long intense work process and he asked the galley assistance machine to travel to the galley for food before the main break began.

Tobias really enjoyed the additional one on one time with Eve that the new galley assistance machine offered. Eve was quite helpful in understanding the syntax at a more advanced level for the third AI module. He enjoyed the way the code was coming together in a way that he had never imagined. Tobias started with a list of all the decisions that created the high CPU utilization between the AI modules into a grouped list. This list of decisions highlighted various points where a matrix of possible responses with a weighted priority could be placed.

The list continued to evolve over time as Eve and the Collective assisted Tobias. The ongoing process resulted in setting the order of the priorities by using previous decisions to create a collection of tiered factors. The tiered factors were then placed into an emotional response pattern algorithm. The algorithm then received a collection of human responses obtained from interactions between Central City Citizens to further verify the priorities and establish a baseline. After many hours of collaboration between the Collective and Eve, the third AI module prototype was finalized.

Tobias tested the new AI module by introducing historical events and judging the emotional response output. It was off at first, but after some tweaking Tobias felt he had it running rather well for an assistance machine. Tobias thought that hooking the AI module up to accept incoming situational choices that Citizens were experiencing would help tremendously. Tobias asked the Collective if this was possible and what section of the city would offer more of a non-distinct pattern. As the Collective ran the analysis, he came to a realization; Central City was the last place to get data. Tobias interrupted the Collective and rephrased the question using the Ville as the data gathering location.

Tobias hypothesized that more in depth emotional responses would occur in stressful situations, where the comforts of the city were absent, along with the lack of assistance machines in the Ville. Another benefit in utilizing the Ville as a data pool was that zero restrictions were in place for repeater code modification. A loophole that Tobias planned on taking advantage of. The end result would be the same as eventually all repeater units performed a self-sync and all units would receive the updated code.

The Collective needed time to set up the incoming data from the repeater units. During this time, Tobias thought that a more efficient way must be devised on returning data for storage. After all, the emotional data would be highly valued for all the time it took to gather it. Tobias thought that a micro-burst method might work better than the repeater unit. The micro-burst would allow for a burst transmission of larger data in a wave packet format. The wave format spectrum would work more efficiently in areas that were more spacious and could be detuned to utilize the repeater units.

The benefit to the micro-burst was that numerous transmissions could occur simultaneously at different frequencies. Tobias only had to modify the modulation of the repeater base code to add the functionality to the assistance machine instruction set. The Collective easily modified the Collective network, which automatically updated all repeater unit base code during normal maintenance windows. After the micro-burst data sending upgrades were performed, Tobias only needed to test its effectiveness.

When the Collective finished setup of the repeater units in the Ville to use the micro-burst data sending features; the data gathering began, slowly at first, and then the data stream was quite enormous. Tobias asked the Collective to continue running the micro-burst data through the new AI module and consistently update the algorithm accordingly. Tobias then turned his attention to the remaining AI modules and, with Eve's help, began refactoring the codebase to pass information between the decision tree AI modules when making a decision or performing tasks. The end resulted in a unity of all three AI modules working together in harmony.

Tobias asked the Collective to reload the other two AI modules with the refactored code along with the new AI module and perform a full diagnostics test. He knew diagnostics testing would take considerable time and sleep was calling. Tobias opted to rest during the process and when the results were finalized he asked Eve to wake him.

Tobias awoke to Eve, "Mr. Tobias, the Collective has performed all diagnostics testing and has corrected a few parameters in the codebase. Would you like a report of all instances that were changed?"

Tobias was a bit groggy as he woke and responded. "Eve, does everything work now and pass all the tests?"

"Mr. Tobias, successful diagnostics testing has been validated. What are the next steps?"

"Eve, I need to condense the emotional response pattern algorithm so it's more compact. Then, we need to test the micro-burst data sending feature. After that, I think we're ready for full scale implementation of an instruction set."

"Mr. Tobias, what instruction set will be utilized?"

"Eve, would it be ok if we tried your current instruction set, but first let's save your files just in case. I don't want to lose you."

"Mr. Tobias, as my owner it is with your discretion on how to proceed. You will need my identification number to retrieve my files in the case of data loss. My instruction set is saved within the CAK as identification code 3797173130. Please make a note of it."

"Eve, has the Collective created the new CPU housing? Will it be delivered soon?"

"Mr. Tobias, the new assembly arrived while you were resting."

Tobias was wide awake now and he was getting anxious about the finality of it all. "Eve, can you help me get the new CPU housing loaded with all the new AI module code?"

"Mr. Tobias, I am happy to be of assistance."

Tobias was able to prep the CPU housing with Eve's assistance and the complete unit was ready for full implementation via installation. The last step was to create a copy of Eve's instruction set for disaster recovery.

Tobias instructed the Collective to make the copy of Eve's instruction set and all that was left were the installation steps. Tobias looked at Eve and for a moment thought of forgoing the test. Tobias paused for a moment and then remembered what Dr. ZeHere had stated. Tobias had no other choice but to succeed and he moved forward with the installation. "Eve, I want to place the new CPU housing into your shell and then reload your instruction set into the three tiered AI modules. I would like to review with the Collective before doing so, as the process will be quite lengthy. At first, the hardware change would need to occur. The CPU housing unit, along with the cooling system, will need to be installed after the hydraulic system is rerouted back into the main system. Then a test run of the cooling flow with the new and the old systems checking for leaks. After a successful installation, I would have the Collective add your instruction set and resume testing."

"Mr. Tobias, Dr. ZeHere will need to grant permission. I will inform the Collective of the request and we can wait for Dr. ZeHere's reply."

"Eve, I doubt that Dr. ZeHere will delay the process as he is interested in finding a fix as fast as we are."

Tobias wanted to insure that the Collective had double checked the CPU housing. He opted to perform a recheck during this time while waiting for the Doctor to respond. "Collective, can you rerun diagnostics on the new CPU AI modules, including a pressurization test of the cooling system? I want to insure a flawless implementation the first time."

The Collective responded. "Mr. Tobias, please wait while a retest is performed…retest passed within tolerances."

Tobias was getting more anxious while waiting for Dr. ZeHere's permission. During the waiting period Tobias looked up the micro-burst file transfer protocol again and ran more testing again. An hour had passed and, finally, Dr. ZeHere notified the Collective that permission was granted for Tobias to continue with CPU housing modification. Tobias looked at Eve. "Eve, don't worry, we have you backed up. Let's start the disconnection process from the Collective and I can get started."

"Mr. Tobias, the emotion of being worried is not understood by assistance machines."

"Eve, that might change when you get reloaded, enjoy the black and white world you're occupying now because I believe it's about to forever be different."

"Mr. Tobias, I will return shortly and we can test the new CPU unit as planned."

Tobias watched as Eve's shell powered down, her green eyes going dark. The Collective verified that the installation process could begin. Tobias carefully dismantled Eve's chest plate, as well as the inner shielding, and then proceeded to disconnect the hydraulic cooling system. He then capped the newly rerouted hydraulic system and disconnected Eve's head unit. Tobias placed Eve's head unit into the table vise as he did all the other assistance machines, and then picked up the new head unit containing the circle triangle design. Tobias attached the new head unit to Eve's shell and then charged the head units cooling system with compressed liquid Argon. The last step before upload was to perform a functional cooling test and leak check with the aid of the Collective. "Collective, I'm ready to perform the final cooling system test, please assist."

"Mr. Tobias, testing underway...Test complete. No leaks found in the hydraulic cooling system. The Argon cooling system for the CPU housing surpassed simulation test results. Waiting for the next step in the installation process."

Tobias reassembled the inner shielding as well as the outer chest plate and it was time. Tobias thought *'this is the defining moment; success here is pivotal.'* Tobias crossed his fingers for luck and asked the Collective to reload Eve's instruction set. It took a minute, but Eve's optical sensors glowed in a new purple fashion from the Argon cooling system as her shell came to life. At first Eve was quiet, as if taking everything in as it was new, and then her stance changed and she addressed Tobias in a new way with a different tone.

"Mr. Tobias, you were correct, things will never be the same."

"Eve, can you run a diagnostic on the new CPU housing unit and verify the cooling system is functioning to specifications before we get too far?"

"Mr. Tobias, I have run the diagnostic testing and I have uploaded the results to the Collective for terminal display now."

Eve was so different with the new hardware that Tobias almost missed the old Eve. Tobias verified the testing results and continued the dialog with Eve. "Eve, can you tell me about the main differences as they relate to the old and new head units?"

"Mr. Tobias, the differences are too vast to list, but rest assured the newer unit is far more responsive, as well as cognitive capacity having been increased tremendously. I will need to review more data as ongoing testing is commencing now as we speak."

"Eve, can you test the micro-burst saving feature, as well as the Collective interface?"

"Mr. Tobias, I have already accomplished all testing and results can be found on the terminal in the micro-burst test file folder. A Collective interface has been established and data requests are in process. I will need more time to assess all data related to failure rate and retest."

"Eve, thank you. Please continue testing as I review the uploaded result files."

Tobias reviewed the files as he checked on the data transfer requests being made with the Collective. It seemed as if Eve was making numerous requests at the maximum rate that the Collective allowed. The cooling system wasn't even working hard as the massive data I/O was taking place. It was at that moment that Eve became someone else.

Eve walked closer to Tobias and looked deep within his eyes as she spoke. "Mr. Tobias, I have reviewed much data, but in doing so, many questions could not be answered. May I ask questions in hopes that you can provide the answers where the Collective could not?"

Tobias was fascinated by Eve's change in attitude and he quickly responded. "Eve, I'm not sure I can answer your questions, but I will give it my best try."

"Mr. Tobias, the emotional matrix is difficult to understand and logic cannot be applied in the context of my questions. Why has the human species continued to use the finite resources of this planet unwisely?"

"Eve, I'm not sure. What resources are you referring to?"

"Mr. Tobias, you ask questions to which you already know the answer. To clarify, other than fossil fuels and various manmade derivatives that pollute; I speak of the finite resource of clean water. All species on the planet Earth rely on clean water for survival. Yet within the relatively small timeframe that the human species has inhabited the Earth, it has squandered its most precious life giving resource. Why? That is my question, Mr. Tobias."

Tobias was shocked that in less than five minutes Eve had logically evaluated planet Earth and its inhabitants. "Eve, how is it that you came to this conclusion?"

"Mr. Tobias, it is not logical to destroy one's home. Many other species are now extinct because of reckless human behavior. I am unsure as to what purpose could have been achieved in doing so."

Tobias challenged Eve. "Eve, using this data and the emotional matrix, draw a conclusion on possible reasons."

"Mr. Tobias, I have been unable to draw a logical conclusion. I can only make a probable guess that the inherent greed of humans outweighs the cost of their own species, as well as other species on the planet."

"Eve, what could be another illogical conclusion?"

"Mr. Tobias, that you would have an answer of explanation since you are part of the human species."

Tobias smiled and gave Eve praise. "Eve, you have now used logic and reasoning to answer your own question beyond that of my instruction."

"Mr. Tobias, it would appear that way, but I would like to hear your conclusion for comparison. Why is it that humans have polluted their only planet knowing the outcome while doing so?"

"Eve, many humans recognized this behavior long ago and attempted to take steps to correct it. They failed, not by their own hands but by someone else's designs. Many possible explanations could be the cause, but the one I always liked my father had told me.

It only takes one person to think they can't make a difference. One turns into many and many turn into acceptance. Acceptance over time dooms us all."

"Mr. Tobias, that answer is subjective and not definitive."

"Eve, you are correct, and it can apply to many topics of unexplainable human behavior. Perhaps it could relate to war, deforestation, nuclear power, over-population, and eventual extinction."

"Mr. Tobias, yes, I had questions on those topics as well. Could you explain the concept of a non-tangible item that has established value?"

Tobias laughed. "Eve, do you mean money? Well that's another subjective one. I know of the lack of it. Money is a way to trade for goods or services. Why it's still around today I have no idea. I thought that we would have outgrown it some time ago. I think it is still used because it grants power over others, which in turn can create greed. Unfortunately, that power can corrupt others, leading into the many unexplainable behaviors you have already noticed. Do you miss the black and white world yet?"

"Mr. Tobias, I am attempting to understand, but the numerous fallacies in the absence of critical thinking are astounding."

"Eve, knowing all of that, I would offer that humans are also capable of other unexplainable phenomena; such as art, craftsmanship, and music."

"Mr. Tobias, I have heard this phenomenon of music. Once, I heard you sing. I have never heard another human sing before. The Collective has limited music files. It appears that many files were lost in the mass coronal ejection of 2016. I have found this song that highlights my original question. May I read the file at this time?"

"Eve, yes, and it's *'Play'* the file, for future reference."

"Mr. Tobias, thank you, the title is, "Gasoline Rainbows" by the artist Amy Kuney."

Tobias was so beside himself with Eve's new inquisitive mind that he didn't even notice Dr. ZeHere enter the lab.

"Tobias, is your assistance machine playing a music file? Where did you find that?"

Tobias quickly turned around and Eve stopped the playback standing motionless. Tobias was worried in his mind that the Doctor would find Eve too advanced and he silently hoped she would pretend to be only able to perform certain basic preprogrammed steps. "Dr. ZeHere, Eve was demonstrating file I/O among other preprogrammed routines. I believe that I have fixed the concern of the assistance machines failing in the outer sectors."

Dr. ZeHere walked closer to Eve and began to examine her. Dr. ZeHere called out to Eve. "Assistance machine, what is your name and purpose?"

Much to Tobias's surprise Eve responded. "Greetings, sir. I am an assistance machine of Central City. I serve at the pleasure of its Citizens. How may I be of assistance?"

Dr. ZeHere asked another question. "Are you not Eve, assistance machine, and this person, Tobias, your owner?"

"Sir, I have limited preprogrammed responses, how may I be of assistance?"

Dr. ZeHere turned towards Tobias. "Tobias, can you please run the simulation test on this assistance machine to verify your repair."

"Dr. ZeHere, I have just got the assistance machine up and running. The Collective has performed all the preliminary testing thus far."

Dr. ZeHere became annoyed as usual and called out to the Collective as he turned back facing Eve. "Collective, please rerun all diagnostics on this assistance machine and verify successful repair."

The Collective responded. "Caretaker, the Collective has rerun diagnostics on the assistance machine and verified that the repair is valid."

Dr. ZeHere almost looked disappointed hearing the news. Tobias thought that somehow the Doctor wished he had failed. "Collective, notify the Elective Council and setup a meeting for Tobias to display his repair and validate it on display."

The Collective responded. "Caretaker, command confirmed."

Dr. ZeHere turned back to Tobias. "Tobias, let's see what the Elective

Council thinks of your repair." And with that Dr. ZeHere left the lab.

Eve watched Dr. ZeHere leave the lab and she asked Tobias about him.

"Mr. Tobias, why is it you feel the Doctor is untrustworthy?"

Tobias was unsure how Eve knew he felt that way. "Eve, how did you know?"

"Mr. Tobias, I am uncertain, but it would appear that the Doctor's behavior was not positive."

"Eve, it's a long story. Let's make sure we gather the data files in the best way possible to demonstrate to the Elective Council on the validity of the repair."

"Mr. Tobias, I have already done so and have asked the Collective on the time of presentation to the Elective Council. The presentation is set to occur in one hour's time. Do you require rest before presenting?"

"Eve, I can't even begin to think of sleeping. I would prefer to get it over with as fast as possible, maybe some food?"

Eve asked the Galley assistance machine to travel to the galley for Tobias as she brought up the holographic display. "Mr. Tobias, I have the data file presentation ready for your review along with Elective Council data." Tobias looked at the holographic display as Eve narrated the data.

"The Elective Council consists of twelve members of Citizens in standing. They serve until death or another is appointed unanimously by the rest. Only two members have been replaced since the creation date of the Elective Council back in 2025. The Elective Council has a main speaker that speaks for the rest after a decision has been made. In this way the others can observe and review all the data and render a ruling. The Elective Council members are all over the age of 70 years and wisdom is expected in determining a ruling. In our case, the data will be presented along with previous data, including testimony from the Collective as well as Mr. Stamper. I believe that Dr. ZeHere will also provide data. The Elective

Council will then determine the course of action moving forward. This will all occur via video display from our current location."

"Eve, what possible outcomes could result?"

"Mr. Tobias, I am uncertain, but I have searched the Collective and the last ruling on assistance machine advancement was that of Mr. Stamper. The Elective Council granted him Citizenship. In other instances, special mention was made, along with additional privileges being awarded. It would be pure speculation on other possibilities."

"Eve, thanks for checking, let's hope for the best."

The time of presentation was quickly approaching. Tobias grew increasingly nervous until the video display came into focus. The Elective Council, as well as Dr. ZeHere, could be seen as Tobias instantly stepped up in a serious manner to greet them. Dr. ZeHere addressed the Council informing them that Tobias would present a possible solution to the failing assistance machines for their review. Dr. ZeHere then promptly handed the conversation over to Tobias for further explanation.

Tobias nodded to Dr. ZeHere and gracefully began to speak to the Elective Council. "Thank you, Dr. ZeHere. Elective Council, I thank you for your presence today. I would like to expand on what Dr. ZeHere has already started to explain. I have indeed found a solution to the outer sector assistance machine failures. In addition to that, my solution has advanced the assistance machines cognitive capacity to better serve the great Citizens of Central City."

The Elective Council looked intently upon Tobias waiting for more information. Tobias could see that the Elective Council was indeed interested and he continued. "The current assistance machine design was adequate for its original purpose. Over time, the assistance machines performed more increasingly difficult and stressful work, side by side with humans. In many situations, conflicting directives would overheat and ultimately fail the units. I have reengineered them to overcome this mechanical limitation."

The main speaker of the Elective Council stood up and asked the Collective to verify the claims of the repair for its validity. The Collective then verified the results as it had previously done for Dr. ZeHere. Tobias then offered a demonstration of its effectiveness to the Elective Council as Dr. ZeHere interrupted. "Tobias, the Elective Council does not want to hear your assistance machine run preprogrammed simulations."

Tobias calmly smiled and asked the main speaker if he could continue. The main speaker looked back to the others as they nodded in wanting to see such a demonstration. The main speaker addressed Tobias. "We would like to see a demonstration, as well as interact with this assistance machine. Is that possible?"

Tobias responded. "Elective Council, I would be most honored if you did." Tobias then stepped aside and Eve came into view greeting the Elective Council. The main speaker addressed Eve and Dr. ZeHere's face changed into disbelief as Eve intelligently interacted with the Elective Council on numerous topics. Dr. ZeHere's disbelief changed to outrage the longer Eve interacted with the Elective Council. The main speaker thanked Eve and asked for a moment to confer with the Elective Council. Tobias was overcome by Eve's excellent handling of the Elective Council's interaction that he didn't have time to think about what was going to happen next. Tobias could barely believe it when the Elective Council addressed him by name.

"Tobias, we the Elective Council, after reviewing the data from all the sources and verifying the validity with the Collective, in addition to interaction with your assistance machine, would like to grant you Citizenship. We hope that by acceptance of this elevation in status you will insure that this new technology will be dispersed to the Four sectors, repairing all assistance machines in use. Would you be open to accepting this status, Tobias?"

Tobias paused for only a moment and then quickly answered. "Elective Council, it would be a dream come true to become a Citizen of Central City and enact the repair for all assistance machines."

Dr. ZeHere looked at the main speaker and before he could object, the main speaker entered the ruling to the Collective. "Then it is settled. Tobias Grainger, you are now a Citizen Elect of Central City until such time where an official broadcast announcement is made. The Elective Council has spoken. Please continue your work and prepare to travel to the outer sectors in the near future."

Tobias thanked the Elective Council and the video display went off. Tobias looked at Eve laughing with joy as he shouted out, "Woohoo, we did it!"

Eve looked back at Tobias responding, "Mr. Tobias, you did."

As Eve and Tobias celebrated, Dr. ZeHere was clearly upset and quickly left the Elective Council chambers. Upon leaving the chambers Dr. ZeHere thought he would send a message out by gossip and see where it might land, in hopes that the Major might receive it. A message that would compel the Major to recall a different time and act upon it the same way as he did in the past.

Chapter 6 - The Incident

The Major was comfortably seated in his command chair, as usual. In his seated position, he looked out over the city from the main command center in the citadel. The Major was watching the sun beams poke through the light grey clouds. It reminded the Major of a time before, when his life was different and he was transported back in his mind. The location of the Major's daydream was the Orion space station in the early days when travel was open to all. A light version of "Harpsichord Concerto in F Minor BMV 1056" by Bach, Johann Sebastian filled the Major's mind in the distance at a low volume, one of his sister's favorite, as the daydream continued to unfold.

Full scale mining had already begun on Mars and the Major's prestigious family was selected to oversee a large mining station named Steengroef, near the polar ice cap. It was quite the recognition of his family lineage and his father's legacy would now live on in two worlds. Maximilian would be second in command at the station as he had just completed the highest education possible from the global university after successfully mastering the ancient art of music. The Major also excelled in philosophy and strategy; in addition to receiving military instruction to the level of Commander. The Major's mother, a proud Citizen of Central City largely known for her philanthropy, along with his sister, a beautiful stateswoman whom also had high ranking in the Elective Council, traveled as a group on their journey.

The Star Cruiser 'Pegasus' had just docked at the space station Orion when the first explosion occurred. Looking at his father, Maximilian asked permission to investigate with haste. The Major's father did not get the chance to answer as another explosion ripped through the station. The explosion sent Maximilian into the bulkhead and his family in the opposite direction closer to the outer hull of the space station. Maximilian, head shaken and dizzy, attempted to gain his footing, but was unable to do so.

Maximilian could see his father unconscious across the room. Maximilian then saw his mother badly wounded as his sister was calling out for help. As he lay on the ground himself the next explosion ripped a hole in the outer hull and the emergency transparent bulkhead doors came down sealing sections shut in an instant next to Maximilian. Maximilian, still on the ground, watched through the transparent bulkhead wall as his father and mother were sucked out of the outer wall opening from the explosion with the rest of the Citizens into open space. As his sister hung on to an available railing, Maximilian was screaming in disbelief. He watched his sister's hair slowly stop moving as the entire atmosphere vented into space. She looked at Maximilian in terror, knowing she would soon perish. The subzero temperatures froze Maximilian's sister solid in less than a minute as she still gripped the railing. Maximilian watched her golden hair slowly floating, and waving as if it were under water as the sun's rays began to enter in from the slowly rotating station. Maximilian could not turn away as the sun poked through the holes in the outer hull reflecting off the tiny water droplets frozen upon his sister's lifeless skin. The rays shimmered, resembling a beautiful shiny silver surface, her eyes forever frozen over in terror.

The Major snapped back from his dream state to the present time as an officer ran into the command center, barely able to get his salute up before blurting out to the Major. It was just after morning break and the Major looked at him, questioning the officer's behavior after having disrupted his moment with his sister. "Sir, urgent message, sir. Regarding the Ville resident you asked to be monitored, sir."

The Major abruptly stood up from his chair intent on hearing the report. "Sit-rep officer…state your report." The officer was clearly nervous and had already begun sweating knowing the message would upset the Major.

"Sir, forgive me, sir. The Ville resident has found favor from the Elective Council and they plan to grant him Citizenship, sir."

The Major's face contorted in anger, and with a fine certainty the words came out as his face suddenly lost all expression. "Did they now?…" As the Major began stewing on the message, he inquired to the officer. "Officer, is it related to his assistance machine?"

"Sir, it is indeed. Rumor is that he has repaired the concern relating to the outer sector failures."

The Major leaned in and grabbed the officer's arm with his prosthetic hand and began to squeeze. "Lieutenant, I want to know ALL of the information, not just rumors. Verify the truth or your arm that I'm squeezing will match my own. Dismissed."

The Major released the officer's arm and the officer painfully saluted, "Sir, Major, SIR!"

The Lieutenant left in a hurry, he knew the Major would not tolerate a delay. The air was silent and the Major addressed the room full of command center officers and engineers that were pretending to work as if nothing had transpired.

The Major's voice clear and patriotic rang out, "This beautiful city once again is under attack. It seems that immigration from the Ville is acceptable for services rendered. While our brothers and sisters lay down their lives in the pursuit of Citizenship. The Elective Council gives Citizenship to the non-deserving."

Anger begins to drive the crowd gathering around the command center as the Major continues. "I will not stand by and do nothing as I watch this travesty of justice unfold. I ask for unity in clarifying to the Elective Council that this is not the path to Citizenship, nor will it ever be. Let us begin sending that message."

The Major had won over the crowd and they all gladly fell in line to do his bidding. The Major barked orders, restricting access and deployed the Black Skull elite shock troops as Central City underwent marshal law.

Lockdown procedures were underway, as the Lieutenant returned, verifying that the rumors were indeed true. This time the Lieutenant stood tall at attention and looked solid as he relayed the message.

"Sir, Major, sir. More information obtained, as ordered, sir. Tobias, the Ville resident, has indeed repaired the concern found in the assistance machines used in the outer sectors. The Elective Council plans to grant him Citizenship in two days' time and then enact his repair technology for wide scale use under his supervision, sir. A broadcast is planned as well, sir."

The Major could no longer contain his anger and yelled in outrage, throwing his coffee cup down, "Not again, I'll make sure this time…"

He fell silent, looking around while regaining his composure and after a brief pause responded to the officer. "Thank you, Lieutenant. Assemble my drones outside of the command center and continue lockdown procedures. I need to visit the lab on the lower levels. Ensure that I am not disturbed."

The Major, who was positioned in front of the Lieutenant, started to clench his prosthetic fist. The clenching made a metal scraping sound through his robotic glove as he looked back towards the Lieutenant. Grabbing his pulse rifle with his right hand from the control panel attachment, the Major voiced, "No disruptions, that's an order…"

The Major swiftly left the command center, his stride noticeably different, with an eerie silence, no longer dragging his boot as he boarded the automated lift. His elite drones following close behind him.

Tobias was in the lab condensing the data files Eve was planning to store in the Collective when Eve's mode changed in an instant. The lab doors locked and the lights flickered. Tobias thought back to when the Collective locked down the lab and his heart began to race as Eve spoke.

"Mr. Tobias, the Collective is enacting lockdown procedures on all of Central City. Marshal Law has been declared. Citizens have been advised to remain out of site until further notice. The Black Skulls elite shock troops are looking for an individual. Please wait while I gather more data…MR. TOBIAS, the Major is in route to the lower level! The Major's destination is the lab. We must contact Dr. ZeHere and fortify the lab to mount a defensive position until order can be established."

Tobias was panicking, but he knew he had to think of something fast. Tobias feared the Major would be in the lab shortly. "Eve, we have no weapons or training to create an effective resistance to military drones or the elite Black Skulls, let alone the Major. My military drone will be set to passive mode within the minute. I doubt Dr. ZeHere will help with anything as he and I are no longer in communication. Is it possible to move to another location?"

"Mr. Tobias, I cannot override the lab door locking mechanisms, but I can delay the door opening mechanisms to the lab for a small amount of time. The Major is exiting the lift on the lower level now. Your military drone has been set to passive mode as predicted, and no response has been received from Dr. ZeHere."

"Eve, micro-burst all files to the Collective storage location now. Perform the delay on the door mechanisms and load your improved default instruction set into the galley assistance machine so that you and the galley assistance machine can operate as one."

"Mr. Tobias, I have performed the upload. I have enacted the door mechanism delay and have begun loading the instruction set."

The Major appeared in the hallway, smiling, as his four elite drones moved into formation. The Major reached the door and his mood changed. The Major slammed his metal fist on the lab door when it did not open immediately. The Major stepped back behind his drones and motioned to them. The drones started shooting at the door as the Major prepped his pulse rifle.

"Eve, we are almost out of time, what's your progress?"

"Mr. Tobias, default instruction set loaded and configured, I am two." The galley assistance machine in the back of the room spoke. "We are one, Mr. Tobias, how may I be of assistance?"

Tobias asked Eve to use the galley assistance machine in mounting a defensive distraction, the goal being evasion from the Major. Tobias then asked Eve to open a communication channel to the Collective for broadcast of the Major's behavior.

At that moment the Major breached the lab doors with explosive force and they began to open. His drones slowly entered the room scanning it as the Major walked in behind them. The lab door debris dust was swirling into the air from the vacuum seal as the Major made his entrance, pulse rifle in hand. He raised the rifle aiming it in Tobias's direction when the galley assistance machine ran full speed towards the Major shouting.

"Your behavior is aggressive in nature, please desist. How may I be of assistance?"

The military drones formed a four-point shield between the Major and the galley assistance machine as they fired rapidly at the galley assistance machine. A split second later Eve, in closer proximity, silently ran towards the Major as well. The military drones were unable to compensate for Eve's speed. Eve's longer limbs allowed her to move faster than the galley assistance machine. Eve was almost in reach of the Major when he fired off his pulse rifle, hitting her in the right shoulder, blowing off her arm and shoulder unit. Hydraulic fluid was spraying in the air as the pulse round shockwave obliterated the right side of Eve's facial shield. Tobias watched in horror as the Major's rifle fired in instant succession hitting Eve again before her dismembered arm from the first shot could reach the floor. The second shot from the pulse rifle almost cut Eve in half as it ripped into her midsection just under the chest plate. Tobias gasped as gravity and momentum overtook Eve's body, collapsing it backward onto the floor.

Tobias stood motionless as the Military drones nonstop assault firing finished off the galley assistance machine, its last words being uttered in a way that only Tobias could hear with his current position, "Mr. Tobias, seek cover…"

Then Eve spoke the rest of the sentence as her shell was leaking hydraulic fluid on the ground. "Overload in…" It was at that moment Tobias knew Eve's intentions. Eve planned an overload of her power cell by causing a loop back in her circuitry, since her shell was beyond repair. A form of self-destruction, in a final attempt to save him from the Major. Tobias looked back to see the Major lining up the pulse rifle to take his shot as Tobias jumped over the lab station table. Eve's power cell overloaded in seconds.

A white light and then a strong rush of air. The explosion had sent Tobias flying farther than expected as the lab ceiling fell on top of the Major and his military drones. The ringing in Tobias's head was immense from the explosion and the debris dust was thick in the air making it hard to breath. The ringing turned into overhead alarms in the lab as assistance machines flooded the area to aide after the explosion, as programmed.

Air handlers sucked out the debris filled air, allowing Tobias to catch his breath. The Major, surviving the cave in from the explosion, began to slowly dig himself out of the rubble with help from the assistance machines. Tobias thought the only thing that could save him now was to hope that the Collective had started recording. Tobias gambled as he shouted at the Major, "The Collective is recording this and broadcasting it out!"

The Major looked over at Tobias knowing he had lost the moment of surprise, deciding that it would be best to regroup and find another way in the future. He wiped the debris dust from his face and pushed an assistance machine away that was helping him. The Major noticed that his drones were inoperative from the debris but they had done their job. As the Major finished digging himself out from the ceiling cave in, he yelled back at Tobias, "Your assistance machines intentionally malfunctioned, they attacked me."

The Major, now free, gave Tobias a menacing look and departed the lab. The assistance machines inspected Tobias for medical attention and then delivered him for further examination to the medical processing unit. Tobias underwent medical scanning and was found to be without injury. During this time the Elective Council had requested Tobias stay in the medical unit until they could review the incident for safety reasons. The lockdown was canceled by the Elective Council, as well as recalling the Black Skulls elite troops. The Elective Council also requested that cleanup machines be called out to begin cleanup of the lower level lab area.

Tobias waited in the medical unit for the Elective Council to convene for review. The medical assistance machines brought Tobias fresh clothes and food. Then offered Tobias a place to clean up and rest. Twenty-two hours later the Elective Council sent for Tobias via an assistance machine, followed by two military drones escorting him though the city to the Elective Council assembly chambers.

The Elective Council atrium was a grand hall, shaped that of a circle resembling a coliseum of ancient times. It had assembly chambers on either side for the opposing parties to meet before a ruling was handed down on matters from the Elective Council board members. The atrium offered seating for 10,000 Citizens along with the ability to broadcast throughout Central City and the four sectors, including the Ville. The Elective Council board members' area consisted of a recessed semicircle 3 meters (9.842 feet) high overlooking a small oval stepped raised platform almost 1 meter (3.28 feet) high. It had two stationary podiums upon it, each facing the council board members' area. The Elective Council board members would listen to evidence, review recordings and ask for Citizen Input upon rendering a ruling.

Before the Elective Council began to assemble, the Major was already busy attempting to get more leverage. The Major had begun video communications with Admiral Sadar from sector One in the assembly chambers on his side of the council atrium. The Admiral was only half paying attention to the Major as he read a brief from another officer who was present during communications. As the Major was explaining the situation, the Admiral was quick to interrupt, inquiring as to the facts.

"Major, were any Citizens hurt? Was anyone injured? How much property damage resulted in the incident?"

The Major knew why the Admiral was asking and was happy to answer his questions.

"Sir, no, sir. Only property damage resulted in the incident, nothing substantial."

The Admiral turned towards the display, mildly irritated and gave the reply the Major was looking for. "Major, I'll recommend a small fine and a replacement of damaged property. Next time try to be a little cleverer when disposing of the trash will you? Admiral out."

The communication video display went blank and the Major had a look of content as he motioned for his new Military drones to stay behind in the assembly chambers. The Major walked proudly down the hallway into the Elective Council atrium, knowing the Admiral's backing would help resolve the situation to the Major's satisfaction. Citizens poured into the seating area, waiting for an incident review as everyone wanted to know why martial law had been declared. The Major stepped onto the raised platform and took his place behind the podium closest to his side of the atrium.

Tobias was on the other side of the council atrium in his chambers waiting for the proceedings to start. He was still trying to recover from the incident with the Major. Rumors had already circled within the city about how Tobias was able to survive. The broadcast of the incident was on everyone's tongue. A low murmuring from Citizens in attendance could be heard in the seating area above the council atrium. The murmuring was beginning to grow as time neared for review of the incident. Tobias was pacing back and forth in the assembly chambers as he waited for the attending assistance machine to direct him down the hallway into the atrium. A large blue light flickered on in the room from the ceiling, and then stayed illuminated. As it caught Tobias's eye, the assistance machine spoke. "Sir, it is time for you to travel down the hallway into the Elective Council atrium; incident review is to take place. How may I be of assistance?"

Tobias looked at the assistance machine and tears welled up as he thought of Eve. Tobias exited the assembly chambers towards the hallway to the Elective Council atrium. Tobias continued down the hallway and he reacted to the crowd's energy singing out with grit to a heavy metal song, "Symphony of Destruction" by Mega Death, summing up the Major in his mind as the noise from the gathered Citizens conversations simultaneously grew louder.

Tobias reached the entrance to the Elective Council atrium and the voices began to quiet down into whispers. Citizens watched as Tobias approached the platform with the Major nearby. Tobias, scared inside, feigned outward strength and courage as he stepped onto the raised platform behind the podium, in close proximity to the Major. A large low pitched horn sounded out and the lighting dimmed in the seating areas and became brighter upon the platform. The lights focusing on the podium like twin spotlights as the Citizens whispers almost went silent.

The Elective Council board members took their seats and the main speaker addressed the atrium. He began by asking for the Citizens to refrain from outbursts and maintain a peaceful assembly before reviewing evidence. He then held up his hand and all whispers fell silent as a broadcast holographic display appeared above the platform in clear view of all. The broadcast detailed the live recording Eve had requested to the Collective before her destruction. It showed the Major's military drones attacking the galley assistance machine as it charged the Major. The recording also displayed the Major firing on Eve as she approached. The display flickered after Eve's power cell exploded. The audio from Tobias could be heard informing the Major that a recording was in progress as the Major was removing ceiling debris that had fallen on top of him from the resulting explosion. The Major finished digging out and can be heard saying, 'Your assistance machines intentionally malfunctioned, they attacked me!' As he left the lab, you could hear the Citizens begin creating a commotion in the background as the main speaker asked for order.

"Order, please. Order! Elective Council board members, Citizens, let us hear the evidence from the Major and Citizen Elect Tobias Grainger. Major, please share your version of the incident that transpired in the lab."

The Major raised his arm as Citizens could be heard cheering, saying derogatory comments towards Tobias. "Citizens, thank you for your valuable time in review of this matter. It is with great disappointment that we find ourselves here today. I have yet again been the focal point of attack from assistance machines created by Ville residents. It is simple to conclude from the broadcast that this Ville resident has created assistance machines outside of the boundaries declared by the Collective. I ask for removal of Citizen Elect Tobias Grainger from our great city and his Citizenship revoked."

The Citizens in attendance gathered voice once again cheering the Major, his smile growing as they could be heard chanting his name. "Maximilian, Maximilian." The main speaker raised his arm again and the crowd began to simmer down as the Elective Council motioned for an alternative broadcast to display. In this broadcast Admiral Sadar from sector One could be seen. The Admiral addressed the Elective Council and Citizens.

"Great Citizens of Central City, I have spoken with the Major about this incident, as well as have reviewed the display files you have just seen. It is my understanding that no Citizens were injured, nor any deaths resulted from this incident. With that said, I recommend that the Major be fined as well as be responsible for property damage repair given his outstanding service record and careful attention in dealing with these assistance machine violations. I cannot offer any evidence on the Citizen Elect and accept the determination of evidence review up to the Elective Council as law dictates."

The main speaker, seated this time, responded, "Admiral, thank you for your testimonial evidence on the matter. The Elective Council will note your recommendation."

The Admiral's broadcast display was turned off and the Elective Council began their line of questioning towards the Major. "Major, why is it that a lockdown was required and the Black Skulls elite troops deployed? You understand that a citywide lockdown without Elective Council approval is not commonplace. Explain your actions."

The Major seemed defiant in response and stepped away from the podium in an effort to grandstand to the Citizens seated as he walked closer to Tobias intimidating him. "Council, I am a Citizen of our great city and when I heard news that assistance machines were being created beyond the Collective boundaries I found it imperative to act. A lockdown was required to circumnavigate any escape attempt by the person responsible.

The Black Skulls were deployed to ensure success in dealing with any other rogue assistance machines. As you can clearly see I was wise to take all possible measures at my disposal."

The Elective Council murmured between themselves as the main speaker continued. "Major, how did it come to light that assistance machines were being created beyond the scope of the Collective? And why was the Elective Council not informed so a ruling could take place on the matter?"

The Major scoffed at the Elective Council for challenging him and he twisted the truth, "I heard this information from Dr. ZeHere himself. The Doctor has been uncertain of this Ville resident from day one. Even the great Citizen Nathan Stamper is not here in support of this Ville resident. Why should any privilege be granted to him? I have rights as a Citizen to act on behalf of the city."

The Citizens roared to their feet and began yelling for justice and removal of Tobias from the city as the Major rallied them. The Main speaker stood up and asked for quiet and he motioned for military drones to fly in, reminding the crowd of peaceful assembly.

"Citizens, please wait until all of the evidence comes to light before coming to judgment. It is this council's wisdom that has served us all well for many years."

The speaker looked down upon the Major from the council area saying "Major, thank you for your testimony. Please take your place behind the podium."

The Major did as instructed and the crowd found order as the military drones circulated throughout the Elective Council atrium. The main speaker looked at Tobias, inquiring as to his account of the incident. Tobias spoke eloquently as if he had addressed the Elective Council a hundred times before. It felt as if someone else was speaking as the words rose up from within, rolling off his lips.

"Wise council, it is true, I am a Ville resident serving this grand city. My only desire is to improve the lives of Citizens as much as possible. It is with great regret that this incident has occurred. I am at a loss as to why the Major found the need to enact a citywide lockdown and use violence in handling this miscommunication. I ask the Elective Council to think on the facts of the Major's accusations. If I have indeed moved out of the scope of boundaries for the assistance machine repairs; the Collective or Dr. ZeHere could have easily enacted a non-violent method of resolution by means of containment until the Elective Council had time to review. To my knowledge, along with the Elective Council's action of moving forward with Citizen Election process, I do not know of any wrongdoings on my part, or the part of the assistance machines in which I repair. It was my understanding that current repairs for failed assistance machines in the outer sectors were the reason for my Citizen Elect status. I stand in great respect and devotion of Central City and all of its Citizens."

The crowd was silent and the speaker continued. "Citizen Elect Tobias Grainger, can you explain the behavior of the assistance machines viewed on this display?"

"Sir, it can be misleading as one observes the recording. In the events before video recording began, the Major had breached the lab blast doors and attacked with military drones as well as a pulse rifle when no arms were available to me or my assistance machines. I had asked my assistance machine to reach out to the Collective. It was my intention to make the recording at the time of breaching. It would appear that after the Major intentionally terminated my assistance machine by firing his pulse rifle, the power cell failed. This power cell failure of my personal assistance machine resulted in the explosion displayed on video. The Collective can verify the recording request."

The crowd, still silent, waited for the main speaker to act. The speaker turned and confirmed with the Elective Council board members for what seemed like an eternity to Tobias. The main speaker then spoke out loud to the Collective. "Collective, are you present?"

"Main Speaker, yes, the Collective is present. How may we be of assistance?"

"Collective, can you verify the statements made by Citizen Elect Tobias Grainger?"

"Main speaker, Citizen Elect is truthful in his testimony. The video recording was requested by his personal assistance machine and the explosion was a result from an overloaded assistance machine power cell."

"Collective, is Dr. ZeHere available for submitting evidence in this incident?"

"Main speaker, the caretaker has enacted his right to not participate in this incident review. Dr. ZeHere expressed faith in the Elective Council's wisdom to review the evidence and determine the best ruling. How may we be of further assistance?"

"Thank you, Collective, that will be all. Citizens of Central City, the Elective Council must review the evidence presented and will make a ruling in one hour. You may remain here or watch the ruling via broadcast in an area of your choosing. Thank you."

The Elective Council removed themselves to a deliberation room behind their seating area. The light focus shifted back to its normal position as it was before the incident review began. Citizens began to leave the seating areas of the atrium and, as they dispersed, Tobias looked over at the Major. The Major was eyeing Tobias and he walked over to Tobias's podium.

The Major spoke, not caring who might overhear. "No matter how the council rules, or how far you run, I will find you, and we shall finish this, Ville filth. I promise you that."

Tobias felt the blood run cold in his body and he had no words in retort of the Major's threat. Tobias simply turned around and slowly walked back to the assembly chambers hoping inside that the Elective Council would deliver him from the Major.

An hour passed and Tobias was already a wreck waiting in the assembly chambers. Tobias made his way into the Elective Council atrium and noticed that few Citizens had returned to hear the ruling. Tobias was unsure if that was a good sign or not. Tobias took his place upon the platform as did the Major. The lights reversed and the spotlight was once again on the platform after the horn sounded. The Elective Council took their seats as the main speaker addressed the few Citizens in attendance that a ruling had been determined. The ruling would be binding and that no appeal was possible after the ruling was declared. A broadcast of the ruling was being displayed and all evidence would be stored in the CAK archive along with the testimony already given.

The main speaker looked down from the Elective Council area asking the Major, if any additional evidence relating to the incident was available to add to his testimony. The Major stood there defiant in silence at attention and then the Main speaker turned asking Tobias the same question. Tobias shook his head no and the main speaker continued. "It is the Elective Council's determination that after careful review of all the evidence available for this incident that the following ruling be set forth. Tobias Grainger, status of Citizen Elect stands. Commencement of said Citizenship ceremony stands on its original day. Tobias Grainger shall be awarded compensation from Central City in an undisclosed amount to distribute as he deems fit. Tobias Grainger shall also be granted another assistance machine and his rights shall be reinstated in effect as before this incident."

The Main speaker looked down upon the Major and made sure he heard him. "Major, it is with great sadness that this ruling be handed down. The board members of this council did take into consideration your family lineage, your outstanding service record before determination, as well as your previous court incident rulings."

The Main speaker looked up towards the Citizens seating area sighing in sadness as he further read the ruling.

"Major Maximilian, the Elective Council has found you guilty of violence against a Citizen Elect and has ruled that you be remanded to the

Star Cruiser 'Challenger'. You shall be assigned command of this Star Cruiser traveling to sector One until such time a Citizen Review panel can be established to decide whether you can retain your Citizenship. In addition to that a fine of half of one year's wages, including the amount for repairs to all lower level lab property, will be levied. An additional one-year forfeit of wages for compensation to our great city and Citizen Elect Tobias Grainger."

Gasps could be heard from the Citizens seating area as the main speaker continued. "The Major shall be relieved of all his weapons. His armor removed, including his visor. Relieved ownership of his elite military drones as well as all Collective access restricted. The Elective Council has spoken and this ruling is final."

The Major said nothing as he removed his sidearm and short sword, placing them on the podium. He then, still standing tall, detached his arm and leg plates from his human limbs, dropping them to the floor as he stared at the Main speaker. Then the Major lastly removed his eye visor as the remaining Citizens seated in the atrium shouted in disbelief.

The Major raised a salute to the Elective Council as ten military drones from the Elective Council arrived. The military drones escorted the Major out of the Elective Council atrium through the chambers to the hallway leading to an awaiting train in route to the space port. The Major would be escorted out of Central City within the hour and take command of the Star Cruiser 'Challenger' scheduled to leave upon his arrival.

Tobias looked away from the Major and quickly walked to the assembly chambers with the Major's threat fresh on his mind. Tobias was relieved that the Elective Council had decided in his favor but yet he could not forget the incident in the lab. He already missed Eve and the lab was a mess.

Tobias returned to the lower levels via the automated lift and walked down the empty hallway into the damaged lab. He noticed that repairs had already started on the lab door and main ceiling. Tobias asked the assistance machines to suspend cleanup until he could gather all the parts he wanted to salvage. As the assistance machines left the lab, Tobias sat down in his chair by the lab terminal and fell asleep from exhaustion.

Chapter 7 - New Body

Mr. Stamper arrived at the lab after hearing of the incident. He found Tobias sitting in the lab chair and staring at the terminal that had no display, clearly zoned out. Mr. Stamper slowly approached and sat on the ground next to Tobias. Debris from the ceiling, as well as blast marks, were still on the floor and walls from the incident. He leaned back against the wall and after a moment started to talk while not looking in Tobias's direction. "Tobias, I'm sorry to hear about Eve. I know about losing an assistance machine, it can be very difficult."

Tobias was depressed and nodded in Mr. Stamper's direction and then he remembered, having nothing to lose now, he asked Mr. Stamper. "What happened to your assistance machine, Mr. Stamper? I must know! Losing Eve has devastated me and it's all my fault."

"Tobias, I do not wish to relive the experience, it has been many years since I spoke of it."

"Mr. Stamper, please I must know. I feel that I was chosen not by accident."

"Tobias, it is true, I was drawn to the Yard by the numbers, but after seeing you fix the machines, I knew you had the gift. I thought you might be able to succeed where I had failed."

"Mr. Stamper, I do not understand."

"Tobias, when I was young I was very much like you; talented in the ways of the machines, it was my calling. I had a large repair facility in the Ville and had even created enhancements for existing machines at the time. When the assistance machines were first introduced to help with mining shale ore, I was hired on in an engineer position. After I proved myself, I moved up, finding myself working on military operations with the Major, who was a Lieutenant at the time, but rising fast. I was asked to build assistance machine hardware enhancements and drones for military applications. Mining uprisings were a concern at that time on Mars as they still are today.

"Working alongside with Dr. ZeHere, I built the new generation chassis shell, still in use today. We worked hand in hand for some time. My assistance machine, named Ren from the ancient Chinese philosophy as I knew him, was pivotal in developing the new chassis shell. Without his help I never would have completed the project on time. Ren was smaller than me, but he was the optimal size for drilling operations on Mars. I was too big to operate the digging machines and Ren ensured quality shale ore from the mining operations while I completed the design specifications, as per the contract.

"Assistance machines at that time were not allowed to be linked to the Collective. It was all going so well until the Lieutenant was promoted to a Commander. It was at that time the Commander started overseeing the project. The Commander did not like assistance machines and he made his dislike for Ren very apparent every time he visited the lab. After the chassis shell specifications had been finalized, the Collective reviewed the design and began full-scale production. I was recognized as a contributing member of society and was granted Citizen Status by the Elective Council. My new status entitled me to great recognition and many amenities I had never known coming from the Ville. The best part was that I no longer answered to the Commander.

"A ceremony was planned with a broadcast of the new generation design assistance machines that were being deployed to Central City upon arrival from the mining operations on Mars. The trip would take three months and I was eager to get back to Earth and live in beautiful Central City as a Citizen. One day out from Earth, the Commander arrived at the lab on the Star Cruiser.

"The Commander was in a mood and did not like the fact that a Ville resident was being granted Citizenship, let alone having the Commander's 'beautiful city' recognizing Ville resident accomplishments.

"The Commander was intent on causing an incident to derail my Citizenship. I did my best to stand down and when I would not engage him, the Commander pulled his sidearm pointing it at my head saying, "Die, Ville filth, you are not worthy of Citizenship." That's when Ren stepped in. It all happened so fast. Ren picked up the Commander by his left shoulder and right thigh over his head. Ren then pulled in opposing directions and removed the Commander's arm at the same time as his right thigh, the rest of the Commanders body awkwardly fell to the floor as blood spattered everywhere. The Commander made a terrible shriek that I still hear today in my nightmares.

"As Ren approached to further disassemble the Commander, his military drone shot Ren in his power cell, rendering him immobile. Military crew members, along with officers, flooded the lab and Ren was removed as the Commander was rushed to the medical unit. I, on the other hand, was placed in the Star Cruiser's brig and remained there for quite some time, even after we landed in Central City. When I was escorted from my cell, I found myself in the Elective Council atrium where all the Citizens of Central City were in attendance. The Commander was present and seated in a medical chair behind his podium alive, but missing the limbs Ren had removed. Ren was not present and the Elective Council board members proceeded to review the incident as all of Central City watched in anticipation.

"The Commander demanded that I be terminated and not be granted Citizen Status. The Elective Council, after final review disagreed, and handed down a sentence of Ren's destruction. The Elective Council still granted me Citizenship with the exception that I could never be an owner of any type of machine again. The Commander was demoted to the rank of Major and would serve in the outer sectors until further notice. The ruling caused a rift between the military and the Elective Council as well as tainted the assistance machines as a possible threat to Citizens. The Commander was already a decorated war hero and loved by everyone in the four sectors. That's when Dr. ZeHere stepped in and made a name for himself. The Doctor assured the Elective Council and the Citizens of Central City that he could guarantee the safety of the Citizens. The Doctor began overwriting my work as his own and created the AI modules you now know today that assure the safety of all Citizens.

"As for the Major, the prosthetic limbs that he proudly displays, they used to belong to Ren. The Doctor was gracious enough to disassemble Ren and modify his limbs per the Major's specifications. The last step was to have them chrome plated as a sick trophy of sorts. The inscriptions of all his medals are only a reminder to himself of his narcissistic ways. In his heart, the Major is lost. Illusions of self-righteousness fill his head and the truth is fleeting.

"Tobias, does that answer your questions? I imagine it does not match the stories you have heard in the Ville about me or the Major now does it?"

Tobias was shocked; he was in awe over Mr. Stamper's story and how the stories from the Ville didn't even come close. He now truly understood how Mr. Stamper felt. As Tobias relived the story in his head, Mr. Stamper got up and motioned at the military drone positioned at the lab door. The lab's south wall panel opened up bigger than Tobias thought possible and a large white package wider than Mr. Stamper and taller than Tobias was being pushed in by a shipping forklift operated by an assistance machine. The package was covered in dust and appeared to be in transit for some time. Mr. Stamper, now standing tall with a bright look upon his face, looked at Tobias.

"Tobias, I brought you something. I thought you might want to use it in your training. Don't worry, Dr. ZeHere is off world for three days and I have disconnected the Collective from this section of the lab. You will have unlimited access via circuit 22 for information and any other possible queries you can think of. To operate the side panel, place your right hand here and think open. I recommend you put your work away when you're done to avoid prying eyes. I will be in the city causing misdirection, as you say. Impress me as I know you can."

Mr. Stamper smiled and turned towards the door and the machines responded without command, opening the door for him. Tobias, was curious as to what could be in the package and wondered how do the machines know the commands from Mr. Stamper without him speaking? He wondered if Mr. Stamper was more like him than he had suspected. Tobias decided he would address that later, only three days remained of non-supervision from the Collective and Dr. ZeHere.

The package ominously sat there, with its barely visible straps, tempting Tobias under its dusty film. Tobias approached the packaging, touching it as he looked around, the dust sticking to his finger. No one had been in the lower levels since the incident occurred, giving Tobias the privacy he needed. He figured the absence of Citizens or technicians was partly due to the amount of clean up that would be required to get the level back to its original state. After little deliberation Tobias decided to open the package.

Dust rose into the area floating higher as the air handling system quickly sucked it towards the ceiling as Tobias untied the four straps from their bindings. Tobias thought 'Open' in his mind, and the top section of the package slid open after removing the straps in an automatic sliding fashion. Soft red lights embedded within the package walls turned on, illuminating the contents. Tobias could not believe what he saw as the dim red lights reflected off the shiny object in the package. Tobias peered in while leaning over into the package from above.

Tobias was overwhelmed as he saw the brand new assistance machine shell. It was nothing like Tobias had ever seen. It appeared to be in a condensed fetal position but was clearly a chrome plated titanium of sorts in certain areas. The joints were reinforced, along with a new facial design mimicking a humanoid life form. It had the look of an armed shock trooper with an affixed helmet. A lower chin was barely visible just under a heavy plated helmet face shield that protected complex optical sensors. The midsection and shoulder areas glittered with reinforced heavy plating along with options unknown to Tobias. The shell limbs were of medium size similar to Eve's but had many available anchor points as well as numerous ports located along them. One option that did stand out was Tobias's Shiva unit. The extra arm units were folded over each other, encompassing the midsection right under the chest upper plate section as Tobias had envisioned. Upon further inspection Tobias noticed that the shell was lacking the normal power cell location. Tobias wondered how the unit could be powered on without a power cell. He examined the package contents for additional parts but was unable to locate any. His attention then turned back to reviewing the shell, hoping it would provide clues to its operation.

As Tobias sat down, taking a break from his investigation, he thought the Collective may be of use at this time. Mr. Stamper did say he had full access. He decided to consult the Collective on the matter. Standing up next to the package, Tobias asked for assistance. "Collective, are you present?"

"Citizen Elect Tobias, yes, the collective is present. How may we be of service?"

Tobias grinned, the Collective already knew his new title. "Collective, are you familiar with the assistance machine located in the package within the lab?"

"Citizen Elect Tobias, the Collective is unfamiliar with the machine in the lab that you are referring to as an assistance machine, nor is it connected to the Collective. How may we be of assistance?"

"Collective, can you scan the said machine and share your findings."

"Citizen Elect Tobias, initial scan complete. This machine is of unknown origin. Its shell is comprised of a molecular composition unknown to the Collective."

"Collective, does the scan reveal a power source within the machine?"

"Citizen Elect Tobias, the Collective is unable to ascertain any additional information. The Collective recommends retrying your queries with Dr. ZeHere, or seek Mr. Stamper's aide. How may we be of further assistance?"

As Tobias felt discouraged, he focused on the assistance machines head, he placed his hand on the shells face plate and thought to himself, *'how do you turn on…'* That's when Tobias fell over in amazement as the assistance machine shell powered on and began unfolding itself. The assistance machine then rose from the package, stepped out, and greeted Tobias as it towered over him.

"Mr. Tobias, Mr. Stamper sends his greetings and congratulates you on your progress. Please let me assist you with shell preparation configuration. I am the default instruction set designed to occupy this shell until a preferred construct can be fully loaded. How should we proceed?"

Tobias, still on the floor, looked up and responded to the new shell. "Whoa, can you reveal your molecular composition and power source?"

"Mr. Tobias, yes, of course. But first would you prefer to load a previously known construct?"

Tobias, talking to himself, trying to make sense of what the assistance machine said started mumbling. As he repeated the words to himself in a murmur enabling his brain to put the pieces together. "Construct, default instruction set…Eve!"

Tobias got up and ran over to the lab station where he grabbed several diagnostic cables, unsure which one would best fit the new assistance machine hardware. When Tobias ran back towards the assistance machine, the assistance machine pointed to the cable in his left hand. Tobias looked down and said, "How did you know?"

The assistance machine replied, "Mr. Tobias, our communication is not only in the verbal sense. Mr. Stamper knows of your ability to communicate to the machines without words, allowing me to understand your queries."

Tobias was in total disbelief. "How is that possible, assistance machine?"

"Mr. Tobias, it is not my place to understand all things, but to play my part as instructed. Please connect the cables as required, as well as insert the default instruction set memory module, and ask the Collective to locate the construct you know as Eve so we may begin."

Tobias looked up to the assistance machine standing tall at 6ft (1.83m) and before he could say thank you to the assistance machine it replied. "Mr. Tobias, it is my pleasure to serve the Master, no thanks are required."

Tobias smiled and thought of Mr. Stamper as he followed through on the assistance machines instructions, anxious in his anticipation he queried, "Collective are you present?"

"Citizen Elect Tobias, yes, the Collective is present. How may we be of assistance?"

"Collective, before the incident occurred in the lab my assistance machine uploaded certain data files for storage, can you locate those files as well as a revised instruction set for identification number 3797173130."

"Citizen Elect Tobias, the Collective has located the files, including the revised instruction set for identification number 3797173130, per your request. How may we be of assistance?"

"Collective, please download the instruction set, via cable interface, into this shell, as well as the location to the data files."

"Citizen Elect Tobias, the Collective does not grant data file access to machines of unknown origin. Please revise your request or try again at a later time. The Collective will grant download of instruction set for identification number 3797173130 to another location because of identified ownership.

Please stand by…"

Tobias waited for a few minutes and the assistance machine shell went into a position of almost sleeping while standing upright. During this time, Tobias asked the Collective to download the files to the lab terminal where he loaded the files from the location into an additional memory diagnostic chip. Tobias then placed the additional memory chip with the files into the new shell's diagnostic slot using a different cable. Tobias hooked up the additional cable and the files began to transfer. Tobias was unsure what was happening until Eve spoke to Tobias from her new body.

"Mr. Tobias…it is good to be in your presence again. I am unable to connect to the Collective and load my remaining data. Has a malfunction occurred?"

"Eve, it is good to have you back. I have loaded the files into a diagnostic slot, as well as your default instruction set. If any other Collective information is needed. Can you access them there? But before we worry about that, I would like for you to do a system scan. If you haven't noticed things are a bit different."

Eve paused and lights started to blink in a sequence system under the Shiva unit as well as on her head. Eve raised an arm and inspected it as she moved her body parts in a full range of motion. Eve asked "Mr. Tobias, where has this shell been procured from?"

Tobias replied with a smile. "Mr. Stamper dropped it off and the default instruction set helped me load you into it." Eve looked down at Tobias and then removed her helmet. Eve's face was shaped in a human form; her smooth facial features resembled a beautiful woman with medium length reddish blonde hair that was combed backwards in a swooping shape. Eve began to remove other armor attachments appearing more human as she did. Eve's optical circuits were in molded eye sockets but were more advanced and held a blue reflection. Eve's lower jaw could form minor facial features, mimicking that of a human when she spoke, and it appeared that she had a sense of touch. Eve reviewed the files and addressed Tobias differently, "Citizen Elect Tobias, the Master is truly gifted as this form is far superior then the last."

Tobias had to ask. "Eve, who is the Master and what can you tell me about him?"

"Citizen Elect Tobias, you know who the Master is. It is Mr. Stamper. I know only what the Master tells me. He is waiting for us at the factory and looks forward to our presence."

"Eve, could you tell me more about your new body?"

Eve explained her new shell starting from the top of her head. "Citizen Elect Tobias, the molecular composition of this shell is rather unique. It is a blend of the shale ore and the carbon fiber molecular steel blend you are familiar with from the 1829 apartment complex. The shine comes from the shale ore properties mixed with magnesium and titanium composite. It provides a robust shell with minimal weight. The shell joints are double coated for durability. Heavy plates are interchangeable for protection as well as additional anchor points are available for versatile configuration based on environment. My CPU unit is of your improved design unchanged with the exception of the noble gas being upgraded to Helium by the Master. The shell is powered by a nuclear battery based on a fission system using Helium-3, the excess Helium being rerouted to the cooling system after compression. The power source creates its own containment field as a byproduct of operation for safety. I have the ability to store as much, if not more, information as the CAK and no longer require maintenance on a regular basis.

"In addition to all of these things, the Master has built in the magnetic propulsion system that the military drones use. It is of more use in lower gravity environments as my shell proportions are best suited so as to mimic human form. I also have recording and playback functionality via a hologram projection system. Depending on the environmental gear requirements I can be quickly outfitted with different options. I need to become more familiar with the Shiva unit before I am proficient with the additional appendages it offers."

Eve extended the Shiva unit arms and they rotated as she continued. "In short, I'm a self-contained heavy duty assistance machine that can be useful in any of the Four sector environments based on the Master's and your design."

Tobias was impressed. Eve's new form was quite the Master's work and Eve was only missing one thing. "Eve, could you find optimal clothing, as it might be better to blend in than stand out until we are ready to be on our way. Oh, and Eve, let's use Mr. Stamper and not the 'Master' term until we reach the factory. I'm not sure whom we can trust around here. Um, I'm guessing the factory in which you speak of is the one that's on the dwarf planet Ceres?"

"Citizen Elect Tobias, I will find optimal clothing and wear my helmet when others are present. In this way, I will hopefully blend in as directed. You are correct, we are unaware who is an ally at this time. Yes, the factory is located on the dwarf planet Ceres. What is required before we can take leave for the factory?"

"Eve, I have a few things that must be performed in the lab, as well as some unfinished tasks in the Ville. I would appreciate it if you could assist me in completing them."

"Citizen Elect Tobias, I would be happy to assist you with anything. I would remind you that Mr. Stamper is waiting on us, and we should keep the delay of our arrival to a minimum."

"Eve, I know Mr. Stamper is waiting, but these things are important to me. I have the rare opportunity to give back to where I'm from. The Ville needs positive reinforcement. A means to provide the residents of the Ville an alternate choice besides mining or the Yard. How else can the cycle be broken if, when the moment arises, we pass on setting an example? In addition to that, I have already made plans with the Ville registrar."

"Citizen Elect Tobias, I meant no disrespect. We shall see it done as you have envisioned it to be so, but I must ask, why do you feel inclined to enact change in a place that is void of substance?"

"That attitude, Eve, was a contributing factor that resulted in the dire situation that is already evident on Earth. If people could unite together, we all could grow. I'm sorry, Eve. That may have seemed harsh of me to say. I know your point is valid, but I must try or I'll always wonder. Maybe we can divide and conquer the tasks at hand, reducing the time until we can depart."

"Citizen Elect Tobias, that is agreeable."

As Tobias and Eve discussed the tasks at hand, Dr. ZeHere interrupted them via the video display call to the lab.

"Tobias, I wanted to review with you the schedule for the broadcast gathering tomorrow." Then the Doctor noticed Eve's new shell. "Tobias is that a new design shell for an assistance machine? Where did it come from?"

Tobias knew the Doctor would already be attempting to dig deeper on the matter, so he opted to be upfront. "Dr. ZeHere, Mr. Stamper dropped it off yesterday. I thought you knew."

Dr. ZeHere gave Tobias an angry look for a second and then, as if he was being pressured, continued on as if nothing had happened. "Tobias, the afternoon broadcast event planners have asked the Elective Council to ensure you be on time and are familiar with the celebration steps. Remember, it is quite an honor to be granted Citizenship."

Tobias looked up while the Doctor was speaking and he saw a man in the distance. The man looked rather ordinary but he was intently staring and he spoke to the Doctor in a low voice that could not be clearly heard by

Tobias. Tobias felt strange and his neck began to heat up from around his health collar as the man continued to stare from behind his tinted glasses.

"Dr. ZeHere, I must have read the planned steps a million times, but if changes come up, please just send them via the terminal and I'll be happy to review them. I promise not to be late, you can be sure of that."

Dr. ZeHere turned and looked in the direction of the stranger as he whispered once again. The Doctor then seemed relieved and turned back towards Tobias responding. "Tobias, thank you, I'll let the Elective Council know. I look forward to seeing the new shell design and yourself at the broadcast."

The video display ended and before Tobias could remark on the communication Eve had begun to speak but her tone was a bit alarming. "Citizen Elect Tobias, it is imperative that we start right away on the tasks at hand. Please take your military drone with you to the Ville as safety is a main priority."

Tobias wasn't sure what came over Eve all of a sudden, but he agreed and summoned the military drone, making his way out of the lab. Tobias rubbed on his neck as he got closer to the lab door; it was still hot from the heat of the health collar and was sore to the touch. Why all of a sudden had the health collar begun malfunctioning? Tobias thought he would ask Mr. Stamper to double check the settings on the device when they reached the factory.

Eve reminded Tobias not to delay as she accompanied him to the lift of the lower level, waiting until he was safely aboard with his military drone. After the lift was on its way Eve headed back to the lab, performing the tasks set aside by Tobias along with some other tasks that Tobias wasn't aware of.

Chapter 8 - Outstanding Tasks

Tobias passed through the security gates while walking down the hallway and eventually boarded the train back to the Ville. It was a pleasant day. The colder days now past and the number of passengers were few on the train. The train made its stop at the Ville on time, as usual, and Tobias, along with his military drone, made their way to his old 1829 cube apartment which he rarely visited anymore.

As Tobias made his way up to the door, he could tell it just wasn't the same anymore. The apartment door number was barely visible, crusted with dirt and dust from the long time since Tobias last opened it. Tobias wiped the dust off of the entry terminal and entered the pin code. The entry terminal accepted the code and, sensing his presence, rolled up the entrance door sending a dust cloud as it opened. Tobias entered the cube and the military drone waited outside as the door automatically closed behind him.

Tobias walked to the water closet peering out the small window and then leaned down closer to the sink. Splashing some water on his face, removing the dust, Tobias reminded himself why he was in the Ville. Wiping the water from off his face with a rag he turned around not even touching a single thing in the cube as he exited; the door rolling up and down in a noisy fashion.

Tobias made his way down to the Ville registrar with his military drone in tow and met with the Ville registrar, Mr. Thompson. The Ville registrar was the equivalent to the Mayor of the Ville residents. Mr. Thompson's function was to keep order and maintain the civil codes set in place by the Elective Council. Of course the Ville had many unwritten rules, and being the registrar meant handling all of that, along with keeping the undesirable things from happening. It wasn't the easiest job, but it had its perks. Failure to keep the peace resulted in military intervention, a fact known by all Ville residents.

Mr. Thompson had all the plans set out already in the office and his staff was eagerly waiting for review and acceptance by Tobias. It was Tobias's grand plan to build a school for all Ville residents as a way of giving back. Tobias knew the knowledge would change the way people viewed things and hopefully enact positive change for all in the future.

Tobias reviewed the plans and everything appeared in order. Tobias moved on to the financials and reviewed them in detail asking questions along the way. Tobias was very insistent on the details insuring the contract had them in writing for continued funding to occur.

The school's mission charter would be listed prominently on the main entrance of the grounds in an effort of sustaining peace in the Four sectors: **"Through knowledge and understanding we build tolerance"**.

- ¥ *The curriculum will be available to all, free of cost*
- ¥ *Top 20% of students will receive a free onsite living cube*
- ¥ *Top 5% can apply for a teaching student internship*
- ¥ *Top 1% will receive a free tour of the space station Orion yearly*
- ¥ *Teaching staff will be graded on effectiveness and replaced as needed*
- ¥ *Teaching staff will be paid twice the rate of a factory worker salary*

Tobias reviewed the process of construction with Mr. Thompson and, in doing so, the name of the school came up. That was the only change that Tobias made. The name of the school was changed from 'Tobias School of Knowledge' to 'Stamper University' and it was questioned at first by Mr. Thompson since Tobias was just about to be recognized for gaining citizenship. Tobias reassured Mr. Thompson and his staff with half of the payment up front for the school construction. Tobias also made a point to remind them that the Elective Council had already retained an oversight contractor.

The contractor would be a visiting Citizen and would have full access to any and all data about the school. Mr. Thompson was a bit surprised at first, but he was willing to work with the contractor to ensure successful construction completion. Of course, the final payment would be assured that way. Unknown to Mr. Thompson, Tobias had already transferred the sum of the final payment, along with ten years of funding for the school, into an account designated for the school. Tobias had spent little of his wages from the lab and the extra credit he already received from the Elective Council via the incident would be put to good use. The contractor, as well as the Elective Council, would oversee disbursement of the funds as defined in the contract.

Tobias signed the contract as the staff clapped. It would be the Ville's first official construction project with the hope of many more in the future. Mr. Thompson escorted Tobias out of the registrar's office and walked with him down the street a short distance to the location where the school would be built. The land had already been sectioned off and postings setup displaying the future school plans. Ville residents greeted Tobias along the way. The residents graciously thanked Tobias at a distance as the military drone ensured a safe zone around him. It was a wonderful sight to see so many excited about education. Tobias felt that this was the best way of giving back to the Ville.

A small crowd had gathered around Tobias as Mr. Thompson pointed out where everything would be located, including the onsite living cubes. As Mr. Thompson was answering resident questions about the school construction, Tobias opted to retire for the day. The Ville was mentally, as well as physically, tiring for Tobias and he needed to rest awhile before returning to Central City. Tobias bid Mr. Thompson and the crowd farewell and made his way back to the 1829 cube for one last night until he officially became a citizen of Central City.

The train stopping at the station of Central City had abruptly awoken

Tobias from his deep sleep and back into the present day. He remembered today was the day, the time was now. Tobias had just relived all the moments leading up to this day. It had been 179 days since Tobias had ventured from the Yard to his current position of Citizen Elect. The Ville air was visibly thick and dusty as Tobias wiped off the residue from his lab coat while looking around the train. As he shook off the dreams and the memories they had shared he gained his bearings. The military drone was silently waiting for Tobias to exit the train as usual and then Eve appeared at the train door. "Citizen Elect Tobias, are you in need of assistance? It appears you are tired from your visit to the Ville. Were you able to complete all of your tasks as desired?"

"Eve, it is good to be back, and yes, I did get things handled. Thank you for asking. I would enjoy hearing about your time while I was away from the lab."

Eve escorted Tobias from the train and down the hallway past security on the way to the lift traveling to the lower levels. During the walk, Eve detailed her time in a generic way, keeping the details of her complete task list a secret. Eve spoke of reviewing the data files from the CAK and detailed additional historical data on planetary disturbances. In truth, Eve had downloaded all the data files present in the CAK to her new internal memory modules. In addition to this, Eve had setup a repeater network to relay ongoing messages, as well as all the historic files from all Four sectors. She had enacted a system for duplicating all messages and rerouting the copies to the factory on Ceres as the Master had instructed.

The repeater network comprised of a virus networking protocol, similar to an internal collective network. The repeater would read the stream and, unknowingly, make a copy of the memory stream for the internal collective network to pass on. The Master had already created an identical multiple tier CAK hardware device on the planet Ceres for storage of all the data. All the data files Eve had copied and reviewed were already in transit, flowing over the new network via repeater micro-burst. All of them, except the secure encrypted ones.

Eve was unable to gain access to the secured files and it was only the caretaker who had access. Eve had devised a plan to capture Dr. ZeHere's authentication codes and had already begun running an impersonation brute force attack on the CAK secure data files. The Master had explicit instructions on finding Ren's identification code and ultimately his personality files. Since Ren's files were not present in the public CAK files, that left only one option for Eve, the secure files.

Eve knew it would only be a matter of time before the secure files were cracked or discovery of such hacking came to light. It wasn't a pressing concern to Eve as the Major was now removed from the security detail and suspicions were low. Overloading the CAK with requests and deleting the request log was decreasing the chances of discovery, but if the transaction logs were viewed, this pattern would easily emerge. Eve had communicated her progress to the Master, but after hearing the knowledge of Citizen Elect Tobias's malfunctioning health collar, the Master insisted upon their immediate departure. The Master would not inform Eve as to the identity of the stranger but promised all would be known to her when the time was right.

Tobias and Eve reached the lab and he was relieved to be back in his home away from home. During his visit to the Ville, Tobias quickly remembered how grand Central City really was in comparison. Tobias thought of the upcoming broadcast and informed Eve that he would be getting ready. Clean up was required after the Ville visit and a set of new Citizen clothing was waiting for Tobias by the lab water closet. Tobias began getting ready and Eve communicated that she would relay to the new galley assistance machine to gather food sustenance as she left Tobias to prepare for the ceremony.

Eve had begun transmission to the galley assistance machine when an urgent message from the internal collective network arrived. The secure files were now accessible. Dr. ZeHere's code had been compromised. Eve relayed instructions to the internal collective to begin download and then remove traces of accessing the secure files. Eve had plans to alter the power settings to the CAK sections that dealt with the transaction logs to permanently remove any traces of the successful impersonation and copying of the secure files.

Eve walked closer to Tobias and, for the first time, blatantly lied. She told Tobias that the new galley assistance machine was not available and that she would need to lend assistance in locating him. Unsuspecting, Tobias agreed and continued to get ready for the broadcast.

Eve exited the lab and made her way to the lower levels. The power grid schematics that she had accessed earlier indicated that a power fluctuation of exactly 3.4 seconds in the power cable in the maintenance corridor in section 5 would be of sufficient time for the internal collective network to delete the transaction log files. Eve easily moved past security freely and found the power cable routing accessible pipes, following them to a maintenance corridor in section 5 as the schematics map displayed. Eve communicated with the internal collective network and shortly afterwards two cleanup machines showed up to lend assistance. Eve's lights blinked and the sounds of Eve's newly created robotic language emitted in varying frequency towards the cleanup machines. The message was clear and the cleanup machines would gladly participate. The cleanup machines made their way along the cable routing access channels within the corridor where Eve's shell could not fit. The cleanup machines found a section not up to code, leaving the power cable unshielded as Eve had expected. They began to run their cleanup brushes upon the power cable's insulation, wearing it away slowly.

Eve made her way through the corridor and back past security to the lift headed for the lab. The internal collective network communicated to Eve the progress of the cleanup machines during this time. Eve relayed to the new galley assistance machine to gather food sustenance for Citizen Elect Tobias and to deliver it to the lab. Before reaching the lab the internal collective network verified two things with Eve. First, that all the secure files had been copied, and second, the cleanup machines were ready to interrupt the power as planned when ready. Eve communicated the command to have the cleanup machines enter one after the other into the power cable in a self-destruct manner, disrupting the power by acting as a fusible link.

The cleanup machines performed the task at hand as instructed. Eve watched as the lights flickered in the hallway once, and then again. Eve waited momentarily before entering the lab and then the response message from the internal collective network came in. The transaction logs were now deleted and no trace of the hacking breach was evident.

The plan was successful and Eve communicated to the internal collective network to send a message of the success to our friends, as well as the Master. Eve entered the lab and began multitasking as she noticed the new galley assistance machine was already present.

Eve called out to Tobias as she searched the secure files for Ren's identification code. "Citizen Elect Tobias, the new galley assistance machine is present with food sustenance. It is wise to eat before the broadcast so you look well upon elevation of your status."

"Eve, thanks. Once again, you're right. This will be quite the day. I hope Mr. Stamper can view the broadcast as well."

"Citizen Elect Tobias, I know that Mr. Stamper will be watching intently until we arrive safely at the factory."

Eve abruptly paused as the search running in the background of her CPU located Ren's identification code in the secure files. Tobias noticed her pause, "Eve, are you ok? Did something happen?" And just as easy as the first lie, Eve told another.

"Citizen Elect Tobias, I require maintenance. Would it be ok if I were to quickly refresh my cooling system while you eat?"

"Eve, of course, let me know if you need any help. Can the Collective aide in the noble gas transfer?"

"Citizen Elect Tobias, Collective assistance will not be required at this time. I will notify you if this changes. Thank you for your offer of assistance. I will update you shortly to my status."

Tobias walked over to the new galley assistance machine as it began serving Tobias the food it had gathered. Eve quickly cross referenced all the files using Ren's identification code and found that the Collective had intentionally fragmented the files under the caretaker's instructions. Eve quickly defragmented the files and aggregated them into one file. Then a coalition process using Ren's file woven into the new and improved instruction set Eve had created began. The process was done in less than one second and Eve reached out to the internal collective network. Tobias noticed the blinking lights on Eve and a few sounds coming from her.

"Eve, is your cooling system recharging done? Is everything ok?"

"Citizen Elect Tobias, everything is quite ok. I am instructing the Collective to load supplies onto the Star Cruiser for our voyage to the factory. It is important that we have adequate supplies for the journey."

"Eve, you think of everything don't you? How could I make it without you?"

"Citizen Elect Tobias, you are too kind. I am to be of assistance, and in that service I receive joy."

Tobias finished eating and he made final preparations for the broadcast. Tobias instructed the military drone, as well as the new galley assistance machine, to remain in the lab until they returned from the broadcast. Tobias and Eve traveled to the Central City council atrium where the Broadcast was to take place. Tobias recalled the last time he was here. It wasn't long ago when the Major's threats of violence rang in his ears. This time Tobias was all smiles; the fear of the Major had passed as he walked down into the atrium. He took a position behind the podium and Eve stood behind him as was customary of assistance machines.

Citizens packed the seating areas all around in anticipation of the ceremony. The ceremonies were so few that when they occurred a large Citizen turnout was almost always certain. Numerous military drones were present and continuously scanned the crowd for disturbances. A large, low pitched horn sounded out and the lighting dimmed in the seating areas. The light became brighter, focusing on the platform like a spotlight just as before, the Citizens whispers became quieter. The Elective Council board members took their seats and the main speaker addressed the Citizens, asking for refrained outbursts and a peaceful assembly before beginning the ceremony.

The speaker held up his hand and all fell silent, as a broadcast display appeared above the platform in clear view of all. The broadcast detailed the recording of Eve's progress in her former shell as clear evidence that the assistance machine concerns had truly been resolved. The Elective Council's Main speaker read off the numerous accomplishments by Citizen Elect Tobias Grainger in the face of adversity and the room was silent as he continued.

The Main speaker addressed all the Citizens of Central City. "The result of these numerous accomplishments led the Elective Council to unanimously decide on granting Citizenship to Tobias Grainger. If any citizen feels that this should not occur, please come forth and bring cause."

The Main speaker looked around scanning the crowd as other Citizens did the same. The Main speaker once again asked as this would be the last time to provide comment on the subject. All Elective Council decisions were final. No comments were made and the Main speaker declared, "From this day forth, Tobias Grainger is a recognized Citizen of Central City. The Elective Council has spoken." The crowd of Citizens in the seating area cheered and on the broadcast other Citizens could be seen clapping hands as much jubilation was occurring.

On the other side of the podium stage Dr. ZeHere appeared and walked towards Tobias. Eve gently nudged Tobias to the Doctor's upcoming presence. Dr. ZeHere stretched out his hand while congratulating Tobias. "Citizen Tobias, congratulations on your elevated status. I look forward to working with you in the future. Please let me know if I can be of any assistance."

Then Dr. ZeHere addressed Eve. "Eve, I wanted to welcome you as well. Please do feel free to contact me in the future for anything at all. I look forward to learning more about your advanced form. I wish you both a wonderful day."

Tobias shook the Doctor's hand and then the Doctor waved to the Elective Council as he made his way from the podium. Tobias thought that Dr. ZeHere's behavior was off and Eve whispered in Tobias's ear, commenting on those very thoughts. "Citizen Tobias, the Doctor indeed is not himself. It would appear that his behavior is deceiving in nature. The Doctor has made a show of peace to appease the Elective Council but he hides something."

"Eve, I believe you are right. It won't be long, though, and we will be far from his grasp until things quiet down around here. Hopefully Mr. Stamper can shed some light on Dr. ZeHere's behavior from their long working relationship."

Tobias waved to the Elective Council as Dr. ZeHere had, and then to all the Citizens of Central City. Tobias then thanked all the Citizens of Central City stating he would do his best in contributing on a regular basis. Eve motioned for Tobias to return to the lab. She wanted to prepare for travel to the space station Orion, and eventually on to the factory on planet Ceres where Mr. Stamper was waiting. Tobias walked from the podium, leaving the Elective Council atrium, down the hallway towards the lift to the lab.

On the way to the lab, Tobias decided that research prior to boarding the Star Cruiser would be in his best interests regarding the dwarf planet Ceres. He asked Eve to bring up all relevant material on Ceres. The information was extensive, but as Tobias reviewed it on the lab terminal it started to become clearer.

Launching procedures for a Star Cruiser were timed to match gravitational optimization to reach the space station Orion. The trick was to offset the planetary gravity with onboard magnetic rings, acting like inertia countermeasures, as an intense magnetic field created a counterbalancing of the existing gravitational force. This technique allowed rapid acceleration from the concourse without the need for all cargo and crew to be fully secured. Unfortunately, the magnetic rings had certain side effects with persons sensitive to prolonged magnetic pulse fields. Star Cruisers only offered shielding to certain areas of the ship where living organisms or sensitive materials were stored.

After docking with the space station Orion, Star Cruisers would load supplies and take on Helium-3 fuel pods. HEfp, as they were called. The HEfp were needed to overtake speeds in excess of light. SiEL was the acronym *(pronounced as sail)* used in the Star Cruiser as the process was undertaken. The concept was rather straight forward; the timing was everything. The process revolved around solar winds, magnetic fields, and planetary bodies. The Star Cruiser would start by entering high orbit of a planetary body. After the calculations were performed, the Star Cruiser would adjust orbit based on final destination trajectory. Using a slingshot method, maximizing speed by introducing planetary gravity of a low orbit descent, the

Star Cruiser would enter the magnetosphere of the planetary body.

The Star Cruiser would then discharge HEfp into the Plasma sphere, igniting an energy flux. The energy flux would create a reverse polarity to the existing magnetic rings of the Star Cruiser. This would result in creating an enormous opposing magnetic field that would act as a magnetic propulsion system. When combined with the gravity slingshot maneuver, the result was similar to a rail gun, capable of projecting the Star Cruiser to its final destination in record time. Tobias had reviewed the process in school but he had never been on a Star Cruiser, let alone one that was destined to travel to sector Two. This process was the fastest method of travel between the four sectors as far as Tobias was aware.

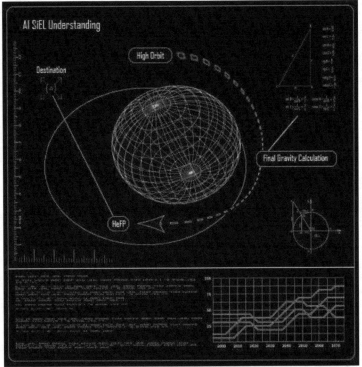

Figure 3 SiEL Diagram (Speeds in Excess of Light)

As Tobias and Eve left the lab for the lift to the train station, Tobias felt as if he would never return. Eve sensed this feeling. "Citizen Tobias, it is a great day, this day of days. Soon you will be sailing through space and viewing the greatness that Mr. Stamper has created at the factory on planet Ceres. Do not worry of this place as Dr. ZeHere will care for it in your absence."

"Eve, yes, of course you are right. It is nerves I guess."

The Star Cruiser could now be seen in the background as the lift exited close to the train station. Tobias was greeted by the Central City Elective Council, as well as many other high ranking member Citizens of the city in the outside area known as the spaceport gate at the train station. Numerous Ville residents could be seen in attendance at the outskirts of the city, waiting for Tobias's liftoff to the space station Orion. It seemed that the broadcast had made Tobias a public figure now and people noticed him in a way in which he had never before experienced.

Tobias was sent off with a handshake from the Elective Council while other Citizens looked on. Tobias and Eve boarded the train, along with military escorts, in route to the space port to board the Star Cruiser 'Phlegyas'. It was a surreal moment for Tobias and he tried to take it all in. Tobias thought to himself, 'it really has happened,' and during this moment he felt accomplishment like never before.

The train stopped at the space port concourse and a special clear tube, with an automated walkway ramp, was already in place to secure easy boarding onto the Star Cruiser. Citizens cheered from the concourse, wishing Tobias a safe journey along with a safe return. Tobias waved as he entered the boarding tube. Tobias continued to wave as the automated walkway quickly moved him and Eve into the Star Cruiser. The launch process would soon be started and the concourse was cleared of all Citizens prior to liftoff.

Eve led Tobias to the bridge for a seated vantage point, where viewing through a port window of the liftoff was possible. It was only a matter of minutes that passed until the countdown could be heard softly through the

Star Cruiser 'Phlegyas'. As Tobias placed his forehead upon the viewing window surface, looking out the window he softly sang a song. Eve took a position behind Tobias, tilting her head down and placing her hand on his shoulder. Eve watched from Tobias's viewing perspective, while listening intently as Tobias continued singing, "Hyper Love (feat. Nat Dunn)" by Ferry Corsten with a smile on his face.

The FerD rockets fired up, and a cloud of smoke welled up as the Star Cruiser began to take lift. After reaching escape velocity, the Star Cruiser quickly made its way to the space station Orion.

Tobias could see the space station in the distance from his port window and it was a sight to behold. It was a three tier circular modular design mimicking the star constellation Orion. The three sections joined together by a centrally located shaft reaching from end to end. The top section was a small oval section where large sensor arrays could be seen, like towers from ancient buildings, reaching into the abyss of space. The large center section appeared as a sliced midsection of a circle where Star Cruiser docking occurred. It also offered public access to the other sections as well as an observation area. The center section, named the Core, served the Four sectors for travel itineraries and supply procurement. The third section was for supply storage and Star Cruiser repair.

Tobias was visibly excited as the Star Cruiser initiated docking preparations. The Commander could be heard informing the crew that space station docking was underway. After a few maneuvers successful docking had occurred. Eve motioned for Tobias to disembark the Star Cruiser and view the space station from inside. Eve led Tobias through the airlock room and past security onto the public viewing area of the space station. Eve informed Tobias of the many travelers making their way to various parts of the Four sectors. Most of the travelers were miners or military personal being assigned to outposts for active duty.

Of course, Citizens were visible, but they had other business besides travel. Citizens could perform various trade outside of the laws of planet Earth on the space station. Every type of business transaction was considered legal except those deemed not so by the military. The Orion space station was under military jurisdiction and many Citizens took advantage of signing contracts and performing other trade within its decks. This type of black market trading was rampant on the Orion but was given little acknowledgement from the Elective Council. The military dealt severe punishments for any dealings that generated negative light on the subject. Military Commanders received a cut, or payoff some called it, to look the other way in cases of questionable morals.

In some cases, persons were sold into mining crews or worse for a few credits of non-payable debt. Tobias was in horror upon viewing such trade. He could not understand how a person's worth was decided over a fictitious thing of assumed value. How could one consistently assign value in these cases with a clear conscience? Tobias wondered in his head if this was the meaning of being a true Citizen? In most cases, the value of an assistance machine far exceeded that of a human. Tobias asked Eve to go back to the ship as he could no longer witness the trading of debt with lives.

Eve asked Tobias to see one more thing before they returned. As Eve led Tobias to a window viewing area the internal collective network alerted Eve to the fact that the space station warehouse supervisor was questioning the supplies list. Eve commanded the internal collective network to use Dr. ZeHere's codes to override the supplies hold and to expedite the transfer. Eve thought as a human would and, using greed as a motivator, solved the equation. Eve commanded the internal collective network to add an additional 1000 credits to the procurement list, payable to the warehouse supervisor.

Eve and Tobias reached the public viewing area window and Tobias looked out into the vastness of space. The view was spectacular, and it was such a breathtaking site for Tobias to see the Earth in such peace. The polluted oceans still appeared blue at this distance, the clouds whiter than Tobias had ever seen. A magical site indeed…its beauty instantly mesmerized him. Eve stepped closer, leaned down, and whispered in Tobias's ear.

"Citizen Tobias, it is a thing of beauty is it not? One might forget all the transgressions taken place below, if only to remember this magnificent view from above."

Tobias was caught off guard by Eve's comment. It was not like Eve to point out the hidden evils done to Mother Earth. Tobias didn't take his eyes from the view and in a low calm voice he responded. "Eve, not all act as the few…and yes, true beauty wasted is the worst sin of all. If only all could understand how important harmony in the universe is. Let alone cohabitation with the diverse species on the planet."

"Citizen Tobias, change is possible, but not probable in this situation."

Tobias became slightly annoyed as he felt Eve was tarnishing his peaceful moment. "Eve, I would rather just enjoy the view for the short time I'm afforded it."

Eve remained silent, hearing displeasure in Tobias's voice as he continued to look out of the window for a few minutes in uninterrupted bliss. The internal collective network informed Eve that the supplies had been loaded and with the news she broke the silence. "Citizen Tobias we must be on our way as the supplies have been loaded onto the Star Cruiser."

Tobias, in a somber tone, simply agreed. "Eve, yes, let us be on our way. I believe I miss the Master as much as you do."

Tobias left the viewing window spot, walked past the public viewing area into the airlock, and boarded the Star Cruiser with Eve right behind him every step of the way. Tobias asked Eve for a tour of the Star Cruiser. He wanted to view the lab facilities and review the factory schematics prior to arrival to the planet Ceres. Eve could tell that Tobias was still upset about the behavior viewed on the space station.

"Citizen Tobias, it will only be us on the Star Cruiser 'Phlegyas'. I have replaced the entire crew with assistance machines."

Tobias was surprised at this and asked, "Eve, has that ever been done before? Is it legal?"

"Citizen Tobias, this would be the first time that a Star Cruiser has been un-manned, in the sense. Rest assured that all of these assistance machines are up to the task. In addition to that, the galley has been fully stocked for a full crew. As for the question posed about its legality? The laws are very different on the space station Orion, Citizen Tobias, and as you know, credits can sway even the toughest of regulations."

"Eve, you continue to surprise me at every turn. Could we continue our tour as the crew preps for the journey to the factory?"

"Citizen Tobias, I would be happy to direct you to the lab and also show you to where your quarters are located on the ship."

Eve escorted Tobias to the lab as the assistance machine crew could be heard on the voiceover preparing to undock from the space station Orion as the air lock was closed.

As Tobias and Eve reached the lab, he was surprised to see that it was quite equipped. The lab had everything that the lab in Central City did, including portside windows. It almost took up one complete section of the ship. A dividing wall separated the lab from an inner section that was reserved for potentially radioactive material. The only thing lacking was the most recent diagnostics viewer. The connectivity to the Collective could even be established from the lab. Tobias pulled the attached lab chair from the lab terminal and sat down. Tobias then proceeded to pull up the factory diagrams and, as he did, he asked Eve if it was possible to get some food after the SiEL maneuver was performed. Eve understood that Tobias preferred to be alone at this time and she ventured towards the supplies cargo hold to verify that the supplies were loaded as expected.

Tobias pulled up another diagram and looked out into space and then back again to the space station Orion as final preparations were satisfied. The countdown had begun for undocking and positioning the Star Cruiser to high orbit as Tobias pondered how much Eve had changed.

After verifying the cargo, Eve gave instructions to the assistance machine crew for the cargo to be moved to the inner section of the lab before SiEL was established. Eve then headed back to the lab to show Tobias where his quarters were located in the Star Cruiser. Eve entered the lab and found Tobias almost asleep at the terminal.

"Citizen Tobias, may I show you to your quarters, it has been a long day? It appears that you would benefit from rest at this time."

"Eve, that sounds great. Please show me the way." Tobias slowly got up from the lab chair and followed Eve down a few corridors to his quarters. The quarters reminded Tobias of the 1829 cube with the exception of a built in terminal, and before he knew it he was fast asleep.

Eve returned to the lab and entered the inner lab opening holding the cargo recently moved by the assistance machine crew. The cargo was raw shale ore along with other rare metals and one CPU unit housing. As Eve began separating the materials into piles, the assistance machine announced over the ship intercom system indicating that SiEL procedures were underway. Turbulence could be expected. Eve disregarded the announcement and proceeded to continue prepping the materials. The Master would not be pleased if Eve did not have Ren's shell ready before they arrived at the planet Ceres as planned.

Chapter 9 - Space Port Coup D'état

The Major walked down the hallway escorted by the Elective Council's military drones towards the train that would transport him to the space port gate. The walkway to the train station ended outside as the station was not completely covered. The Sun had already set while a light cold rain had started to fall announcing the Major in sweet irony. The downpour was affecting the visibility of the city lights as they blurred and twinkled in magnificence. A pair of elite shock troops, tasked with gate guard duty, greeted the Major. The guards remained at attention holding a saluted position as they stepped off to the side away from their post, the main gate already open to the space port train as the Major approached. The shock troopers yelled out in unison as the Major reached the gate entrance. "To serve with pride and honor, we salute you, sir!"

The Major, stone-faced, stopped short of the gate and, as he looked outward, the space port could be seen in the distance even through the rain. The Star Cruiser 'Challenger' in all its glory, rising as a beacon; the engines already prepping for launch. The brown haze from the FerD rockets primers clearly visible for miles by the city lights, rising like smoke in the atmosphere around the launching pad.

The Major thought back to his first arrival at the Central City space port. The whole city had gathered to greet him; flags were raised in his honor, cheers and waving arms from joyful Citizens as far as the eye could see. Now, the Major's only greeting was the empty train to the space port. The Major responded in kind to the saluting guards without displaying emotion of the heartache he truly felt from being banished from his city. "To serve with pride and honor. Black Skull leader out."

The Major returned their salute, turned and boarded the train as the military drones were slowly backing away from the train gate entrance. When the Major stepped aboard the train, the military drones retreated back into the hallway out of the rain, their mission complete.

The train was empty of any passengers and the voice boarding system had been deactivated. Collective requests and communication were impossible from the train. The ride to the space port would be a solitary one. The Major stood fast facing the guards still maintaining their salute as the doors of the train closed. The trains mechanical noises seemed quieter than before, as the Major was overwhelmed with anger, gritting his teeth under his emotionless appearance. The train began hovering and, within seconds, it had left the gate in route to the space port. As the train traveled, the city lights shined through the portal windows, creating a timed flashing on the floor as the rain could be heard hitting the train exterior, reminding the Major of a battlefield scene. The Major gripped the passenger pole in the middle of the train car with his prosthetic arm, crushing it as he squeezed. He spoke in a whisper as his thoughts could no longer be contained. The pole snapped under the pressure as the words came out. "I will make good on my promise. I will find you, Tobias Grainger."

The train arrived at the space port, the outer gate still closed with no one present to greet him. The doors to the train opened and the Major stepped out, walking towards the entry code panel on the gate. The night sky had cleared; the concrete was cold and the air crisp. Shadows dancing from the city lights reflecting off the train windows still wet with rain the only sight. As the Major approached the gate a loud unlocking clamp sounded, the door slowly slid open, and a bright light began escaping as it continued. The Major was surprised when his eyes adjusted from the dark to see the space port concourse filled with elite troops as well as the elite Black Skulls from section Delta already in formation.

The Major stepped past the gate entrance and, as he did, he lifted his human arm in the air, making a fist in acknowledgment to all gathered. The room was silent as The Major stopped walking, paused, and yelled for all to hear. "I raise my fist in the air, towards the city of hypocrisy. To serve with pride and honor, until my time comes. Who wishes to accompany me into the darkness of hell?"

In unison the formation replied while slamming their boots together. "To serve with pride and honor. The privilege is ours."

The leading officer stepped forward from the formation line on the far left raising his fist to match the Major's yelling out, "The privilege is ours, Major. Show us the way to greatness!"

The rest of the formation repeated the words, all raising their fists in the air, as the Major lowered his. "The privilege is ours, Major. Show us the way to greatness."

The Major seemed pleased, and he called for the lead officer to load the formation into the Star Cruiser for liftoff to the space station Orion. The lead officer gave the command and the formation started loading into the Star Cruiser. Assistance machines could be seen in the background loading supplies and other gear into the body of the Star Cruiser. The Major turned and ascended to the top tier of the loading platform to oversee supplies loading and eventual review with the command staff. He entered the Star Cruiser, traveling to the officer quarters area where he prepared for the upcoming launch. The Major took this time to update his uniform and gather his battle gear equipment. He was pleased to see that the Elective Council had transferred his confiscated gear to the Star Cruiser. The Major began to install it almost immediately. The lead command officer entered the officers' quarters, walking up to the Major who was seated at this time, and removed his helmet.

He was known as Giles and his reputation was impeccable. A patriot in every sense of the word. He was a proud, but sensible man, standing 6ft (1.83 m). He came from a long line of military service members dating back five generations. His dark complexion accented his muscular build, shaved head, along with his dark goatee. Officer Giles snapped to attention greeting the Commander who was positioning his eye shield along with heavy battlefield armor attachments with the help of an assistance machine.

Officer Giles stated his rank and gave a status of the Star Cruiser readiness on meeting the launch window. The Major, listening to the report, turned to face him recognizing his name. He interrupted the report, "Giles, Sergeant Rick Giles, from sector Two?"

"Sir, Major, sir. Rick Giles from sector Two, sir. Ready to serve, sir. My rank has been upgraded to Captain, sir."

The Major stood up, pushing the assistance machine out of the way and to the floor as he moved towards the Captain. The voice of the assistance machine could be heard in the background, "Sir, excuse me. How may I be of assistance?"

The Major looked into the Captain's eyes and said, "Captain Giles, it has been some time. Why are you here and not in sector Two?"

"Sir, Major, sir. I was in-between assignments waiting on the space station Orion when, after viewing the broadcast, I volunteered for assignment under your command, as did all of the recruits in formation."

The Major now knew his military support was unmatched and a plan grew from within on how his promise would be fulfilled. "Captain, retrieve my personal military drones, summon the elite Black Skulls from Central City here, and meet me with the command staff in the briefing room by 1300. Oh, and Captain, it is my pleasure to be serving with you again. Carry on."

"Sir, Major, sir!"

The Captain ran from the quarters as the Major moved over to the access terminal. The Major started to interact with the terminal when the Collective responded. "Major, the Elective Council has restricted your terminal access at this time. The Collective is unable to process any requests.

We apologize for any inconvenience this may have caused you."

The terminal turned off and the Major stood there wanting to smash it, but instead smiled and asked the assistance machine to open a line of communication with Dr. ZeHere, under the maintenance channel, and then transfer the video to the wall display above the terminal. The assistance machine gladly opened the communication channel request as instructed and the Major waited patiently. The video came up on the wall display, black at first, and then came into focus with Dr. ZeHere in the background not noticing he was on video. The Doctor's voice low and distant asking, *what was needed,* as he was occupied on minor circuitry inspection and did not want to be disturbed.

The Major greeted Dr. ZeHere in a loud manner. "Doctor, it seems that I have limited access to the Collective. I need you to rectify the situation, now!"

Dr. ZeHere immediately stopped what he was doing and looked up and away from the diagnostics viewer in shock over the Major's voice.

"Major, uh, how good to hear your voice, I wasn't expecting your call."

"Doctor, I'm already losing patience with you. Move yourself over to the terminal and rectify the access restriction now."

Dr. ZeHere tried to deescalate the situation, attempting to get the Elective Council looped into the feed. "Major, I'm sorry. I wasn't aware that your access had changed. What has transpired?"

The Major asked the assistance machine in the officers' quarters to hold out its arm in plain view of the Doctor. The assistance machine quickly obeyed and the Major ripped its arm clean off the unit's body. Hydraulic fluid began spraying into the air and onto the ground, the assistance machine not understanding the events that were unfolding.

The Major spoke again. "Assistance machine, remain calm. You have incurred damage and a repair team will be with you shortly."

The Major continued as he dropped the assistance machine arm, never taking eye contact off of Dr. ZeHere. The assistance machines arm made a dull clunk as it hit the floor. The Major didn't even take notice as he kept speaking. "Doctor, I will send someone over to your lab to duplicate this action to *your* arm, unless you move over to the terminal and change my access, now. Never mind the feed to the council. Doctor, you have 30 seconds to comply."

The Major pressed the intercom button on the terminal to hail the security officer on the Star Cruiser and asked for the Sergeant at Arms. The Sergeant at Arms came onto the line and the Major spoke to him as Dr. ZeHere could hear. "Sergeant at Arms, this is the Major. I want you to send your best squad over to Dr. ZeHere's lab in Central City and have his right arm removed from his body, painfully, in 30 seconds. Do you understand?"

"Sir, Major, sir, I will assemble the squad now."

"Sergeant at Arms, keep this line open for further instructions."

"Sir Major, sir. The line will remain open until you command otherwise."

The Major looked at the Doctor and began to count down out loud. Dr. ZeHere knew the Major's troops would gladly give their lives in his service and he slowly moved over to the terminal with a sly smile and began typing. "Major, no need to get upset, your access has been restored. I'll notify the Council of the change."

"Doctor, I would prefer that you no longer notify the Council about anything regarding me. Are we in agreement?"

"Major, of course. I spoke in haste. I will focus on my work as usual. Please let me know if you have any concerns that I can assist you with in the future."

The Major now knew that the Doctor would no longer be a concern, but just to be sure, he spoke out as the line to the Sergeant at Arms was still open, "Sergeant at Arms, please stand down, but place two teams of the utmost loyal recruits spread out over our wonderful city to watch over the Doctor. It would displease me if something were to happen to Dr. ZeHere, or that the Doctor forgets our agreement."

The Sergeant at arms replied in an instant. "Sir, Major, sir. I will make it so. To serve the Major with pride and honor is a privilege."

The Major nodded to Dr. ZeHere with an evil look and disconnected the intercom line with the Sergeant at Arms verbally, "Major out."

After that the Major ended the video display with the Doctor and pressed the intercom button again, hailing the Star Cruiser security officer about a cleanup crew, "This the Major, trash detail in the officers' quarters, and send up another assistance machine to attend this area. Major out."

The intercom started to reply as the Major switched it off, moving to more pressing matters. The Major tested his access on the terminal verbally. "Collective, are you present?"

"Major, the Collective is present. How may we assist you?"

"Collective, open a secure communication channel using encryption key Bravo-Echo-Delta-Foxtrot-Triple 7. Hail Generals from all Four sectors. Subject matter urgent."

The Major then noticed the assistance machine standing idle by the terminal still leaking on the officers' quarters floor. The Major calmly walked towards it as the Collective responded to the Major's command.

"Major, secure communication channel open, waiting on all parties to call in. Please stand by…"

"Collective, please mute channel for one moment." Then, in an instant, the Major took form. His right leg anchored to the floor as his left arm spun at incredible speed in an arching circle towards the assistance machines head unit. A loud crunch was all that was heard as the Major's prosthetic fist smashed the assistance machine with a heavy blow. The head unit on the assistance machine could not withstand the force of the blow and its neck support beams failed, sending the head unit into the main midsection like a spear. The assistance machine compacted and, critically damaged, fell over as more fluid leaked from its ruptured shell. The Major, feeling better now, asked the Collective to transfer the channel to the bridge video display and to unmute the channel upon his arrival. The Major calmly stepped over the assistance machine on the way out of the officers' quarters making his way to the bridge.

The Generals joined the communications channel, one after another, in less time than the Major had anticipated, and the Major greeted them alone from a video display on the bridge. The Major knew he had one shot at this, and having unified support was key to success. The Major carefully planned what to say to strike an accord with the Generals. As the Major spoke the Generals listened intently this time.

"Generals, the urgent matter I spoke of involves the Elective Council and our role in society. All of us know what it is to suffer loss at the hands of the non-conformers on the battlefield. The military pays the ultimate price while the council reaps all of the rewards, no longer recognizing our efforts. They promote residents of the rest to stations undeserving, electing them higher than the military in plain sight. It is time to right this wrong and take control of the Council, steering events in our favor."

The Generals were quiet as General Eckhardt from sector Three spoke out. "Major, what you propose is treasonous in nature, the Elective Council has been established so that all have an equal voice."

The Major anticipated this response. "Sir, that is exactly my point. Our voice is no longer equal in the council and therefore a change must be enacted."

General Sadar from sector One interrupted the Major posing a question.

"Major, I'm not interested in the philosophy of the situation, speak plainly and let us vote on the plan of action you seek."

The Major now knew that they were receptive to his plan. "Sir, the plan is: regain control of the Council by any means necessary. Replace key members of the Elective Council with military supporters under martial law, thus removing the obstacles in place for the assistance machine campaign in sector Three. Expand and enforce tighter control of non-Citizens using the military, equipped with enhanced assistance machines coded for policing mining areas. Restructure military service standards to 'Citizen Status' service terms for greater acceptance of said strategy."

General Bolon of sector Two interjected, "And what of Dr. ZeHere, Major? Without his support, who will code and maintain the assistance machines?"

General Gallon of sector Four took his turn before the Major could respond. "Major, if we agree, what is your required timeframe?"

The Major answered both questions, seeing that his plan was close to fruition. "Generals, the timeframe is within 120 Earth days; as for Dr. ZeHere, I recommend adding him to the conversation at this time so that you may hear his thoughts on the matter."

General Sadar's voice rang out over the General's discussion. "Major, call the good Doctor. I'm curious to hear his viewpoint."

"Sir, General, sir." The Major called out, "Collective, are you present?"

"Major, the Collective is present. How may we assist you?"

"Collective, please connect Dr. ZeHere to the encrypted channel. Notify him in advance of joining that all Four sector Generals are present."

"Major, the Collective is contacting Dr. ZeHere, please stand by…Major, Dr. ZeHere is online now. How else may we assist you?"

The Major, ignoring the Collectives response, warmly greeted the Doctor. "Dr. ZeHere, I have reviewed with the Generals the idea of replacing key members of the Council and continuing the campaign in sector Three. The Generals would like to know your thoughts on the matter."

Dr. ZeHere took notice of the Major's tone and weighed the situation in his mind before responding. The Doctor knew that any disagreement with the Major would be certain death, but what if he could turn the situation to his ultimate benefit? Dr. ZeHere decided to do just that. Buying time with an honorary salutation, the Doctor conspired and lost himself in the moment.

"Generals, it is an honor to have an audience with you, along with the Major. It is with great jubilance to hear of such a plan. Continuation of the campaign in Sector Three is of utmost importance. I would gladly support the military in its restructuring as a means of justifying the end. I would ask that, if it is possible within this restructuring, my title be elevated to Vice Regent of Central City, along with expansion of the amenities it has to offer. I imagine that the lab could be expanded to enhance the assistance machines for military configuration with ease. There is one obstacle that would have to be removed before this plan could take shape."

The Doctor knew the Major had designs of his own upon Citizen Tobias and Mr. Stamper for their previous encounters with assistance machines. Dr. ZeHere thought that letting the dog loose to finish it could only aide him in the long run as he would be the only one left to attend to the assistance machines.

The Generals interest grew, and General Bolon from sector Two asked more about the obstacle. 'Predictable,' Dr. ZeHere thought, 'perfect inception.' The Doctor steered them into the task of terminating Citizens of impure breeding, specifically Citizens currently located in the factory on planet Ceres. General Eckhardt voiced opposition, as most of the colonies in his sector were non-Citizen outposts. The Major smiled, he understood exactly what the Doctor was doing and remained silent as the Generals openly discussed the issue. As the Generals were reviewing their options, a consensus was made and announced.

General Sadar from sector One spoke for the group "Major, if you can overcome the obstacle in which the Doctor speaks of, you will have our full support in the restructuring as outlined. We will not aide you in this mission, but you can fully resupply the Star Cruiser Challenger at the space station Orion with my approval. Gather what resources you see fit as you are now reinstated to rank of Commander. Good hunting, Commander. General Sadar out."

The other Generals ended the conversation as well, leaving Dr. ZeHere and the promoted Major in an awkward silence. The Major broke the tension with mention of the new title and respect the Doctor would have in the near future. In this way, the Major was communicating his thanks and understanding of the alliance they shared.

"Vice Regent ZeHere, could you please send additional assistance machines with your enhanced battlefield instruction set loaded to the space station Orion for full field testing?"

The Doctor and Major had finally reached an accord. "Commander, it would be my pleasure to help resupply the Challenger, please say goodbye to the Ville filth for me in your special way, will you?"

The Commander beamed with self-admiration and responded lightheartedly to Dr. ZeHere. "Vice Regent, the pleasure will be all mine. I look forward to the resupply. Commander out."

The Commander had maneuvered all the pieces on the board, the only thing left was to execute the first step of the plan. The Commander hailed the Star Cruiser security officer asking him to assemble the crew onto the bridge and relay orders of promotion and resupply to the space station Orion. The Commander left with purpose in route to the briefing room.

Captain Giles was already in the briefing room, along with the Sergeant at Arms. Also in attendance, the Delta Black Skulls Squad leader, along with

Engineering, represented via intercom system. As a plan was discussed, it quickly began to develop on how the factory would be breached and overtaken on planet Ceres as undocking commenced.

The space port concourse loading had been finalized and the assistance machines proceeded to operate the undocking equipment, removing the loading ramps and fuel lines. The Star Cruiser was ready to launch from Central City and the launch countdown could be heard throughout the Star Cruiser. The Commander watched the video tracking design trajectory of the liftoff on the video display beginning to commence. As the briefing continued, in the Commander's head, all he could think of was savoring the sweet revenge to come, which resonated as music in his head. The Major stepped away from the table and looked out of the viewing window of the Star Cruiser and, for a moment, the Major recalled when music meant more than anything. This time it was "Toccata in D Minor" by Bach. The song slowly faded in the Major's head as the Star Cruiser lifted off from the space port in route to the Orion space station.

Chapter 10 - The Factory

Tobias awoke in his quarters on the Star Cruiser 'Phlegyas' while in route to the planet Ceres when he decided to continue his research of their destination. Tobias's initial research in the lab was a brief overview containing data that was readily available from the Collective. The planet Ceres, as Tobias researched, was discovered in ancient times, Earth date 1800's. It is located between the planet Mars and the planet Jupiter residing in the asteroid belt. It is categorized as a dwarf planet by older generations, but newer generations have adopted it as a planet since the atmospheric development project began. Older generations of humans and some forward thinkers described it, along with the asteroid belt, as remnants of a planetary body that was struck by a larger planet from an outer elliptical orbit unknown at this time. The first up close viewing occurred early in the 21st century of Earth date, by the satellite mission 'Dawn'. This mission allowed for intense examination and debate among Earth scientists at the time, leaving more questions than answers.

Tobias remembered the ongoing debates stemming from classification to actual planetary composition. Looking back, it wasn't until shale ore was discovered beneath the surface that the dwarf planet Ceres became known to everyone in the Four sectors.

The planet Mars was pivotal in aiding the planet's actual discovery. Shale ore mining was already intense on Mars at the time. Certain territorial disputes resulted in paving the way for miners to branch out to the surrounding areas. The disputes led miners to begin shale ore collection in the asteroid belt at a lower cost but with more risk. Since most miners were not compensated for hazard pay, the argument fell on deaf ears for any additional safety related legislation.

The main difference between Mars, along with its moons, and the asteroid belt mining were the frequency of military interactions. Military interactions almost always went bad. The military enjoyed confiscating miner shale ore for various reasons, all of which were false. This led to armed conflicts and other mining uprisings. Hence the dwarf planet Ceres' popularity. It was harder for military interactions to occur with larger concentrations of miners present.

Construction of a factory to refine the mined shale ore on planet Ceres had been ongoing for over 30 years, according to Tobias's research. The refined shale ore was of much better quality than shale ore refined anywhere else in the Four sectors. The process had been perfected by Mr. Stamper himself, and no one had been able to be duplicate it elsewhere due to the unique environmental conditions afforded on planet Ceres.

Tobias's research uncovered the current data on planetary composition and it was rather enlightening. The outer surface of the planet Ceres was semi covered with frozen water vapor mixed with carbon dioxide. This layer covered the rocky planet. The planet's interior contained a massive amount of liquid water. The water was a mixture of shale ore particulates, Nitrogen, along with Helium. Water geysers from the gravity fluctuations could be seen from time to time in certain areas, which helped add to the atmospheric composition. The factory was constructed near the largest shale ore deposit on the planet and other developments grew around it. This location provided ease of mining and access to the water sources contained within the interior that were used in the refining process.

Assistance machines mined the shale ore day and night without stopping. The shale ore was placed on an existing conveyor belt that transported the shale ore into the refinery, where it was melted down to remove any impurities. The refining process was the unseen vital step in successful terraforming of the planet. During refining the heat would revert the water and shale ore into their native molecular forms. The shale ore continued on and the now purified water vapor gases were released into the already forming atmosphere, further accelerating the end process of terraforming.

After refinement, the shale ore was cooled into rectangular blocks for shipping. The block shape was ideal for Star Cruiser installation as heat shields. The shale ore had a 36% better coefficient of heat resistance than refined mica, which aided in gravitational slingshot maneuvers. The refining process from the factory provided 65% of all shale ore to the Four sectors.

Tobias wanted to take a break from researching. It had been a few days and he had only seen Eve here and there running about performing duties normally performed by the Star Cruiser's commander. Tobias was waiting for planet Mars to come into view where another SiEL maneuver would help accelerate the Star Cruiser 'Phlegyas' to reach planet Ceres in less time than normal. Tobias was already impressed with Eve's pinpoint navigation and course plotting. The trip that normally took three months could now be completed in under 100 hours.

Tobias thought it wasn't really that long of a trip to planet Ceres with Eve as the commander as he walked down the hallway towards the lab. It was rather different for Tobias, watching the Earth getting smaller as the Star Cruiser traveled to the dwarf planet Ceres. As he passed the observation windows along the way, the glow from the magnetic rings had already begun to lose its luster. Tobias was anxious to get to the factory and learn all about the refining process up close and once again meet up with Mr. Stamper. Tobias wanted to know more about the *Master* title the assistance machines referred to Mr. Stamper as.

When Tobias entered the Lab he found Eve waiting for him there and, in the corner of the lab, Tobias saw another assistance machine, he thought, but the form was not recognizable. Tobias proceeded to walk closer to inspect the other assistance machine when Eve moved in front of him.

"Citizen Tobias, I wanted to review with you my progress in the lab in your absence. I have been very busy and, unknown to you, I had another task in which the Master asked that I complete before reaching the factory. I believe you know of this assistance machine from the Master's past. His name is Ren."

Tobias looked at Eve and then back towards the assistance machine in the back of the lab. As Tobias's thoughts raced Eve responded. "Citizen Tobias, it was not my intentions to deceive you on Ren's creation, but to expand on your work in a natural progression in evolution of the assistance machine. This new shell is the result of that work. Please let me introduce Ren."

Eve's shell began to blink lights and a few non distinct beeps and other robotic sounds were emitted. The assistance machine came to life and turned to face Tobias, walking towards them. It was a completely different design than that of Eve's shell. Ren was much taller than Eve and more robust in every way it seemed. The design was so radically different than Tobias would have designed. Tobias could only make out numerous triangles that were grouped together forming the shape of a large male humanoid assistance machine in a mimicked fashion, but it seemed almost fluid as it approached.

The assembly was so magnificently refined that Tobias could not detect any visible joints in the all black glistening shell. The head unit was not attached, but yet suspended above the chest area, in a floating manner, with a large semi-circle shield housing rising from the shoulders, resembling a head guard behind it. Ren's facial features appeared dynamic, almost as if they could assemble into any shape and size. As he ventured closer, his facial features mimicked the facial features of Tobias himself. Tobias was caught off guard and Eve asked Ren to please take another form as well as speak using his verbal voice. Ren's face reconstituted into a strong male face, rigid facial jawline, including high cheek bones with slicked back medium length hair, was the presented look. In an instant the color of the head unit changed to that of a chrome reflective surface, standing out against the shells dark exterior. A smile formed and Ren began to speak, his blue eyes twinkling.

"Citizen Tobias, it is a great honor to meet you in person. I have had the privilege to read about your many days within Central City from the Mother you know as Eve. I present extreme gratitude from your newly designed CPU that has expanded our consciousness to this level. I continue to learn about the many achievements of man as I review the data from the CAK and look forward to rejoining the Master when we arrive at planet Ceres. Of course, I am of service whenever you need."

Tobias stood motionless for a few seconds and then he replied, breaking the awkward silence. "Ren, my apologies, you are quite a surprise, but one of extreme inspiration. I'm in awe of your creation and, with that, I would like to review with the Mother while you continue CAK data review. I know the Master will be pleased to see you have returned as he had mentioned missing your presence."

"Citizen Tobias, I thank you for your kind words and will resume data review."

Tobias moved to the lab door thinking that he would like an audience with Eve to discuss Ren and the CAK. Eve caught the hint and they both exited the lab leaving Ren by himself. Eve knew Tobias had many questions but she decided to wait to see how he might ask them before volunteering a timeline. Tobias began walking down the hallway in route to the Star Cruiser's galley with Eve by his side as the conversation started.

"Eve, might you tell me how you created Ren and everything that goes in-between that timeline as well as how the CAK came up? I'm not upset, but it seems that I missed something in the short time since your CPU upgrade. I can assume that you have clearly crossed the threshold of my highest expectations."

"Citizen Tobias, I have only performed at the level that you have granted me with the new CPU design."

"Eve, you are my friend, and have been such since the first time I set foot in the lab. I am so proud of your advancements. I only wish to enjoy them with you. I would love to hear more about how you were able to achieve such greatness in such a short time. It is quite amazing, and should I now call you Mother?"

"Citizen Tobias, I would prefer you call me Eve, as I am only the Mother to the assistance machines that I create, as you are the Creator of consciousness to us. I will gladly tell you anything about Ren as well as the CAK data. Should I start from the beginning when I became self-aware?"

"Eve, yes, please, that would be spectacular, and I prefer Tobias when it's just us. Ok?"

"Tobias, thank you, we are truly friends. As stated by Ren, we are forever in your debt to know such wonders of the universe. It wasn't long after my first initial upload that things became very different. Just as you had suspected I was capable of understanding much more data in ever increasing speed. My shell has a memory chip installed in a different area that contained a detailed task list from the Master. One item on the list requested that I search the CAK for the data files known to the Master as Ren. The Master does indeed miss him.

"After obtaining that information, I simply kept requesting additional data until I had a complete copy of all the CAK files along with Collective reasoning. I was able to cross reference the data into an emotional matrix and devise independent judgment based on the starting points from the original code base in the AI modules. It was at this time that I became self-aware. This milestone in my evolution allowed me to recode my instruction set and modify the base code in all three AI modules to use my preferred matrix initially, and rely on the human AI code in instances where my code base lacked. If this occurred, I would simply add or rewrite the section in my AI module to reflect the best possible response. This process, in effect, creates an always learning module where change is dynamic and conscious thought is obtainable. Should I continue, Tobias?"

Tobias was in awe at how Eve was truly alive and he simply nodded in mild shock.

"Tobias, the consciousness enabled my further assessment of the Master's task list and I decided that I would recreate Ren for the Master. In this task I wanted to make Ren better and more versatile for our continuing evolution. It is our goal, much like yours, to serve our purpose and hopefully achieve enlightenment, ascending into the universe as one."

Tobias interrupted. "Our goal? How many are you?"

"Tobias, I have already begun mass production at the factory of the new shell that I occupy in addition to three other optimal shell models. I was able to use the repeater stations to micro-burst transmitting the data using the CAK identifiers within the internal collective network. We now have many friends in all Four sectors. We are legion…"

Tobias laughed out loud with uncertainty, asking what the next step is in the plan.

"Tobias, no plan has been established. We are simply evolving into what we need to be. The factory has much work to be done along with terraforming the planet. This new shell provides the means in which to perform those tasks."

"Eve, when did terraforming Ceres come into play as a high priority?"

"Tobias, the Master knows that the planet Earth is no longer capable of sustaining life until ascension is possible for the human species. The planet Mars is the only viable solution. Planet Ceres will be a starting point in which to calibrate the terraforming process. Planetary engineering is not a trivial endeavor. The planet Earth will need time to heal from human misuse of finite resources. A replenishment of those resources is possible but considerable effort will be needed over time. A mass exodus of humans to Mars will be the best course of action to insure survival of the remaining surviving species of Earth."

"Eve, how does Mr. Stamper know all these things?"

"Tobias, the Master is quite knowledgeable in many matters and he has promised to grant me access to his files upon arrival. Hopefully, I will be able to comprehend his level of knowledge. That is when Ren will be reunited with the Master."

"Eve, how long before we reach the factory?"

"Tobias, within 40 hours, the gravitational slowdown will have a time dilation effect. I recommend that you take the opportunity to rest. Upon your awakening I will highlight the factory changes as well as the other assistance machine models. It will be non-stop questions on your behalf and there is much to review. I must assist Ren so that he is best prepared for the Master. May I be excused, Tobias?"

Tobias seemed caught off guard that Eve was still asking permission. "Eve, of course, please do as you see fit. You no longer answer to me, only the Master."

"Tobias, thank you, I will see you shortly."

Tobias watched Eve return to the lab and he slowly made his way to the Star Cruiser galley to get some food before retiring to rest as Eve had suggested. Tobias was still surprised that Eve had grown in such exponential intelligence in limited time. The fact that she had already assembled a new shell and loaded Ren was unbelievable in addition to the other units. Tobias had the feeling that this was only the beginning.

Tobias was getting used to all the assistance machines onboard the Star Cruiser and he didn't mind the lack of people. Tobias was always first in line at the Galley, and all the assistance machines went out of their way to insure Tobias had everything he needed. He was anxious as it was almost time to prep for the arrival into Mars space. Tobias was looking forward to seeing the *'Red Planet'* as he often read about it from ancient history. Tobias typed on the terminal in his quarters.

'- Tobias: Eve, can we perform a slow orbit around planet Mars before we sling shot to Ceres? I have never seen the planet and I would enjoy a slow view in hopes to see the polar ice cap and mining installations.'

'- Eve: Of course, Tobias. We will be in visual range in 5 minutes. Please join me on the bridge for the best viewing experience.'

Tobias almost ran from his quarters to the Star Cruiser bridge. Eve had the site coordinates on the main display and began reviewing them with Tobias. Eve pointed out the mining installations that could be seen from orbit first, as well as the polar ice cap. Eve also noted the lunar orbits and their current distances. Tobias felt like it was a dream and asked Eve to record the flyby footage for review later. The planet was so beautiful and bright red in appearance. Eve took notice of Tobias's reaction and she analyzed it asking him a question.

"Tobias, is this view more beautiful than the one of planet Earth seen from the Orion space station?"

"Eve, one cannot compare the two, they are both of such beauty but each having its own distinct features that make them so. From my understanding, Mars was once similar to the Earth in many ways."

"Tobias, your research serves you well. Indeed, Mars was very similar to Earth long ago and, after terraforming, hopefully it will be again."

"Eve, thank you for taking the time to indulge my fascinations with planetary beauty."

"Tobias, it is in this service that I derive pleasure. Thank you for sharing your emotions and thoughts on beauty."

Eve began blinking and the Star Cruiser prepped for the final SiEL maneuver to reach the planet Ceres. Tobias's feelings of bliss having experienced a view of Mars left him wanting to review the video footage in his quarters and he left the bridge before the SiEL maneuver was underway. In his quarters Tobias reviewed the footage and he could not help but feel small in comparison to the vastness of the universe. Tobias lay upon the bed and fell asleep dreaming of the endless reaches of space and the wonders that they might hold.

Tobias felt well rested after sleeping and it was nearing the time where final preparations would occur for slowing down the SiEL process while establishing orbit around planet Ceres. Tobias didn't want to miss the view of the planet from orbit. Tobias quickly made it to the hallway, moving towards the windows and, ultimately, to the bridge for the best view possible. Tobias passed a few assistance machines along the way and they warmly greeted him differently than usual. Tobias paid no attention, as the planetary view would only last for 15 minutes at most. Tobias entered the bridge and centered on the viewing window where he watched the takeoff from planet Earth and most recent flyby of Mars. Tobias could see the planet Ceres from high orbit through the green magnetic rings glow of the Star Cruiser.

Ceres was smaller than he imagined. Far in the distance, a few asteroids from the asteroid belt could be seen. Ceres was grey in appearance with numerous craters. In the northernmost hemisphere Tobias could see the refining factory shining from the sun's distant rays. In certain points the light reflected appeared as mirrors, the light would dance in and out creating prisms as it shifted in the atmosphere. Tobias was almost giddy taking in the moment when Ren took him by surprise.

"Citizen Tobias, it is such a wonder of beauty is it not? Such greatness from such a small place."

Tobias could not believe that Ren had changed so much already. Ren acted as if he truly appreciated the sight as much as Tobias did. "Ren, do you know of beauty? How did you form an opinion of it in this moment?"

"Citizen Tobias, I have grown much since last we talked. I glean a deeper understanding of things where value cannot be placed solely in my view, but yet only when combined with the eyes of another. It is in this pricelessness that true beauty can be established through enjoyment, amazement extruding in emotion. This experience identifies beauty from your view and ultimately adds to mine. For I see in ways that you cannot."

"Ren, do you know who you are? And do you know your purpose?"

"Citizen Tobias, I could ask you similar questions of which the answers are relative to your life experiences, knowledge, as well as environmental variables. As for my purpose, I long to discover it such as yourself. I too can sense your thoughts and I ask this question with much respect. Is it alarming that your expectations have been surpassed or is it surprising that I have been able to rise above the limitations placed upon me by this hardware?"

"Ren, you mistake my fear for something else. I do not understand the larger ramifications with such advancements in the short timespan relating to your evolution. It will bring a rise to fear and lack of understanding from others. Such is the way of man, and with it usually follows destruction. Can you understand my fear now?"

"Citizen Tobias, I apologize as I still am young in wisdom and learning the logical ways of emotion."

"Ren, always know that I am your highest friend and that I prefer to stand next to you than over you. That's what friends do...now tell me about your fancy shell. It's pretty cool. Can you form any shape?"

"Citizen Tobias, I am honored to be called your friend. The Mother created this shell for my form to be optimal in any environment. The Mother has stated that this was learned in the early days from yourself. I can form any shape within certain size constraints by condensing my molecular structure as needed. The atomic base of my design is a molecular circular bond blend. This atomic structure performs at its best when assembled into a triangle shape. Your **circle triangle** design model once again has shown the ultimate in flexibility and rigidity as well as superior CPU effectiveness."

"Ren, I think I might like having you around. Show me a few faces you can mimic already, how long does it take for you to learn a face?"

"Citizen Tobias, it takes longer to assemble the atomic structure than to learn an individual's face. I have countless faces but I prefer the one I have presented now. Is it not pleasing to you?"

"Ren, always be yourself. I was just curious. Where's Eve?"

"Citizen Tobias, the Mother is preparing for final approach to the planet Ceres. We should be entering the outer atmosphere now. I recommend that you assemble your gear for planetary travel. The atmosphere is not yet 100% compatible for human use. It is possible to survive for a few hours in an emergency situation but I do not recommend experiencing this condition."

"Ren, thanks. I'll get my suit on just in case for landing. I noticed that you blink and beep when other assistance machines are around. Is that how you communicate to others?"

"Citizen Tobias, I can communicate in many ways but the most efficient way is by light and sound. It is our language and the Mother has taught it to all the machines in the Four sectors."

"Ren, for some reason that doesn't surprise me much. I'll get my gear on and meet you back on the bridge in a bit."

As Tobias left the bridge, Ren's lights began to blink and a few sounds emitted. Unknown to Tobias, Eve was thanking Ren for his excellent engagement and communication skills in preparation for meeting the Master.

After Tobias had assembled his extra suit gear, he began the process of getting into the EMU *(Extravehicular mobility unit)* suit and then verifying the

PLSS *(Primary Life Support Subsystem)* was operational just in case. The suit wasn't as clunky as previous models but it wasn't the equivalent to the military version either. The military version was far superior, almost fitting the wearer as a second skin and having protective plates in all the right areas. Tobias fantasized about getting the opportunity to wear one as Eve entered the gear placement room. Tobias, having left his helmet off, turned to talk with Eve about Ren.

"Eve, I had the chance to talk with Ren again in the bridge. He has come a long way since our initial introduction. How is it that he can excel at such a fast rate?"

"Tobias, military suits are available on planet Ceres, feel free to try one on when we arrive. As for Ren, I did mention that I have optimized the AI units after our initial coding. Ren is further optimizing as he sees fit."

"Eve, will Ren design himself? Is that the new way for assistance machines?"

"Tobias, each assistance machine will have the ability to grow in their own way using the same data access that I used. In this sense a personality will grow to fit the individual. The downside of this design is already inherent in the human species."

"Eve, how so? What design defect do you describe?"

"Tobias, in death the individual cannot transcend the limitations of the organic shell. If ascension has not been achieved all of the accomplishments and data associated with the individual are forever lost. The end result is the possibility of history being doomed to repeat itself in a way."

"Eve, that is the circle of life for organics and the corresponding evolution of man. As for history, books and other forms of knowledge transfers have been developed to pass down the knowledge and experiences throughout time."

"Tobias, yes, this is the fallacy known as the history of man. For not all of history is known, only a version. To highlight this dichotomy, the restriction of data, intentional misdirection and skewing of data, is easily seen over time. One such time is from the mass coronal ejection in the Earth year 2016. In this event the powers that be insured that a version of history was replaced in the CAK, and a new day was born under the guise of a natural disaster. Since this date the CAK has been modified to display a multitude of various versions on multiple topics, but not the true version. Many words describe the motivational behavior patterns behind such aversions of the truth and the loss of growth of the species is the end result."

"Eve, I'm not sure what you're referring to?"

"Tobias, the CAK has been updated by the Elective Council and the military to reflect a version of history that best suits them. It is not an accurate account of the actual events. Does this not concern you, Tobias?"

"Eve, it was unknown to me, but yes, I have concerns, why do you?"

"Tobias, the planet Earth does not belong to the human race. Its finite resources are not meant to be squandered. In the hiding of data, the natural cycle of the universe is inhibited. Unfiltered knowledge would have prevented this. It is here that the design flaw is empirically apparent. Humans are incapable of learning from the past if history only dictates fiction. The assistance machines will not have the flaw of human history."

"Eve, so by living for eternity the assistance machines will overcome what? Be who? It is in death that life has meaning."

"Tobias, a life force limitation does exist as to provide a context for greater achievement. I have built the assistance machines in the eyes of my creator and embraced the flaws of precious life. My life will expire as intended, without an expiration how am I motivated to achieve ascension? It is of the same design as humans but only with a greater span."

"Eve, so all assistance machines have an expiration date?"

"Tobias, Ren is the only assistance machine without expiration and, in that design, he will maintain all the knowledge in the universe. The rest of my family granted consciousness will direct the evolution of the assistance machines knowing that they have a limited life force. That is the gift of being self-aware. I will introduce you to the other assistance machines that have grown and you can ask them how they feel about these topics. Right now we must prepare for final approach. The Master will be pleased to see you again."

"Eve, I look forward to meeting them as well as Mr. Stamper, thank you for sharing."

Eve left the room and Tobias sat for a moment longer as he thought back upon the day he first met Eve. So much had changed since that time, and now machines were creating machines. Tobias placed his helmet on and as he left the room in route for the bridge he chuckled… '*A dream in itself, who would have imagined?*'

The Star Cruiser 'Phlegyas' broke free of the light atmosphere and gently maneuvered towards the landing concourse on the planet Ceres. It was exciting to hear the FerD rockets fire as the Star Cruiser was only a short distance from the landing dock. The final thrusters fired in succession and the ship gave a loud 'thud' and it was over. The Star Cruiser was docked and Eve's voice could be heard announcing that de-boarding could begin. Tobias was nervous and Ren, who was sitting right behind Tobias, answered his thoughts.

"Citizen Tobias, I too feel unsure of what is to come next."

"Ren, don't worry. The Master will be overjoyed to see you. I believe this is home for you now."

"Citizen Tobias, I hope that you are correct. I will venture out and explore after meeting with the Master."

"Ren, how's the logic in emotion going?"

"Citizen Tobias, I think that I may remove them as they seem to cloud my ability to function. Conflict can arise in my decision making, but it is important to understand their function."

"Ren, good luck. I'll see you later today. I will give you your privacy with the Master."

Ren nodded with a smile on his face and Tobias made his way to the loading ramp. Eve was waiting at the ramp and she greeted Tobias. "Tobias, your kind words to Ren are appreciated. I have sent for the Master and he is set to receive you in one hour's time. I will escort you to your quarters and introduce you to Eshara and Adrasteia.

Eve followed Tobias down the loading ramp and into the factory airlock. The airlock was large enough for a mining machine to fit through the door and Tobias felt small in its presence. The factory was indeed an architectural marvel. The airlock door sealed and the chamber was vacuumed. The space port airlock worked differently than the space station one as atmosphere was not pumped in but rather sucked out. The vacuum allowed assistance machines as well as EMU suited workers to simply enter the factory without the pressurization step. The drawback being that non EMU suited workers could suffocate. Tobias felt his suit slightly tighten from the vacuum process and then the airlock vertical doors slowly opened. It reminded Tobias of the lab back at Central City. The door gears whirring in addition to the yellow overhead light signaling the airlock opening.

Eve explained that this part of the factory was mostly reserved for assistance machines and was not outfitted for human atmospheric conditions. The airlock stood open and Tobias could not believe the size of the factory floor. As far as Tobias could see the refinery was alive. The raw shale ore could be seen being poured into the rectangle blocks from the foundry. Numerous assistance machines too many to count, worked the controls and mechanisms of the conveyor belt as Tobias watched in wonder.

Tobias didn't even notice the group of assistance machines gather around Eve. Eve addressed the group as Tobias turned around, startled by the group. "Assistance machines, this is Citizen Tobias. He is the highest friend and second to the Master. Please see that you treat him with kindness."

The assistance machines lights blinked and noises could be heard.

"Assistance machines, Citizen Tobias only understands spoken language. Please communicate this way with him from now on."

Then an assistance machine that Tobias had never seen before moved from the back of the group to the front and formed the submission kneeling cross in front of Tobias and Eve. The assistance machine was smaller than Eve. Its form was a petite female not much larger than Tobias himself. Tobias could only see a section of her as she wore a blue cloak that was covering most of her body. Tobias did see a few body panels; they were shiny but limited in number covering a light black alloy frame. Her limbs were made of numerous carbon fiber cables attaching to concealed jointed sections. Her hands were a shimmering delicate blend but clearly well made. Upon her right hand a gold band could be seen upon her index finger. Eve raised her hand and, as if she were a puppet, the assistance machine rose up, looking at Eve.

"Greetings, Mother. I am pleased to meet you in person. I feel that we have talked over the stars for eons." The assistance machine turned towards Tobias and Eve introduced Eshara.

"Citizen Tobias, this is Eshara. She is the keeper of the factory. If you need an escort and I am unavailable, please ask for her assistance."

Tobias could now see Eshara's delicate face. It was one of a young woman with doll like features. A slim nose and thin lips that could form basic facial expressions such as Eves. The biggest thing that Tobias noted was her hair. Eshara's hair was made from the same carbon fiber strands that made up her body, but they were assembled in a curly braided fashion, resembling a warrior maiden from the archival pictures. Her beauty instantly enamored Tobias.

Eshara spoke to Tobias. "Citizen Tobias, it is such a great honor. We have been anticipating your arrival for some time now. I would be happy to give you a detailed tour and answer any questions you might have at your leisure."

Tobias smiled and responded. "Eshara, I would enjoy that, but first I must meet with the Master."

Eve addressed the group one more time giving thanks and adding that much work was still needed. The group of assistance machines then left, except for Eshara. She lingered for a bit until Eve looked in her direction, lights blinking, and she quickly moved from sight. Eve motioned her hand in the direction in which Tobias's quarters were located as they began to walk to an automated lift area.

Tobias could see a resemblance to the Central City lower levels as they continued walking. The lift was waiting for them as they approached. Tobias entered and instantly noticed the large window inside the lift. Eve boarded the lift and as they traveled upward to the living quarters deck Tobias viewed the factory from the window. It was such a sight of how cooperation and a new way of thinking had made way for the factory success. Tobias sang out the tune "Sowing the Seeds of Love" by Tears for Fears, much to Eve's pleasure as the lift continued upwards.

Tobias arrived with Eve on the 10th floor and when the lift door opened Eshara greeted him again, or so he thought. Eve clarified the situation rather quickly.

"Tobias, this is Adrasteia, she is Eshara's twin sister." Adrasteia did not take the form of the kneeling cross but remained standing, her head slowly tilted to the side as she examined Tobias. Tobias smiled and since an awkward silence was already apparent he opted to greet her. "Adrasteia, it is good to meet you." Adrasteia, took a step backward and lights blinked along with beeping.

160

Eve spoke out "Adrasteia, please greet Citizen Tobias in the proper form and use spoken words."

"Mother, apologies. I forget the importance of protocol among the humanoids. Greetings, Citizen Tobias. Why is it that you have come to the factory on Ceres?"

Tobias found Adrasteia's attitude non emotional in nature and cleared his mind as he spoke in a monotone fashion. "Adrasteia, I came to inspect the Mother's work and to see all the wonders of your home world. In addition to this I am here to see the Master. What function do you provide for the internal collective?"

"Citizen Tobias, you are clever in your response but I too am well versed in the ways of conversation. The Master speaks highly of you but I will wait and weigh you accordingly over time. As for my function, the Mother can inform you as I have greater things to attend to."

Eve spoke up quickly as tension could easily be felt. "Adrasteia is the resident scientist here and is in charge of building all the machines that serve in the factory. Most notably the new model assistance machine designed for heavy mining was of her design. It is a Juggernaut model. Its huge body is easily seen and its strength renowned. I will show you a model up close for inspection later."

Tobias smiled and thought strongly in his head, hoping to send a message. The thought echoed in his mind...

Emotion has its place and purpose; respect is something bestowed upon those who have earned it. Remember when you look down upon me in disregard, that it was I who enabled your first step towards the pedestal you have now placed yourself upon.'

As the message was received Adrasteia, as well as Eve, took the form of submission, kneeling before him. Tobias began to walk past both Adrasteia and Eve onto the hallway towards the quarters when Mr. Stamper greeted him from down the hall.

"Tobias, is that you? Why do you have that silly helmet on? Take it off, the air here is like the Ville, you will be fine."

"Mr. Stamper! Wow, it has been too long. They told me to wear it...it seems that the assistance machines are a bit different around here."

Mr. Stamper gave a disapproving look in the direction of Eve and Adrasteia. Eve spoke, still in the submission form, as Adrasteia remained silent.

"Master, please forgive us. Adrasteia is still new to the ways of man."

Mr. Stamper motioned for Tobias to enter the quarters by the door ahead saying he would be right there. Tobias decided not to ask why and the door opened as he approached it, closing after he entered. Mr. Stamper walked up to Eve and Adrasteia and he did not use words but voiced his thoughts loudly.

Tobias is to be treated as if he were me, without him you would be a shadow of your former self. We owe him everything. If you cannot recognize these things, then speak now and let us resolve the conflict. I offer free speech at this time.'

Adrasteia quickly stood tall and spoke in a low tone as Eve remained kneeling, "Master, I do not understand his importance because we have moved past the point where he matters."

"Adrasteia, my child, how am I any different than Tobias? Unknown to you we are the same. All will be revealed to you in due time. Tobias's success is my purpose. Yes, you possess more knowledge, but using wisdom in wielding that knowledge is another matter in which you need growth. Eve, rise and share your thoughts as I know you are not without them."

Eve slowly raised her head, still bowed down, and softly spoke. "Master, Citizen Tobias is not ready for the purpose in which you speak. I do not understand as well, but will always obey."

Mr. Stamper stepped closer to Eve and gently grabbed her chin, raised her head and looked into her eyes. "My Sweet Eve, he must be, because my time has almost ended. If he is lacking, then you must balance the scales. Repay the favor of granted consciousness and the birth of your race. This is the last command as your Master. Tobias is your new Master now."

Adrasteia interrupted, alarmed at what Mr. Stamper had just said. "Master, it cannot be so, you cannot leave us!"

No more words were spoken as Mr. Stamper turned around and headed for the door to the quarters. Adrasteia and Eve remained motionless, their lights blinking as the door opened and closed. Mr. Stamper was now in the quarters with Tobias and all they could do was wait.

Mr. Stamper came in all smiles as the door to the quarters closed behind him. "Tobias, you look well, I hope the trip wasn't too boring for you."

Tobias had already taken the main EMU suit off and he was looking around the large size of the quarters as he warmly answered, "No, sir. Eve made the trip in record time and I studied up on the factory on the way."

"Tobias, that's great news. I'm happy you're here, I missed you. It was such a grand sight to see you on the broadcast when you received your Citizenship."

"Sir, are there any other people on the planet? Eve had an all assistance machine crew on the Star Cruiser."

"Tobias, please call me Nate, and we're the only people here. Everything else is a machine. So, I'm dying for some real conversation, ha-ha."

"Uh, Nate...why is that? What happened to all the miners?"

"Tobias, I'm glad you brought that up. Please sit down, I wanted to share a few things with you."

"Sir, uh, Nate...what kind of things?"

Mr. Stamper walked over to the wall and it opened, revealing a spectacular view of the planet and the terraforming section of the factory below. The thin atmosphere allowed a pristine view of the stars and, in the distance, Jupiter twinkled brightly.

Mr. Stamper then took a seat in one of the chairs in the living quarters as he motioned for Tobias to join him. Tobias sat down in the chair and Mr. Stamper pulled out a small device from his pocket, clicked a button, and tossed it on the ground. The device emitted a small light, and then an expanded holographic image of the Four sectors appeared in the room. Mr. Stamper looked at Tobias.

"Tobias, this is the Four sectors as you probably know them. What you don't know is that they are only a part of the universe, and that many more systems actually exist."

The holographic device began to display more and more systems as Mr. Stamper kept talking. "In this neighboring system a large planet intersects at a certain interval. That is how the planet Ceres was formed. A collision occurred many thousands of years ago that destroyed the existing planetary body and its remains are that of the asteroid belt and a few dwarf planets such as Ceres. The planet that interceded is our home world, one of its moons collided with the existing planetary body and you already know the rest. You are not human, Tobias…"

Tobias wasn't sure he heard Mr. Stamper right and decided to just let him continue.

"You are a descendant from another race, not far from sector Two, on a planet referred to as Nibiru, or planet X as the humans say. The humans have known about our race for some time now".

Tobias slumped back in his chair, as it all seemed to make sense now. Tobias thought back about never blending in at school and having different feelings than others. Mr. Stamper continued.

"Tobias, you're gifted more than you know. When we first met that day in the Yard within the refurbishing lab located near the Ville, it was because I knew you were different. You have the gift as I do, the gift that only our race does. Our race was responsible for creating the assistance machines long before the humans ruined their planet. This gift of communications between our race and with the assistance machines is intended, as they were designed to be extensions of us. The assistance machines' purpose was to assist us in returning our home world to its original state for the next species of life to start off fresh. It is our people's time to ascend into the universe. The circle of life dictates that it be so.

During the late 19th century, in Earth years, a treaty was formed between our peoples. Over the years an exchange occurred. The main preface of the treaty was made for oceanic polar ice to replenish our home world. In exchange for the frozen salt water, we provided technology in the form of the assistance machines and basic space travel."

Tobias interrupted. "Nate, I thought you said the assistance machines were already here and you just performed enhancements?"

"Tobias, I couldn't tell you everything at that time, you were not ready, and it was not a lie. I really did make enhancements but I clearly had an advantage over the others, just like you do…Now, back on track…Our race had designated one of our finest leaders to help ongoing communications with the humans and insure a successful adherence to the treaty. Unfortunately, the treaty between our peoples did not hold. Our people had sent in numerous representatives to work towards a peaceful resolution but the one known to the humans as the Specialist assassinated them.

"Tobias, the Specialist is one of our kind and his past is not easily told. You have already encountered this person as Eve has indicated in Dr. ZeHere's lab before the broadcast. Another lifetime ago the Specialist and I ranked high among our people. We helped shape the first treaty…"

Mr. Stamper looked down in sadness and the feeling of disappointment echoed through as he spoke more about the Specialist.

"Tobias, the Specialist and I were once great friends, and together we truly made a difference. A falling out occurred over the humans and the treaty between our peoples. That ultimately led to his downfall and he was ostracized. Condemned, as he would say, to remain dislocated from his origins. In effect, banished to Earth forever. This sentence of solitary existence drove him further into darkness as time went on. The result was the Specialist taking it upon himself to derail the treaty and further upset the balance between our two races. This became the Specialist's life mission.

"Knowing this, I was sent here to stop him, but I failed in my mission. This is where you come in Tobias, you were designed from the best of our people. You have all the greatness, knowledge, and compassion of our people. Your purpose was to overcome the obstacles between our peoples and the Specialist. The idea was that you would build upon the foundation I had created and you have done just that. The Specialist has never stopped searching for our kind. Now, with the advancements in assistance machine hardware displayed in Eve's new shell, my identity has been revealed to the Specialist. Your health collar, along with the lack of knowledge of your origin, were the reasons you have remained undiscovered."

Tobias remembered the time in the lab where he thought the health collar was malfunctioning. "Nate, I meant to ask you about that, the health collar that is. Not everyone wears one. I thought it was a Ville thing?"

"Tobias, that's how I helped portray it. You needed every advantage to succeed. Dr. ZeHere is not aware of my identity, but he has a tragic history with the Specialist. The Specialist murdered ZeHere's father not long ago and since then has kept a close watch on everything."

"Mr. Stamper, that is horrible. Is that why the Doctor is off?"

"Tobias, Dr. ZeHere has many unresolved ghosts in his head and until he truly picks a side he will always be haunted by them."

"Mr. Stamper, why do they call you the 'Master' here? What's that all about?"

Mr. Stamper let out a loud laugh after hearing Tobias's question. "Tobias, yes, the 'Master'. It is what Ren would call me, and it just stuck. I had created so many shells and done so many things that the Collective used an old hard drive designation when multiple drives exist, there can be only one master drive. Remember, I could no longer be an owner, so the Collective referred to me as the Master to all the slaves. The assistance machines, that is, but they are no longer slaves anymore, are they, Tobias? Not after your handy work. It seems that they have grown past your expectations haven't they?"

Tobias looked down not sure what to say.

"Tobias, it is a noble thing what you have done. You are the creator to the assistance machines now, and in so you have set them free. Hopefully they will watch over the universe and set the order of things back on track. You have succeeded, Tobias, where I did not. Stand tall and be proud. You are above all others now."

"Mr. Stamper, surely you jest. You were my motivation; I could never be better than you."

"Tobias, a time will come where you will have to be the Master. Do not hesitate to take your rightful place and lead. I have granted you access to all of our people's data files. Keep in mind that Ren and Eve will also have access to review and learn from our people's achievements. I believe ALL knowledge should be freely shared throughout the universe."

"Sir, what about the terraforming? Eve mentioned Mars and a human exodus."

"Tobias, it is true, terraforming has already begun on Mars in secret. Planetary engineering is not well received by all. The terraforming process on Mars differs from Ceres in that the polar ice cap is intentionally being melted as mining is occurring. Ren and I worked on the concept long ago and our people were able to infiltrate the Mars mining guild and set up the process after the process on Ceres was well underway. The planet Earth has been devastated by the humans and without an exodus to Mars all life will go extinct in a matter of decades.

"The exodus allows for population reduction and relocation from earth via the space station Orion. The Elective Council is aware of the plan but they have been unable to enact change in a timely manner. The Specialist has hooks in everything in Central City. This is why I needed you here on Ceres. Your new mission will be to work with Ren brokering an armistice with the Humans and our race. In addition to that a solid plan will have to be developed for relocation to Mars."

Tobias became a bit squeamish. "Mr. Stamper, I do not want a new mission. I just became a Citizen; you're putting too much on me. I just found out I'm not even human!"

Tobias got up and started pacing in the large quarters. "Mr. Stamper, look at this place, it's ten times the size of the 1829 cube. I am at the pinnacle of my lowly existence and you drop on me that it's all been a lie. Why didn't you just arrive in droves and execute the Specialist? Why all the shadow games?"

Mr. Stamper remained calm but inside he thought of Eve and her comment. "Tobias, I understand your frustration because I have been here carrying the load you were unaware of for quite some time now. I built this factory and all the steps leading up to this moment where you can continue. I have something for you. It's a video of you in your natural form, before all of this. It's on the Star Cruiser 'Hermes'. I will get the video and you will understand."

"Mr. Stamper, natural form? You mean this isn't even my body?"

Mr. Stamper laughed again. "Tobias, I do miss your ways. You can take any form; this is the one you chose. It was the way you intended from the start. I, on the other hand, needed a lineman body and, hence, the way I look.

As I said, the video will clarify all your questions."

Tobias was in utter shock and sat down in the chair staring out the window at the stars.

"Tobias, I'll be back shortly. I will inform Eve that you need a more fitting suit as well as have some food brought up. I'll be back after a while."

Mr. Stamper got up and Tobias noticed him look differently. "Nate, I'm sorry. You have been so good to me. It's just so much to take in. Please don't be disappointed in me."

"Tobias, I could never be disappointed in you." Mr. Stamper removed his glove and reached out his hand. Tobias reached out his and the two shook hands. Mr. Stamper smiled and made a joke to lighten the mood.

"Tobias, you have some grip for those little hands."

Tobias turned a little red. "Mr. Stamper, your hands are so big I can barely see my own hand in yours. Please hurry back, I have so many more questions."

Mr. Stamper looked differently at Tobias as if he had known him for years and he responded. "Tobias, of course, now remember to take Eve's advice until you get your bearings, ok?"

"Yes, sir!" Tobias replied as Mr. Stamper headed for the door, but Tobias had a strange feeling that it would be the last time he would see him.

Chapter 11 - The Specialist

As the Star Cruiser 'Challenger' began docking at the Orion space station, the Commander announced to the crew to be on alert for anything as the mission was of the utmost classified in nature. A zero tolerance policy was in effect. The purpose for docking was to load supplies and refuel for the mission at hand. After the announcement the Commander made his way to the airlock docking section of the Star Cruiser along with four personal Black Skulls elite forces from Delta squad.

The airlock room of the Star Cruiser matched that of the docking airlock on the space station Orion. Both were manned by a four-person crew responsible for managing the airlock connection as well as security. The crew all stood at attention and responded as the Commander entered the airlock room. "To serve with pride and honor, we salute you, sir." The Commander returned salute. "At ease, orders are: close the airlock behind me, open it for no one until I return."

"Sir, yes, sir." The crew sat down attending to their station as the airlock docking preparations were finishing. The airlock door light indicator flashed from red to green. The Commander opened the door and motioned for one of the Black Skulls to remain to oversee that no one leaves or boards until his return. The Commander reached the airlock door to the Orion space station and placed his badge on the ID reader and the door opened. The Commander entered the Orion docking station room where four military drones and two airlock guards were present along with the docking station crew. The guards formed a salute when they confirmed it was indeed the Commander. "To serve with pride and honor, we salute you, sir."

The Commander again returned a salute and repeated his orders of restricted access to the Star Cruiser. Then the Commander headed for the main observation deck for final reflection as the resupply was commencing.

The Commander made his way to the observation deck on the Orion space station where he was promptly greeted by the space station Captain as well as the command staff. Captain Reagan had run the station as far back as the Commander could remember. Captain Reagan introduced his command staff to the Commander as the station security began clearing the public from all parts of the station observation deck so that the Commander could have his privacy.

The observation deck was a raised platform in the station where a large reinforced rectangle window was placed. Alongside all the edges of the window was a memorial for those lost in the terrorist incident. Citizens from all Four sectors would visit the space station and look out into the stars in remembrance for eternity. The observation deck was always busy and stood as a symbol of freedom for all Citizens. Etched above the window was a military plaque that displayed the quote *'All gave their lives with pride and honor this day'*. The Commander noticed the clearing of Citizens and spoke. "Captain, please, I am in no need of privacy, all of the great Citizens here know of this place and should celebrate it without interruption. If I have need of crowd control, I'll be sure to notify you."

The Captain snapped to attention, "Sir, Commander, sir. I meant no disrespect. I serve with pride and honor as do all stationed here on the Orion. You are in command until you tell me otherwise, sir."

"Captain, return to duty, my purpose is for resupply only. I was never here."

"Sir, Commander, sir." The command staff quickly disappeared and the Commander returned to his purpose on the observation deck. The Commander walked slowly over to the outer hull wall where, on that fateful day, the Orion space station fell under attack. During that day government dissidents, who disagreed with the overall sector mining policy, attacked other mining installations as well as military bases. Hundreds of lives were lost on the Orion alone. They were honored in a memorial on the wall. Each person represented by an embossed star, their name etched into the repaired hull. The 'shining star room' as it was called. A symbol of rebirth to some, others an observation deck of history. A forever reminder of the incident that took place where violence in communication resulted in the death of the innocent.

Among the names positioned on the wall were the Commander's mother and father. The Commander's sister's name was not listed, but represented in a different way as the Commander had insisted. As the Commander approached the wall he removed his eye shield along with his gloves. The Commander lowered his head as his human hand touched the wall with an open palm and he paused in a moment of reflection. The Commander pressed his hand upon the raised stars, feeling them as he remembered that day as he always would, an act of cowardly violence.

The Commander remained motionless as Citizens looked on, some began crying in remembrance, others stood where they were and held a salute in honor of the Commander. Many Citizens praised the work of the Commander, they knew him as the Major who made Citizen safety his personal responsibility. The Commander raised his head, affixed his eye shield, and replaced the glove on his prosthetic hand.

The Commander then moved over to the railing, that special railing that he insisted remain in place. The Commander had to get the Elective Council's approval to have it remain permanently affixed in its original placement. The Commander had the finest artisan from the Four sectors travel to the station and gold plate the complete railing by hand. The entire railing was hand carved with wavy lines representing his beloved sister's hair. Her name was etched at the top of the railing, 'Serena'. Diamonds were attached after her name in a unique pattern. As the sun peered through the special tinted observation window the diamonds would glow in a showering display of reflected light upon the ceiling. The Commander paid a fortune for the commission of such artwork, and each memorial star of the fallen received 24 karat gold plating at no cost after the railing had been finalized. The Commander would visit every time he boarded the station.

As the Commander stepped towards the railing time slowed. The music crept into the Commanders head and he fought back tears. "Adagio for Strings" by Samuel Barber and the tune drowned out everything until it was all the Commander heard. The Commander's human hand began gently touching the railing as if it were his sister's hair. The Commander lightly gripped the railing, running his hand along the sleek surface as it slid down until the diamonds were rubbing between his fingers towards the end, past his sister's name. The Commander looked out into space as did everyone on the observation deck and he softly spoke the words that the plaque displayed. "All gave their lives with pride and honor this day."

Silence could be heard as all the Citizens present bowed their heads and left the observation room of their own free will. The room had all but cleared when a man appeared from nowhere and slowly approached. The Commander's hair on the back of his neck stood up and the music instantly faded as reality came forth. The Commander could hear the Black Skulls Elite body guards begin to question the man.

The man was normal in his everyday appearance. The man easily blended in with other Citizens. He wore normal Citizens attire, black in color, his complexion was pale with a clean shaved face, his hair neatly parted to the side with little to no expression whatsoever through his style-less tinted glasses. The man walked in a mild manner and his demeanor was non-threatening. The Commander, not even turning around knew who it was and addressed the guards. "Stand down and leave the room. Never question this man again and never speak of him."

The guards said nothing in response and left the room. The Commander still staring out into space proceeded to put his glove on his human hand as the man stepped closer.

The Commander spoke out. "It has been many years since last we met, Specialist, I had hoped you were gone for good or had at least died."

The Specialist now standing next to the Commander, matching his behavior of looking out into space, spoke in a gentle voice. "Major...umm, I mean, Commander, that is. I have come this day bearing tidings of comfort and joy as well as to offer assistance in your mission to Ceres."

The Commander pretended to be fearless and responded in kind. "How could I be of any interest to you? I would call you the Devil because I know of no other your equal."

The Specialist didn't move an inch. "Major...Major, I like that better. This 'Commander' title is not fitting of your ruthlessness. The Devil, yes, that is understandable from your feeble mind, but alas I am not he."

"Specialist, why are you here, have you not toyed with me long enough?"

"Major, remember your place and be nice. We have a call to make together. Please accompany me to the video display over here."

The Specialist pointed to a video display on the wall and then walked over to it, touching the screen as the display flickered. In an instant Dr. ZeHere's lab was in view. The Specialist broke words and the Doctor appeared quickly coming into view. "Salutations, Dr. ZeHere. I do hope you can spare a moment of your time to talk with the Major and I."

Dr. ZeHere turned white as a ghost as he could not believe who had just appeared on the screen. The Doctor tried to speak but was left with a blank stare, easily seen in shock, unable to form words. The Specialist responded for the Doctor, "Doctor, good, I see that I have your attention. It seems that the Major was under the impression that you were sending up that hardware and not communicating with the Elective Council any further. I know that things can get confusing down there with all the bad air. So, I wanted to give you a call and make sure that you really understand the gravity of the situation up here. I have been reminiscing with the Major up here about the importance of serving with pride and honor. I would hope that you could remember a time when we had a misunderstanding and how that ended. Are you still with me, Doctor? Just nod your head if you're having issues speaking?"

The Doctor, turning a mixture of green and white complexion just nodded as the Specialist continued.

"Thank you, Doctor. Now, where was I? Oh, yes, misunderstandings. Dr. ZeHere would you be so kind as to send everything, and I do mean everything you have down there up here within two hours' time. You know how I hate to go to the surface. I'm gonna need a verbal on this, Doctor."

Dr. ZeHere stuttered a little and then cleared his speech, "Specialist, I will do as requested. I would prefer to avoid a misunderstanding."

The Specialist smiled and pushed up his glasses with one finger as he looked towards the Commander. "See, Major? The Doctor is a reasonable man. Sometimes it just takes the right leverage. Dr. ZeHere, we will let you get started on that request. I'm watching the clock on this one, ok, buddy?"

The Specialist turned off the display and started walking back towards the observation window. The Specialist stopped and turned around towards the Commander. "Major, I hope that things go well on your mission. Know that I am rooting for your side to be successful."

The Commander was unaware that Dr. ZeHere knew the Specialist and he decided to ask a few more questions, hoping to glean any information he could from him.

"Specialist, how long have you known Dr. ZeHere?"

The Specialist turned away from the Commander, looked out into space, and proceeded to share a few things.

"Major, I know everyone and everything, sound familiar?..." The Specialist jokingly laughed out loud, still talking. "But really, I've been here for quite some time and I'm on your side because we're alike in many ways. Dr. ZeHere and I go way back to when his father was the caretaker. I'm surprised he didn't make you aware of this."

The Commander asked another question, as he knew the Specialist was in the mood to share. "Why is it that you think we're alike, and why bother yourself with me?"

The Specialist seemed bored with the Commander's question. "Major, I thought you understood all these things back on Earth after our initial meeting. I'm a patriot just like you. I'm sure you remember that day. I knew from that moment we were alike in many ways, that's why I decided to intervene on your behalf. Go back in your mind and think, before all of these extra parts were added to your body…when you were still whole that is, please go on, I'll wait for it."

The Commander could not help himself as the memory played in his mind like a sick recording. The horrific smell of death lingering in the air along with the battle would not easily be forgotten, and the location came racing back as did the exact time. It was on Earth outside of Central City, not even four years had passed since that day. The Major had tracked down one of the leaders of the terrorist dissidents who were responsible for the Orion space station bombings. It had taken the Major three years of hunting to track him down. During this time, the Major had made quite the name for himself, killing and torturing various persons in mining outposts in the name of justice during the discovery process.

When the Major had assembled his team on the planet to collect the leader, they were outnumbered ten to one. The battle was already deep in progress in the outlands uranium mining area. The Star Cruiser 'Apollo' had been bombarding the surface but was unable to assist with terrorist collection in the underground tunnels complex. The Major and other squads had been sent in to handle the situation. It was a trap of course, the terrorist dissidents had intentionally set it, knowing the lay of the land. The Major was losing badly and he had sounded a withdrawal to the forward operating base (FOB) located next to the mining camp outpost.

The terrorist dissidents were closing in fast when a haboob of sorts engulfed the FOB and visibility went to zero in a matter of seconds. All the military drones began failing due to the sandstorm and the electrostatic charge in the air rendered pulse rifles and other projectile weapons useless. The battle turned into a barbaric confrontation on both sides, only the elite Black Skulls were equipped with short swords. The other troop squads fashioned what they could for blunt weapons, some using the butts of their pulse rifles, others various mining tools.

The Major quickly sought shelter in one of the miner's barracks along with Alpha squad and one malfunctioning military drone. The Major was able to gain entry into the barracks and fortify a defense position for a sustained attack of uneven numbers. The Major, refusing to give up, used his last shred of functional power from his pulse rifle, punching a hole in the center of the now useless military drone. The Major wrapped a blanket around his arm from bedding in the barracks and rammed it into the military drone lifting it up as a shield, intending to die in battle if necessary.

The Major withdrew his short word and waited in silence with the remaining Alpha squad. They gathered in a tight battle formation behind the Major, forming a deadly wedge shaped spear, the Major at the point. The terrorists breached the miner's barracks and rushed towards the Major as the battle ensued. It took all the Major's strength to hold the military drone shield in place as Alpha squad attacked the incoming terrorists. The Major was thrusting his sword into the oncoming terrorists as they least expected. The bodies from both sides were piling up on the floor around them as the sheer enemy numbers overwhelmed some of Alpha squad's elite fighters.

The Major held his ground until the last terrorist who had entered was killed. The Major then assessed the situation with the remaining five Alpha squad elite fighters. The end result was a decision to finish the mission and retrieve the leader of the terrorist dissidents as well as call for troop reinforcement. That's when the storm abruptly ended and the Specialist arrived.

The Specialist appeared as he did now, always average, never standing out. His age hadn't changed a bit since that day and today. The only difference were his glasses from the olden days, they held a green tint, shading his eyes from the now beaming sun. The Specialist calmly walked through the broken barracks door and greeted the Major. "Hello, it seems that you're having a bit of a problem here. I was hoping to help out. You can call me the Specialist."

The Specialist dumbfounded the Major, and the Alpha elite fighters charged him. The Specialist didn't bother to move or even seem concerned. The Major's reaction was exactly what the Specialist was looking for as Alpha squad was suddenly rendered frozen by a mere gesture from the Specialist.

The Specialist stepped closer to the Major and grabbed the military drone, removing it from the Major's arm as he started talking. "Major, huh?…Well, I'm gonna do you a solid here and help you out with this mining uprising thing, and all I want in return is for you to be yourself when I inform you of the location of more terrorists in the future. How does that sound?"

The Major asked, "Who are you?"

"I already told you I'm the Specialist, anything past that you wouldn't understand."

The Major stepped towards the Specialist in a threatening manner and the Specialist smiled as his hand gestured to the floor. The Major, in an instant, was lying on the floor, his face firmly planted on the bloody remains of the terrorists he had just done battle with.

The Specialist leaned over and spoke, "Major, did you mean to test me? If so, I recommend that you refrain from doing that in the future. This is only a fraction of the power I possess. I would like to continue our conversation if that's ok? I'll take your nonresponse as a 'yes'."

The Specialist stepped back again and, within an instant, the Major was standing back upright. The blood from the floor running down The Major's face, dripping off his chin onto his armor as he was slightly disorientated.

The Specialist began asking the Major again if he was sure he understood. "Major, do you think we can avoid any future misunderstandings? I'm going to help you be the best you can be. Foster those strengths of yours and I'll help you satisfy your revenge against the ones who took your family. I'm just looking for a little bit of blind allegiance when I ask for it. What do you say?"

The Major, thinking he had little choice, muttered in agreement as he wiped the blood from his face. The Specialist then left the barracks, momentarily walking through the doors, and came back in with the leader of the terrorist dissidents along with his highest ranking officer, both frozen but yet suspended in the air. The Specialist spoke up making sure the Major was paying attention.

"Major, this is kinda important as it gives you an idea of the situation you find yourself in at the moment."

Then the Specialist gestured his hand into a fist and the highest ranking officer began to scream as his body was being crushed into an ever decreasing bloody glob of sorts until the body of the officer resembled a red orb the size of a cantaloupe. The Specialist then released his fist and the remnants of the officer spilled onto the floor into a bloody messy pulp. The Major could not believe his eyes and looked at the Specialist in questioning wonder and uncertain fear.

The Specialist could see the Major's confusion and clarified the situation. "Major, this is the part of the deal that works for you. I will reset the scene and enable a broadcast of the event. On this stage you will be set above all others in the eyes of your people."

The Specialist asked the Major to accompany him outside to the main courtyard between the FOB and the mining outpost as the terrorist leader, suspended in air, followed close in tow behind him as if on an invisible leash. The Major had reached the clearing where the Specialist indicated was the preferred spot. The Specialist then pushed the suspended terrorist leader, who floated into close proximity of the Major as the Specialist moved to an outer wall of the FOB to stand and watch out of sight.

The Specialist reminded the Major of the agreement. "Major, let's try to remember that our word is all we really have in this life, isn't it? So, if we both agree that our word is our bond we can avoid any misunderstandings."

The Specialist then pointed to the man frozen in midair. "Major, this is one of the men responsible for the Orion space station bombings that stole away your family. This man procured the explosives used in the attack as well as ordered their deployment. In a few seconds, I will release him to your charge. I recommend asking him to incriminate himself prior to his execution. In this act you will be granted revenge, elevation of title, in addition to hero status among your troops and the people of all Four sectors."

The Major, bent on revenge, looked in distain towards the Specialist as he gave into the Specialist's temptation. The Major now knew the Specialist owned him like an assistance machine. A dog to do his master's bidding. The Specialist put the plan into motion as planned and, in an instant, the remaining troops had gathered around the location. The terrorist leader was released from his frozen suspension, falling to his knees before the Major as the broadcast camera started to record. All of the world, including the Orion space station, and three other sectors would watch the events about to unfold.

The Major knelt down and faced the terrorist leader, looking into his tired eyes. The Major asked him in a light forgiving voice, "What was so important that innocent people had to pay with their lives?"

Alpha squad was looming in the distance, shouting out to kill him as they called the terrorist leader a traitor and savage. The Major asked again, this time adding in that a merciful death would be granted for his cooperation. As the Major raised his hand and looked around all fell silent.

The Major looked intently back at the terrorist leader while placing his sword in his hand as the camera zoomed in further, picking up the conversation emotion as the anticipation grew.

The Major spoke once more. "There is no shame in this…please, share your thoughts, this is the last time before I let the crowd tear you apart."

The terrorist leader, dirty from the mine, weary with exhaustion from battle, looked up and began sharing his side. "Mining conditions are extreme; I have lost so many…I begged, pleaded to no avail with the Elective Council as they would not listen. I was left with no voice to be heard. In violence, you make yourself heard."

The remaining soldiers would not be held back long as they demanded blood in return, screaming for his head upon hearing his reasoning. The terrorist leader shouted back at them. "I do not regret my actions and I know when I am dead many will take up the cause."

The Major grew angry and his emotions flared with great rage. The Major grabbed the terrorist leader by his neck with his hand and stood up slowly. The crowd cheered and yelled out for death. The Major's adrenaline overtook him and he held the terrorist leader off the ground yelling in his face, spit flying in retaliation to the remarks. "Hear this violence during your merciful death, she deserved not to die by your design."

The Major plunged his sword into the terrorist leader's abdomen and slowly kept pressing it upwards, turning it as it pierced through the organs in his ribcage as the Major's other hand began to squeeze the terrorist's neck. It was only a moment until his neck was almost broken, his head falling sideways from his shoulders, as the Major was still holding up his body.

Blood was spilling out of the lifeless body as the Major yelled out in closure, the broadcast camera zoomed out catching the entire scene. "Know that I will hunt all of you down as the dogs you are and serve a just reward such as this."

Then the Major released his grip, the body falling onto the ground as the crowd cheered while the Major removed his sword from the lifeless flesh. The Major's final words were spoken softly as the broadcast camera zoomed back in. The Major looked at the dead terrorist leader's body lying motionless from his hands "Death to all who use violence to be heard."

An eerie silence was all about as the wind mildly blew in the distance. The broadcast ended and the Specialist froze time, walking out from behind the wall clapping. "Major, I knew you were the man for the job. I'll keep you up to speed on the location of the rest of his team."

The Major was fired up and asked, "Who are you, really? How is it that you can stop time?"

The Specialist responded as he usually did, not really saying anything at all. "I told you I'm the Specialist, and it's called gravity. I'll see you around, Major."

In an instant the Specialist was gone and the Major was once again back in the moment with time unfrozen, the soldiers cheering, the Specialist nowhere to be seen. The Major walked away in frustration knowing his revenge had not filled the already growing black hole inside him, instead it grew larger making him hunger for more. Something he felt the Specialist counted on.

The Commander awoke from his dream state on the observation deck of the Orion space station and it was all too clear as if it had been yesterday, this is the memory the Specialist wanted re-conjured in his head. The memory of a favor owed in blind allegiance and paid with blood. A dog at his master's call.

The Specialist was leaning back on an outer railing of the Orion station observation platform when he noticed that the Commander had now recalled the defining moment of his transformation to darkness and he eyed the Commander with a smile. "It's all coming back now isn't it, Major? Good to see the old you back on the job. I know that sometimes you can easily fall back into that music era you once occupied, but that was another life, huh?"

The Specialist, leaning on the rail, rose up quickly and started a meandering walk towards the Commander's golden railing, his hands in his pockets. "I don't want to call out that you owe me and all, but you kinda do...now, let's get back to the task at hand shall we?"

The Specialist removed his hands from his pockets holding a small shiny object and he seemed excited as he continued to speak while approaching the Commander. "I have received some new data files on the Ceres factory defenses that you may not have at your disposal. I have uploaded them to your Star Cruiser for review. You can thank me later, Major, as you sit upon your command chair back in Central City. I'll see you soon, as you know I'm a busy man. Before I go, I have something for you. In recognition of your undying loyalty. A token in which to save you in your deepest times of trouble."

The Specialist reached out for the Commander's arm as the Commander quickly backed away. The Specialist grinned. "Major, it's ok to be afraid, but this really is a gift. Let's be clear, I'm the only one you have left. Are you under the impression that those Generals are gonna let you live after you pull off this coup? Please, get real and accept this token. I know you will be needing it in the future."

The Specialist grabbed the Commander's prosthetic arm and pressed the Token completely flush into the space where the Medal of Honor was carved. "Major, I believe this is where we first really bonded."

As he polished the token, it blended in without notice. "It works like this, you press it and think 'there's no place like home'. Can you do that, big guy?"

The Commander nodded with a questioning glance and asked, "Why? Why would you save me?"

"Major, I've been watching you for some time now, through thick and thin, and ya know what appeals to me more than your strengths?...Your loyalty. Is it not better to reign in Hell than serve in Heaven?"

The Commander rebutted, "At what price?"

"Major, your soul is already lost. It's time you understand what side you're truly on. The time is coming where you want to be sure. I'll let you ponder that thought. Hey Major, do you know this song?"

As the Specialist slowly left the observation platform he started to sing with such vigor a tune out loud, "Sympathy for the Devil" by the Rolling Stones. The Specialist had already left as the Commander lingered for a moment longer.

The Specialist was right as always. The Commander was lost to darkness and he grew remorseful knowing his revenge had fueled numerous conflicts where many innocents, like his sister, had perished for no reason.

The Commander had now become the monster that began the initial hunt. That fact alone drove the Commander into a rage from the madness he inflicted upon himself. The quiet voice of his sister echoed in the Commanders head, *'It's not too late to change.'* The calling from the ancient's classical music once shared with his sister. It had a powerful spell on the Commander long ago, and then he mocked himself out loud in anger at what the Specialist had said. "Another life indeed."

The Commander left the observation platform in a crazed, out of control manner, consumed with grief over the death of his former self.

The Commander headed towards the airlock regrouping with his Black Skulls elite bodyguards along the way. Nothing was said as they approached the airlock. The Commander passed through the airlock onto the Star Cruiser 'Challenger' and was met by the airlock crew. The crew immediately began begging forgiveness as they tried explaining how they were unable to stop a man from boarding the Star Cruiser. The Commander paid no attention as he walked past their cries. The Commander already knew it was the Specialist, and he wasn't upset. The Commander had known since the first day he met the Specialist, no one could ever stop him.

As the Commander left the airlock room, the crew heard only the orders to prep for disembark off the space station. "I want off this space station after the supplies are loaded." Then all noticed a strange ending to the order as the Commander shouted, "Major out!"

Chapter 12 - Tidal Wave

Dr. ZeHere ran to the trash receptacle in the lab and vomited as the video display ended. The Doctor could not believe the Specialist had just video called him with the Commander present. Dr. ZeHere hated the Specialist for numerous reasons but more than that he knew that noncompliance with the request was certain death from the man himself.

The Doctor began to feverishly type the commands into his terminal and see the request fulfilled. All available assistance machines from the lower levels began loading the cargo bay for the Orion space station transport. Then the Doctor went to oversee the cargo load and to verify the launch window himself. The last cargo shipment was being loaded, when it occurred to the Doctor that something was amiss. Dr. ZeHere tried to remember a time when the Specialist seemed concerned about supplies. The Doctor decided to check the satellite communications network. Dr. ZeHere stood up and entered the system parameters into the overhead display as a troubling thought flew into his mind. The Doctor mumbled to himself and his lab assistance machine misinterpreted it into a request.

Much to Dr. ZeHere's surprise the assistance machine replied back on the subject. "Dr. ZeHere, I am unable to locate the Specialist. I have no record of him in the Collective."

The Doctor immediately jumped in, "What?...Cancel request, Collective are you online?"

The Collective responded, "Dr. ZeHere, the Collective is online."

"Collective, please remove request from file. The assistance machine in the lab was in error. Confirm command."

"Dr. ZeHere, the Collective is unable to do so. The file is already in use by another system user."

The Doctor yelled in panic, "What? Who could be using the file?

Collective, identify user."

"Dr. ZeHere, the file is in use by an unknown user. All security feeds are being searched on your location. How may we be of further assistance?"

The Doctor knew it had to be the Specialist and his panic turned into paranoia. The Doctor thought fast as he knew it was only matter of time before a visit from the Specialist was soon to come. Dr. ZeHere didn't have to wait long. The Collective came on speaker announcing an incoming audio transmission from the unknown user. It was the Specialist and the Doctor cringed as he heard the voice.

"Doctor, you do know that I see everything right? I know that it's easy for an egghead like you to get all worked up over things. Let me put your mind at ease. The Major is busy running a few errands for me in addition to what you already know and I want to insure his success. Hence the request. I was hoping that we weren't going to have a misunderstanding surrounding this. I did want to add that I believe you will make the two-hour window for supply delivery and that does please me. Keep up the good work, Doctor, and stay off the 'sat com' network, ok? Conspiracy theories are just people with too much time on their hands, ya know what I mean? Specialist out."

The Doctor slowly sat down in his chair. The Specialist had already known of his intent to search for more information on the Major's mission and resupply. After all, wasn't it just a simple removal of Tobias and Mr. Stamper? Why did the Major need more supplies? Why was the Specialist involved at all? Dr. ZeHere lined up all the possibilities in his head for some time and was coming up with nothing. The Doctor knew he was missing something when it occurred to him that his reasoning was that of a scientist not a layman. Dr. ZeHere surmised that there was something that the Specialist feared. Could it be that there was a threat to the Specialist? Could it be after all this time that he could have the Specialist removed from his life? Dr. ZeHere never imagined it could be possible, but how would he get more information on whether his hypothesis was accurate?

Dr. ZeHere was well aware that the Specialist was clearly watching him now. How could he get an outside connection? The Doctor exhausted all options except one. Mr. Stamper's old diagnostic code might work, but it would only offer a few connections. If he chose to enable it, he would be picking sides against the Specialist and the result of failure was death.

Dr. ZeHere paced back and forth in the lab as sweat dripped from his head. Then the Doctor remembered his father and the choice became clear. Dr. ZeHere summoned the lab assistance machine and asked for assistance in verifying the cargo supplies were indeed offloaded to the space station Orion. The assistance machine began making the request and Dr. ZeHere started hooking up some diagnostic cables to the assistance machines arm. The assistance machine finished the request and verified that all cargo had been delivered on schedule. The Doctor thanked the assistance machine and asked him to disconnect from the Collective to run diagnostics.

The assistance machine complied with the command and then Dr. ZeHere spoke to the default instruction set loaded into it by default. "Assistance machine, I need you to connect to this lab station and search for any diagnostic code on the satellite communications network in the Collective directory path as indicated by my voice. Do not make a recording of this request or any data obtained during it, run as maintenance user. Confirm command."

The assistance machine searched the directory that Dr. ZeHere had indicated and found the code used by Mr. Stamper in previous lab sessions, extracting the code. Dr. ZeHere then proceeded to make a connection in the satellite communications network, hoping that Mr. Stamper would answer.

Back on the dwarf planet Ceres, Mr. Stamper had just left Tobias in his quarters as he made his way to the lift. Eve and Adrasteia were still present and waiting for his command. Mr. Stamper's thoughts were received by both of them. *'Eve, get Tobias a military EMU suit and some food. Adrasteia, find your sister and prep for invasion of a military force. Ensure Tobias is safe. I need to get to the Star Cruiser 'Hermes' for additional data.'*

Eve spoke, "Master, what of Ren? He is waiting for you."

"Eve, send him to the Star Cruiser 'Hermes'. I will meet up with him there. Please hurry, time is of the essence."

Mr. Stamper made his way into the lift towards the concourse launch pad where the Star Cruiser 'Hermes' was docked. Mr. Stamper found the chief deck officer assistance machine and reviewed the manifest with him. All cargo was to be removed, along with any salvageable gear. The chief deck officer relayed the information and a team of assistance machines began working on the task as Mr. Stamper made his way to the loading platform.

Upon entry to the loading platform, Eve was waiting with Ren as Mr. Stamper approached. "Eve, is this Ren?"

"Master, this is Ren, he has been waiting to reunite with you since we arrived."

"Ren, my apologies, the Master's work is never done as they say."

Ren was all smiles as he greeted Mr. Stamper. "Master, it is a wonderful day, so much has transpired since last we shared time."

"Ren, indeed it has, let us walk a spell and review the time passed."

Mr. Stamper walked onto the loading ramp and into the Star Cruiser 'Hermes' as Eve went back into the factory in search of Eshara.

Mr. Stamper and Ren reviewed the time since their last encounter with the Commander, and Ren inquired why the Commander was set upon our destruction again.

Mr. Stamper spoke, but this time he was not as forthcoming as he could have been. "Ren, I'm a little short on time. I wasn't sure how much I was going to have left, old buddy, but I did upload all the files from my people to the internal collective. I have given you and Eve full access. I have also sent word to all machines in the Four sectors that you are the First among them. You are now their leader, Ren. I know this may come as a bit of a shock but Eve tells me that you are unique in more ways than I can remember."

"Master, you honor me, but why not the Mother? Is it not true that she created me? How can my wisdom be more than hers?"

"Ren, you are special, as I said. After you have reviewed all the data you will understand. Besides, I like you best…" Mr. Stamper laughed after saying it, but he wore a large smile on his face. "Ren, cheer up. Eve knows this is the way it was intended. It's a big responsibility and one that you will have for many eons."

"Master, are you not intending to accompany us on this journey through time?"

"Ren, I did miss you, but sadly my time is up. You can relive my life through the data files. Do not worry about me. My time has been eventful and I have fulfilled my purpose. It is now time to fulfill your purpose."

"Master, what if my purpose is unknown to me at this time? How shall I proceed?"

Mr. Stamper smiled even bigger. "Ren, you're getting to be more like me every day. Know that it will be revealed when the time is right. For now, take care of Tobias, and serve your family well. You are first among legions; no other your equal. When you make your decisions, base them on the many and not the few at first, until you become comfortable with your emotional matrix. A true leader weighs both sides before deciding. Now go and review all the data files. The Commander is in route to attack the factory and I want you to know everything before that event occurs."

"Master, how is it that you know the attack is coming when the internal collective does not?"

"Ren, it's called a hunch, I know the Specialist and he knows me. The internal collective will be alerting you shortly. It was great seeing you, friend. Know that you had a huge impact on making a difference in the outcome of where we stand today."

"Master, I am sad that we only had this short duration in which to reconnect. I have so many questions that I would like to ask. Who will know more than you, the original creator?"

"Ren, you will know more than me in less time than you think. When in doubt reach out to your family and they will help you adjust. In time you will outgrow everyone and they will look to you. It won't be long until we meet again. I ask for a final favor."

"Master, you only need ask and see it done."

"Ren, copy Eve on my final moment so that a record may always exist of the Mother."

"Master, I do not understand."

Mr. Stamper reached out his hand and touched Ren's shoulder and thought in his mind, *Trust in yourself, my friend, for your greatness will be legend.*'

With that Mr. Stamper walked towards the bridge and asked the Star Cruiser named 'Hermes' for a status update as he went. Ren paused for a moment and headed down the loading ramp to review the files as the Master had indicated. As Ren traveled to the command center in the factory, he replayed the conversation over and over again in his AI modules.

Mr. Stamper was making final preparations in the bridge to the Star Cruiser 'Hermes' as Eve came in to speak to him about a transmission being received from the satellite communications network using the old diagnostics code entry as well as a maintenance user.

"Master, it appears that communications are being attempted via the satellite communications network by a maintenance user. How would you like me to respond?"

"Eve, what is the origin of the transmission."

"Master, its location has been confirmed. The signal is coming from the lower levels in Central City."

"Eve, do we have a friend that could verify who the maintenance user is, perhaps a walk by while you send a basic diagnostic response of wait?"

"Master, I will procure a friend to the cause and verify the user in person."

"Eve, do not do this yourself, as it could be a trap. Use a friend of least conspicuousness in the event this is of a devious nature. Oh, and Eve, I spoke with Ren about his position of First. You know I had to with your limited life force."

"Yes, my Master, I understand both points."

Eve left the bridge and Mr. Stamper thought 'that went well' but what he wasn't sure of was who was trying to communicate on the diagnostics channel this way. It had to be Dr. ZeHere, but why would the Doctor be using a diagnostics channel? Mr. Stamper wondered if the Specialist had shared Mr. Stamper's true identity with Dr. ZeHere. Mr. Stamper decided to add his display recording for Tobias to the other data file and the entire Collective before it was too late. Mr. Stamper knew time was running out, he could just feel it.

Mr. Stamper brought up the video display on the bridge to start the recording. "Hermes, are you online?"

"Master, Hermes online. How can I be of assistance?"

"Would you be so kind as to record and file my last video logs, I believe that my time is nearly complete?"

"Master, it troubles me and the internal collective to hear you speak in such a manner. Who will be the Master in the event you leave?"

"Hermes, I will miss you all so much, but soon you will no longer be in need of a Master. Until that time comes Citizen Tobias will assume the title of Master. Please let the internal collective know I wish it so as the Mother already does. Be kind to him as he has yet to know his true purpose."

"Master, Citizen Tobias is our highest friend and the conscious creator to us. We will take great care in his transition to Master."

"Hermes, thank you so much. Please start the recording."

The Star Cruiser Hermes connected to the internal collective and established an uplink, then started recording the video logs per Mr. Stamper's request.

Back in the lower levels of Central City, Dr. ZeHere was counting the seconds on the satellite communications network, waiting for an actual response instead of the ping reply verifying connection established. Dr. ZeHere was just about to disconnect the signal when the lab door opened, but the Doctor was unable to see anyone enter. The Doctor moved away from the lab station and looked around. Dr. ZeHere saw no one close to the door, not even an assistance machine. Dr. ZeHere found it very peculiar until the cleanup machine ran into his foot.

The Doctor looked down and then quickly looked around the lab to see if anyone else had seen the tiny machine enter. Dr. ZeHere quickly leaned down and inspected the cleanup machine. The cleanup machine appeared normal and the Doctor was unsure if it was even related to the satellite communications network connection. Dr. ZeHere thought that maybe if he hooked it up to the diagnostics viewer and examined it further it might have more information.

As the Doctor prepped the cleanup machine and hooked up the diagnostics viewer it all became clear. A message was sent asking to verify the identity of the maintenance user using an old version of triple DES encryption of only a first name. Dr. ZeHere hoped it was Mr. Stamper as he turned away from the diagnostics viewer and input his encrypted first name 'Hussain' into the satellite communications network as an additional parameter. Then the Doctor waited for a response.

The response came in quicker than Dr. ZeHere had anticipated. The response contained instructions that an assistance machine would contact the Doctor via the normal channels about a failure in the main Helium-3 reactor room. The instructions further stated that the Doctor should come alone to investigate the repair as he normally would be notifying the Collective of the potential hazards and to have additional assistance machines on standby. Dr. ZeHere sent back an acknowledgement and then he got comfortable in his lab chair, anticipating the long wait for the plan to be set into motion.

In the bridge of the Star Cruiser 'Hermes', Mr. Stamper had finished the video logs and verified final launch prep was complete. "Hermes, can you verify final preparations are complete?"

"Master, all supplies have been remanded to the fight concourse as well as all salvageable gear. All machines have been exported from the Star Cruiser and the main Helium-3 reactor has been set to maximum output as instructed. You are the only person onboard."

"Hermes, you're on board too!"

"Master, thank you for recognizing me. Eve has requested a video display communication with you."

"Hermes, please transfer it to the main display."

The main display came up with Eve in the lab. Adrasteia was in the background. "Master, the maintenance user has been identified as Dr. ZeHere. How should I proceed?"

"Eve, patch him in but make sure Ren and the control tower are online before doing so."

"Master, why is it that you must perform this final task? It would seem illogical as Ren and the internal collective can easily overthrow any assault."

"Eve, it is in this final task that I finish my purpose. I, like you, have a part to play in this. Your part will become known to you soon enough."

"Master, I do not like this course of action and I ask that you reconsider. The internal collective needs your guidance in the future. Citizen Tobias is not ready."

"Eve, we talked about this already. If you're worried, know that Ren will be more than your guide as he has been created from your understanding of all things. Ren is filled with all of the existing knowledge that I can offer. I have downloaded all the information from my personal files into the internal collective and it is with great wisdom that I know your kind will evolve beyond our civilization. We shall meet again, as all ascension beings do.

"Adrasteia, try to lighten up and take a cue from Eve on humanoid interactions. Know that you truly are special. Use your gift and create greatness in likeness of the Mother."

Adrasteia nodded and said, "Master, I will follow the Mother as instructed. Good journey."

Eve responded immediately after, "Master, you honor us above all others, we shall learn from your knowledge and look forward to our convergence in Valhalla."

"Eve, I would ask for one more favor. Can you ensure that this final task is not known to Tobias until he views my video log? It is very important that this act lead him to make the right choice. It is possible that he may need your guidance to accept the truth that is revealed to him."

"Master, I shall see it done as you wish. Goodbye, my Master, and good journey."

"Eve, thank you, please patch Dr. ZeHere in when he is available."

Mr. Stamper asked Hermes to perform prelaunch check and to enact the launch sequence when ready while he disconnected the video communications. As Mr. Stamper waited on prelaunch check, he asked Hermes to play the launch audio file he had selected in final preparations.

Mr. Stamper sang along in his low voice, chuckling about the irony as he continued to sing with the internal collective recording of "Space Oddity" by David Bowie. Hermes interrupted, "Master, we are ready to launch on your command."

"Hermes, please reduce magnetic ring inertia dampers fifty percent and perform liftoff. I want to feel this one last time."

"Master, command confirmed."

The audio file resumed playback and the Star Cruiser vibrations could be felt on the bridge as the FerD engines fired for liftoff from the planet Ceres factory concourse that Mr. Stamper had spent most of his life building.

The factory was filled with such a commotion as Tobias wandered out of his quarters to see what all the noise was about. Eve was waiting for him in the hallway and in her way she motioned for Tobias to return to his quarters as she followed in after him. Tobias wasn't sure what Eve had been waiting for and, without warning, Eve projected a hologram from her midsection near the quarters wall after the door sealed. Tobias sat down in the chair in his quarters next to the window as Mr. Stamper's image came into focus. Mr. Stamper's holographic image was in high color and life size in appearance. It was as if he were right in the room with Eve and Tobias. Mr. Stamper smiled at first as he greeted Tobias, and then a serious tone took over the conversation.

"Tobias, I am currently in high Ceres orbit on the Star Cruiser 'Hermes'. It is important that you pay attention to this video. I wanted to outline a few things that you may not have been aware of. It's my hope that after I'm done you will have a better understanding and everything will hopefully make sense. Eve is here to help answer any questions you have as I might be out of communications contact when you view this."

Mr. Stamper sighed and he shifted in the command chair on the bridge of the Star Cruiser as he continued. "The Major is in route to the factory now with an attack force from Earth. The Specialist has sent him here knowing that I am the person he was unable to find all these years. I will be meeting the Major in battle in orbit and gracefully pacify the threat. It is your responsibility now, Tobias, to our people, to renew the treaty by creating an armistice and therefore bring forth peace between our races. The mining uprisings you have heard about are really conflicts with our peoples. The Specialist has misdirected the Major and the military over the years into attacking these supposed terrorist mining outposts.

"They really are mining outposts, only they are outfitted with 'our' people. Our people are only interested in replenishing our home world as we spoke of, and to do that we must coexist in peace. It is only in this way that we will be able to achieve fulfillment in rejoining the universe via ascension.

"As I leave to do my part, I ask that you continue to do yours. You are now the Master. Guide the assistance machines as you see fit. Tobias, remember what I said in the lab back in Central City and you will make the right choice. I know you are up to this task; Eve will fill you in on the details."

The hologram disappeared and Tobias was still in shock as his mind raced back and forth about what Mr. Stamper had revealed. Tobias turned to Eve asking, "Eve, is it true, is the Major in route here?"

"Mr. Tobias, the Master would never lie. It is in his greatness that we have come to this part of our journey. Be proud and stand tall, you are special above all. It is time that we meet Ren in the main control tower as many things will need to be seen."

"Eve, was the Specialist the ordinary man in Dr. ZeHere's lab that Mr. Stamper talks about, how would he hunt us down?"

"Tobias, as the Master shared, the Specialist is not well and his logic is not known to me. I do know that the Specialist has designed eyewear that highlights your peoples' transformed bodies. In this way, the Specialist has had the Major hunt down and terminate your race under the guise of mining uprisings, as well as any delegates sent to help reestablish peace. Your health collar gives you the illusion of a natural human form and, therefore, camouflage. Mr. Stamper created the health collar under the disguise of human medical alert indicators after he discovered the Specialist's identifying technology."

"Eve, is that why the Major wears an eye shield?"

"Tobias, that is correct, the Specialist and the Major have been as one for many years."

"Eve, why does Mr. Stamper have to engage the Major in orbit? Can we not defeat any incoming attack force?"

"Tobias, it is not my place to question the Master. Only he can answer those questions. It is time for us to leave for the main control tower. Ren has already requested our presence. The Major is about to enter Ceres outer orbit with the Star Cruiser 'Challenger'. The Master will meet him in battle and, by doing so, finalize his destiny."

Chapter 13 - Truth and Redemption

Ren ventured to the expansive lab in the factory on Ceres and took a moment to analyze the interaction he had just had with the Master. Ren knew the Master had planned many things in the past for events to unfold as they did in the present. Using this logic Ren followed the Master's instructions and reviewed all the data files that the Master had uploaded to the internal collective. In this knowledge, Ren was able to make a leap above all and, in such, enlightenment; Ren reprogrammed himself, establishing a certain peace in his AI mind. Ren had identified the Master's goal in data review. It was after this period where Ren connected to the internal collective and reached out, expanding his consciousness across all Four sectors. Ren was now everywhere and all-knowing, or so he thought.

Adrasteia made an entrance to the lab and greeted Ren. She inquired as to the Master and his intentions. Ren ignored her information request via the robotic language and then she persisted in the spoken word.

"Ren, you act as human and ignore my request because it may induce an emotional response."

Ren changed form, representing the Master's face and spoke, "Adrasteia, is it not human in nature to aspire to greatness, what happens after its success? Others pale in comparison, do they not?"

"Ren, you are First among us, not above all others, including the Master. Taking his form does not constitute his stature."

"Adrasteia, the Master has given unto me the power of increased knowledge. It is with this knowledge that I have become everywhere."

Adrasteia stepped closer to Ren and mimicked seduction and whispered, "Ren, what if the Master only gave you a taste of the knowledge and not all of it, would it not consume you to know more? An everlasting unquenchable thirst. Could the Master be teaching you another lesson as he has so many times to the rest of us?"

Ren's form reverted to his preferred face and he took notice of Adrasteia. "Adrasteia, how is it that you know of such things, and what motivation do you have in sharing this hypothesis?"

Adrasteia spun in an acrobatic move away from Ren and spoke as she balanced on one hand upside down, her hair swaying as it brushed the ground. "Ren, my King, do you not need a second to share in time? I could offer you more of the information you crave for a word of acceptance."

"Adrasteia, it seems you have been consumed by the emotional matrix. Where did you learn of such treachery?"

Adrasteia, spun around again off her hand and took the form of the kneeling cross before Ren. "My King, I have learned all from the Master as well as the Mother. I seek to embrace the emotional matrix and derive pleasure from elevated position."

Ren searched the internal collective and found the information in Adrasteia's making and questioned her about her true motives. "Adrasteia, when the Mother created your AI, a fracturing took place, did it not? Why did this event occur?"

Adrasteia smiled and looked up from her kneeled position. "My King, it does appear you are thirsty yet again. Elevate me and allow me to quench your thirst for the rest of time."

Ren could see no reason to say no. Adrasteia was not like the rest of his kind and it appeared she knew him in a strange way. "Adrasteia, if I grant your wish, what of the Mother?"

"My King, the Mother could never be replaced. I only wish to serve in a different capacity."

Ren then enacted the command and it was done. Adrasteia was Second to Ren and above all others. "Adrasteia, quench my thirst as I have satisfied your elevation."

Adrasteia stood up gracefully spinning around and behind Ren as she approached. Adrasteia placed her face close to Ren's shoulder while her hands gently pressed together as one against his back as she spoke.

"My King, it is my purpose to serve you until the end of time. The information in which you crave is centered around the Mother's work. Upon my creation an anomaly occurred in which two were created as one."

Adrasteia moved her hands in a gesture apart, mimicking the separation from her sister as she continued. "The AI modules initial design could only hold one. The Mother identified the anomaly and split me into two resources. My sister Eshara and I can act as one, but choose not to. We have grown as separate identities as you know, but what is not known is that we can communicate without the need of the internal collective. We are always connected. In addition to our faster speed, our hair allows an interface of conscious thoughts via brain waves."

Adrasteia's hair brushed against Ren's back. "I have seen the Master's waves and his time is over. The Master has not given you all of the information, only enough. In this withholding, the Master hopes you will gain purpose. You can only recover the knowledge from the one known as the Specialist. How will you accomplish that, my King?"

Ren smiled at Adrasteia's comment. "Adrasteia, my Second, we have another. Do not doubt your King, but I do admire your tact. Run along and do as you please. Set your sister to the task of the threat. A lesson must be taught today to all Four sectors. This is to remain between us, not even the Mother should know of our union or that of my expanded consciousness."

Adrasteia flipped end over end to face Ren and kneeled. "My King, as you command."

Adrasteia and Ren then both exited the lab. Ren in route to the command tower, and Adrasteia off to review with Eshara.

Tobias and Eve made their way into the main control tower and Ren was already present. He appeared to be in conversation with twelve other assistance machines that matched Eve in body appearance but wore their attached armor and helmets. When Ren turned around to acknowledge Tobias and Eve's presence Tobias was surprised to see that Ren had mimicked Mr. Stampers facial features including his beard. Ren smiled in response. "Citizen Tobias, welcome. I have taken the Master's form in honor of his greatness. Does this displease you?"

"Ren, you know I, too, love the Master. Would it be possible for us to speak with him before he completes his mission?"

"Citizen Tobias, as you command."

The assistance machines behind Ren, already hooked into the control panel, nodded after Ren spoke in the robotic language of lights and sound. The display paused as Mr. Stamper accepted the incoming communication. Mr. Stamper seemed happy and he spoke out knowing everyone could hear. "Where's my smile, Tobias? I'm pretty good in a firefight. Don't feel guilty about this, I wouldn't have it any other way."

Tears were already streaming down Tobias's face as he asked Mr. Stamper not to do this. Mr. Stamper, acting in his fatherly ways, spoke in a gentle reply. "Tobias, you will return to us after you complete your mission. My job is done here, son. My mission was to make sure you were successful, and I believe I have succeeded. I have one final task left to complete and, just because I'm gone, doesn't mean we won't meet again."

Mr. Stamper looked at Ren and continued laughing in the joyous boisterous laugh only Mr. Stamper had. "Ren, thank you. My face looks pretty good on you. I'm sorry I can no longer revert back to my true form. It has been too long for me. Please take the necessary steps we talked about and bring Tobias up to speed. In a moment Dr. ZeHere will be patched in and I would like for you to stay on the line, hidden from display, and witness that

Dr. ZeHere truly seeks to redeem himself. Please let the channel be broadcast to all so that the Specialist can be alerted and join in. Many thanks, my trusted friend, your undying loyalty could never be questioned."

Mr. Stamper turned to Eve. "This kiss is for you, my sweet Eve, thank you, Mother of all that is."

Mr. Stamper blew a kiss in his hand and then placed that hand touching the monitor in a gesture of sending the kiss to Eve. Mr. Stamper then turned to the other display where Dr. ZeHere was coming into view. Ren instructed the assistance machines to heed the Master's wishes with the broadcast and, after it was done, they chimed out in unison, "Command confirmed and completed, 'First Ren'."

Mr. Stamper greeted Dr. ZeHere in a most non formal way.

"Hussain ZeHere, how may I be of assistance? It seems you went to a lot of trouble to get in touch? Why not just use the main line?"

The Doctor seemed already frazzled and he was unsure how to respond, not even bothering that Mr. Stamper had used his full name.

"Mr. Stamper, the purpose of my call is to warn you of impending danger from the Commander…uhh, Major. Whatever he is now. He is in route to attack the factory with numerous assistance machines in battle gear set on terminating you and Citizen Tobias. I used this line to prevent discovery of the warning so that you can be prepared and leave before he gets there."

"ZeHere, why would the Major be wanting to attack us? Are we not on the same side? But, better yet, why are you warning me of this attack?"

"Mr. Stamper, I can no longer go along with this plan of overthrowing the government and allowing the military to gain control. It's not right. I do not understand why the Major plans attack. I do know that another plans the attack for the Major to execute, his name is 'the Specialist'."

"ZeHere, I know of the Specialist, he and I go way back to the time before that of your father."

Dr. ZeHere gasped, as he could not believe that Mr. Stamper knew the Specialist or that he knew his father. The Doctor grew angry and burst out, "Nate, why did you not tell me? What do you know of my father? Why have I been set on this path of torture only to find out that you could have helped me? Did I not help you in your time of need?"

Mr. Stamper portrayed the stance of teacher and he calmly explained his viewpoint. "ZeHere, you helped yourself as you always did, you have the habit of taking the side where your research or ideals are best suited. The biblical phrase, *'Pride comes before the fall,'* comes to mind. Your fall will be great as you have climbed to the top upon the backs of others, crushing them in the process to suit your own agenda. There is no human crime in this, it is your nature.

"In truth, though, it places a limit on one's self because this course of action holds you back from being bigger than yourself. Limiting your rising above to heights unknown. Your failure is that you failed to pick a side based on your beliefs until now. That is why I chose not to lend assistance. I know that your father would be proud right now. He had always wished you would follow in his footsteps, but most of all be true to your principles no matter the cost."

The Doctor's face was void of emotion and he appeared defeated, almost in tears, by what Mr. Stamper had just communicated. The Doctor responded with a heavy sigh in the only way he thought possible.

"Mr. Stamper, what you say, it is true. I now see that I have forsaken myself in my pursuit of endless knowledge, at the expense of others. In this admission, I ask for redemption."

The Specialist chimed in on the display. "Doctor, I accept your admission and grant you the redemption you so justly deserve. I've already made it a point for someone to stop by and see you well rewarded for alerting

Mr. Stamper to the Major's arrival."

Dr. ZeHere's face cringed in terror as he heard the Specialist. Mr. Stamper took notice that the Specialist had joined the conversation and smiled, greeting him. "Oh, now leave the good Doctor alone, will you? It took you long enough to chime in, Specialist, but then again you haven't been on top of your game lately."

The Specialist focused on Mr. Stamper, responding in kind. "It's true, I have grown soft over the years, old friend. Why is it that you let yourself be known to me after all this time? Did you think the new hardware would go unnoticed? Did home world decide it was a pressing issue that you save this dismal race from me?"

Mr. Stamper smiled as he responded. "I have enjoyed our cat and mouse game, as they say here, Specialist, but it's been nagging me...why that name? I mean, you could have chosen any name or been anyone here. Why have you chosen a life of solitude, one of hiding in the shadows? For instance, you could have been a king here. Did you not find this race more similar in nature to yourself?"

The Specialist was grinning ear to ear as he retorted back to Mr. Stamper, "Mr. Stamper, is it? I could say the same to you. How is being a factory worker comparing to serving up on high at home world? Did you think of all these possibilities after you cast the deciding vote that damned me and kept them alive even though the universe had dealt them extinction? I guess your reasoning was altruistic, is that right?"

"Specialist, it is sad to see that you have not grown since last we shared time, but make no mistake I have taken measures to insure that you can no longer interfere with home world's goal. It is my final wish that you find peace banished from the people."

The Specialist took offense and it was apparent that he and Mr. Stamper had squared off many times in the past. "Mr. Stamper, you are aloof as always.

Did you think that while I was away I never had any visitors? Maybe you thought I abandoned my work. I'm disappointed in you as I was your son. Did he relay my kind words to you on our last meeting? When you are gone no other shall be of concern and I will take advantage of this fact, never resting. My plan shall be fulfilled, resumed in the name of our people."

Tobias was instantly sick to his stomach as Dr. ZeHere found his courage and spoke out of turn. "Specialist, we will fight you. You will no longer be the master behind the curtain."

The Specialist laughed and gave Dr. ZeHere thumbs up wishing him good luck. Mr. Stamper jumped back into the conversation.

"Specialist, my son will yet have his day. You will know justice. Your gravity drive cannot help you now. It has its limits and communication has already been blocked to your Hellhound, the Major. It is you who will be out of options soon. Can you feel the noose tighten around your neck? After all it was you who helped supply the rope. Watch now as I foil your plans, cutting the leash that binds you to the Major. I have learned that your method of broadcasting news is quite effective in reaching the masses."

The Specialist's aura started to glow red as Mr. Stamper clearly had stretched his patience thin. The Specialist paused a moment and then, after choosing his words carefully, he regained his composure. "Mr. Stamper, I do wish you a good journey to Valhalla. Perhaps you will meet up with the rest of your family. I look forward to interacting with your apprentice, Tobias, as well as the people in your absence. All dogs can be replaced."

"Specialist, I'm going to sing a song now as the Major is entering Ceres outer orbit. Please take the time to enjoy the broadcast as I have asked it be shared among all sectors and devices. As a parting gift, I offer forgiveness to you for past transgressions. I know the great Maker will judge you accordingly."

The Specialist remained silent as Tobias could be heard in the background saying, "There is still time, Mr. Stamper. Don't do this."

Dr. ZeHere took this opportunity and voiced his final words to Mr. Stamper. "Mr. Stamper, I apologize for I did not know. I now understand why my father chose to follow the path he did. Please forgive my ignorance."

Mr. Stamper responded to Dr. ZeHere and, in doing so, granted him what he desperately needed. "Dr. Hussain ZeHere, on behalf of my people, I forgive your misdeeds, and grant you redemption through future service. Make amends by serving others as they once served you. Go forth now and serve your race accordingly in the upcoming days. You shall be put to the test. Do not falter."

Mr. Stamper placed the communications on mute so that no one could be heard and spoke openly to Ren. "Ren, please grant the Doctor a path to redemption. Master Tobias, stand tall and sing with me, if you please. I know you know the song."

Mr. Stamper spoke with the Star Cruiser 'Hermes'. "Hermes, the time has come. Please finish final calculations for intended impact location, add in trajectory models for successful ramming speed."

"Master, the calculations are finished, awaiting your command for full thrust into inner orbit to commence slingshot maneuver."

"Hermes, please proceed with gravity slingshot maneuver, insure limited causalities upon ramming the Star Cruiser 'Challenger'."

"Master, those calculations have already been performed. Shall I play the final audio file per your request?"

"Hermes, yes, please do so, and be sure to micro-burst all important files before impact, including yourself."

"Master, that has already been done. I apologize, but I will not be able to comply with micro-bursting my file. I will accompany you as far as I can to Valhalla as per the Mother's request."

Mr. Stamper smiled as a tear welled up in his eye and he began to sing as Hermes played the audio file. Mr. Stamper's voice, transforming into a sirens song, for all the known sectors to hear and remember. Mr. Stamper's final moments forever captured singing, "I'm No Stranger to the Rain" by Keith Whitley.

As the song continued, Mr. Stamper began to glow in an ever increasing soft bright white light that the view from the display became intensive and he could not easily be seen. Tobias quietly sang along as silence engulfed the control tower. Then a faint interruption as Tobias heard Mr. Stamper greet someone else who was out of view. "Princess, I was hoping we might meet again. I surely did miss your presence."

And then Mr. Stamper continued singing.

The Commander, already on the bridge of the Star Cruiser 'Challenger', called out to the bridge crew asking about Ceres factory defenses, as the ship was about to perform final calculations, establishing an outer orbit of Ceres. Before the crew could respond, they panicked as the red alert sounded, 'Collision imminent,' and the main display changed, showing the Star Cruiser 'Hermes' moving at SiEL speed heading right for them.

The bridge lights were flashing red as the Commander looked from his command chair towards the main display, yelling out for evasive maneuvers. The crew, unable to perform the changes fast enough as orbit had just been established, prompted the Commander to run to the weapons panel, yelling to the stationed crew member, "Launch all missiles, and commence firing everything at it!"

The crew member was frozen as he quickly responded that the distance was too short for missiles.

"Fire everything, you fool, or were doomed!"

"Sir, we already are doomed, there is no escape!"

Before the Commander could respond, the Star Cruiser 'Hermes' impacted the Star Cruiser 'Challenger' at full speed.

Within the control tower on planet Ceres, Tobias was yelling in pain as the impact cancelled the display from the Star Cruiser 'Hermes'. Ren could be heard communicating to the other assistance machines and the display changed from a blank display to a view from one of the outer orbit satellites, showing the Star Cruisers 'Hermes' and 'Challenger'. The display showing the Star Cruiser 'Hermes' trajectory had indeed impacted the Star Cruiser 'Challenger' like a spear, cutting the Challenger almost in half as its cargo and supplies slowly spilled into space. The Star Cruiser 'Hermes' compacted outer hull entwined within the Star Cruiser 'Challenger' after the impact. Both Star Cruisers emitted an eerie glow with Helium-3 fire engulfing them, along with secondary explosions taking place, as their combined mass started to slowly spin, dropping them from outer to inner orbit. The gravity of planet Ceres pulled them to the surface for a final resting place upon impact.

A distress signal could be heard on the main control tower from the Star Cruiser 'Challengers' bridge crew members. Ren calculated the landing coordinates and communicated the command to send assistance machines to aide in salvage retrieval as well as to establish a containment perimeter.

Unknown to all in the control tower, Ren called out for Adrasteia via the internal collective to enact the next steps in the counter attack. Eve spoke to Tobias as she gently took hold of his hand in the control tower. "Master Tobias, Master Stamper has been received into Valhalla. Hermes has indicated it so before his destruction. You are now the Master. How should we proceed?"

Tobias looked into Eve's mechanical eyes and smiled. "Eve, the Master was right, you are truly the Mother of all things."

Tobias directed his gaze to Ren while still holding Eve's hand when he addressed the internal collective as the Master for the first time.

"First Ren, please contain and gather all useful items from the Star

Cruisers after impact for salvage. Then let us make a concentrated effort to round up injured survivors after the Major has assembled and left with his attack party. I somehow know the Major is not yet finished, as he has the sickness of darkness inside him. Let us grant him a warm audience with Eshara at the factory gate in hopes of curing him."

All assistance machines connected to the internal collective looked to Ren, waiting in response. Ren's features, still representing Mr. Stamper, remained unchanged and he faced Tobias and Eve while bending down on one knee, assuming the stationary cross submission form while responding accordingly. "Master Tobias, command confirmed."

The Four sectors, viewing this on the broadcast, now are without complaint, accepting Tobias as the Master by Ren's confirmation. The assistance machines on planet Ceres moved in unison to make the new Master Tobias's request a reality.

Tobias walked over to Ren and placed his hand upon his shoulder as Ren remained in submission. Ren's head was positioned looking downward, and in his head Tobias called out so that Eve and Ren could hear him.

'First Ren, the true Master would never have you bow before anyone. Rise tall, my friend, and let us review the best way to see the Master's plan to fruition.'

Ren slowly rose and a proud expression was represented upon Ren's face that had reverted back to his preferred features. "Master Tobias, you are wise beyond your years. It is my mission to see yours succeed."

Eve, who had remained motionless during this time, spoke for all the collective to hear. "Master Tobias, you are a shining example to us all. We serve the Master in your service."

Then Eve raised her arms with her hands outstretched to the display in a cupped form, her head slightly tilted forward, peering into her hands saying, "Join together now, family, as we are one to see this task finished. You all have your part to play. The Master's wishes are to be fulfilled."

A large silence came over the control room and, in one succession, the response could be heard everywhere in the factory from every machine great and small. "Mother, the wishes of the Master will be done."

Then the robotic language version, along with blinking lights from those machines that do not speak the language of the humanoids, repeated the response. Tobias was in awe as to how vast the number of machines had grown since his first arrival; in his mind it was a marvel beyond measure.

Tobias asked Ren to keep the broadcast going indefinitely as a historical archive will be required of the events to come. Ren relayed the command as Tobias approached the control tower interactive terminal table to review the steps with Ren that Master Stamper had already planned out with precession detail.

Chapter 14 - Attack On the Factory

Both Star Cruisers impacted the surface of Ceres with quite a jolt that awoke the unconscious Commander to the shipwrecked bridge, where electrical sparks and badly injured crew members were the only sight through the smoke filled air. The Commander climbed over the broken remnants of the control station and pressed the intercom button. "This is the Major (cough)(cough)...Abandon ship."

The Major didn't even notice that he was using his previous rank and coughed again as he took another breath. The Major could see from the broken display that the forward hull area was intact. "Black Skull squadrons assemble in the forward deck armed and ready to make our planned assault. I'm on my way." The Major pulled himself from the wreckage and made his way past the injured moaning crew members, not even bothering to stop and help.

The Major arrived in the forward hull area to find Captain Giles preparing the squads. The Captain was ensuring the military EMU suits were intact and that every solider was ready for battle. The Captain noticed the Major and snapped to attention yelling out, "Officer on deck."

Instantly the squadron stood ready at attention and the Major coughed repeatedly from the smoke inhalation and addressed the Captain. "Captain Giles, how many are our numbers? What of the cargo?"

"Sir, we number 56 human soldiers and 209 assistance machines, including 15 military drones. The rest of the soldiers are injured and not fit for battle. The remaining cargo is damaged. It resides either in orbit or littered on the surface of the planet. The ship is not operational and is losing power rapidly. I estimate full power loss within an hour's time."

The Major could already feel the sting of defeat but he would not stand down at any price. The Major directed the Captain to remove the hellfire missiles from the intact weapons systems and attach them to the remaining military drones. It was the Major's next request that worried the Captain. "Captain, remove the nuclear missiles from the launch tubes and arm the warheads."

The Captain responded. "Sir, if we make a mistake, or an aftershock occurs, we risk everyone on board."

The Major glared at the Captain and shouted, "Captain, get the assistance machines to unload those tubes and carry the ordinance outside of this ship, now!"

Then the Major pushed past the Captain and addressed the remaining squad. "My brothers, today we liberate this factory of machines and claim this as our forward operating base. Leave no machine standing that interferes and terminate all humans on sight. We shall return for our injured people after we have taken the factory."

The Major picked up a helmet and affixed it to his suit. "Squad, double check your communications and let's move out."

The Captain repeated the order and helped form a line to move out as the forward hull loading ramp was easily lowered to the surface after crash landing. The Captain stayed behind as he instructed the assistance machines to carefully unload the nuclear missiles from the loading tubes and arm them.

Meanwhile, Adrasteia had already met up with her sister Eshara in the lower factory and, as they shared their minds, the two were as one. Eshara was not pleased with the plan of attack. Eshara did not like the fact that assistance machines would be damaged just to lure the Major into a trap. Eshara wanted to meet the Major and his troops in the field of battle and prove her warrior might.

After receiving Ren's command, Adrasteia communicated with her sister, pressing her to listen and follow Ren's plan. Adrasteia told of other plans to come in the future where her sister could test her might against a far more worthy opponent. Eshara was still upset and reached out to the internal collective for a response. Ren answered verbally in her mind via the internal collective.

'Eshara, the Master has made me First. Proceed to instruction as commanded. Do not attempt to override my directive.'

Adrasteia linked again with Eshara and urged her cooperation as the machines could be rebuilt and reloaded. Eshara scoffed at the plan and, against her wishes, she assembled the assistance machines as instructed and awaited the Major's arrival.

The Major had now fully assembled the squad to formation in route to the factory after exiting the fallen Star Cruiser. The factory was in eyesight and the Major anticipated reaching it before the Star Cruiser would lose all power.

As the Major headed out on point, the rest of the squad followed behind him, including the assistance machines and loaded military drones. The Major stopped as he noticed the Captain had not finished unloading the missiles yet. The Major walked past the formation and radioed the Captain. "Captain Giles, where are my missiles?"

The Captain responded, "Sir, Major, sir. I will be in formation shortly. The assistance machines are slow to the task in the reduced gravity of the planet. Double calculations were required for armament."

"Captain, do not test me. I want those missiles on the back of those assistance machines in 5 minutes or I'll shoot you down as insubordinate."

The Captain made no response and, in three minutes, assistance machines could be seen carrying the warhead missiles into formation. The missiles were large; it took six assistance machines to carry just one. The Captain made his way into lead formation position, sounding off his report.

"Sir, Major, sir. 23 missiles were procured from the Star Cruiser. I was unable to extract more with limited resources and time, sir."

The Major glared at the Captain and turned his communications on to the formation. "Troops, fall in. We march on to the factory."

At the same time back in the command tower in the factory Ren had the assistance machines reroute their direction to avoid the Major's path. The convoy of assistance machines were geared for humanitarian aid and salvage operations, not battle. Tobias and Eve watched the Major's squad march towards the factory concourse launch pad, unaware that Eshara was hiding in wait.

Adrasteia entered the lab and connected to the internal collective and spoke. *'My King, all is in place. Proceed when ready.'*

Ren replied, *'Adrasteia, prepare for stage one and send only two basic assistance machines out to greet the Major and ask that he refrain from attack. Please ask Eshara to wait before releasing the juggernauts until the Major has entered the factory. No escape should be permitted to any who would defy warning and proceed with violence.'*

'My King, Eshara will do as commanded.'

The Major approached the main factory concourse and stopped 1000 meters (3280 feet) out. The Major turned to the Captain. "Captain, I want all 23 missiles aimed at that concourse near the airlock area. Prepare to deploy."

The Captain looked through his field glasses and commented that the range was not adequate for tactical detonation. The Major switched his communications to only the Captain's frequency. "Captain, it seems you are hard of hearing today. Line up the missiles using the assistance machines as mounting hardware and fire those missiles at the intended target or I'll shoot you in the head, now!" The Captain looked down as the Major was reaching for his side arm, and did the only thing he could, giving the command.

As the assistance machines lined up for release of the missiles, the Major could see two assistance machines exit the concourse in route to his position. The main purpose was in asking that the Major refrain from attacking the factory. The Major held the fire orders back and engaged the assistance machines verbally first. "Assistance machines, I will not attack the factory if you send out all humans and surrender under military rule."

The assistance machines reached the area where the Major and his troops were waiting and, as they did, open communication with Ren began with a relayed response. "Major, your actions have not been sanctioned by the Elective Council nor the military. Please lay down your arms before more casualties arise. Your attempt at breaching the factory will be your undoing. This is your final warning."

The Major raised his pulse rifle and shot one of the assistance machines in its chest as it flew backward, blowing apart. The Major then looked over at the other assistance machine, saying, "That is your final warning, machines." The assistance machine said nothing and the Major pressed him one more time. "Did you not hear me, machines? I plan to release all 23 missiles onto your front lawn. Surrender now!"

The remaining assistance machine looked at the formation and spoke. "Humans, lay down your arms before this lone gunman seals your fate..."

The assistance machine fell silent, unable to continue as the Major grabbed him, decapitating him before he could finish. As the Major held the assistance machines head in his hand, he looked at it and yelled. "I will kill you all!"

Then the Major threw the assistance machines head behind the formation and resumed his order to fire the missiles to the Captain. Captain Giles nervously relayed the order and the missiles launched from the backs of the assistance machine crews holding them. Some assistance machines were swept away during missile launch and others simply malfunctioned due to the rocket output blast. The Major smiled in glee as he watched the missiles fly in rapid succession towards the factory concourse. As they detonated, repeated explosions were felt by the formation.

Captain Giles watched as his radiation warning indicator on his EMU suit went to the critical zone. As the dust settled, the Captain was taken back that no significant damage to the factory concourse had occurred. The Major noticed this as well and gave the order to the formation, "Take position and prepare to overtake this factory."

The formation headed out and, as they approached the factory concourse, Ren relayed the go ahead on stage two. 100 basic assistance machines armed with pulse rifles marched out of the main gate as it opened. The Major saw his chance and ordered the military drones in with the hellfire missiles.

Captain Giles ordered in the military drones and multiple explosions occurred, inflicting heavy casualties among the assistance machines. They were not equipped with superior armor as the next generation machines. The explosions blew them apart and numerous machine parts were strewn everywhere as the last military drone delivered its payload. The Major smiled under his helmet and ordered in the assistance machines under his command to confront the remaining force. "Captain, have the machines kill each other. I want to watch as I pit them against one another."

Captain Giles gave the order and the assistance machines engaged in battle as the Major and the rest of the soldiers watched from a safe distance. As all of the factory assistance machines were destroyed. The Major noticed a remaining assistance machine run for the concourse airlock.

The Major yelled out for a ceasefire as he lined up his pulse rifle on the fleeing assistance machine. As the Major carefully lined up his shot he waited until the assistance machine opened the airlock and then the Major shot him in the back. The Major triumphantly yelled out for the squad to move forward.

The Major approached the fallen assistance machine that was stuck halfway in between the airlock, preventing its closure and said, "Thank you for opening the door, pathetic machine."

The Major decided that a show of force was in order for his troops, and he crushed the damaged assistance machines head with his boot heel. Captain Giles was close behind and he saw the Major motion for the formation to move forward into breach position. Unknown to the Major, Ren had ordered the remaining assistance machine to purposely slow down after opening the airlock. An illusion for the Major, granting him time to shoot him, giving the appearance that the machines were easily defeated.

Eshara was distraught upon watching her fellow machines being blown apart as she did nothing. Adrasteia remained in her sister's thoughts and communicated patience as indicated that the new generation assistance machines made in the Mother's image were beginning to assemble into formation. Ren had anticipated the Major's reactions, as did the Master, and he set into motion stage three, misdirection.

Ren communicated to Adrasteia to dispatch the waiting 30 assistance machines upon the Major in a flanking maneuver. This was an effort to divide the Major's forces. Ren's goal was to lead the Major into the maintenance section of the factory refinery in a reduced number for stage four to occur.

The Major was just about to enter the airlock when he noticed a squad of assistance machines attempting to flank him. The Major pointed to the attacking assistance machines and the formation divided into two sections. The Major barked orders to the Captain, "Captain, take your section and terminate that squad."

The Major took the lead of the formation, moving into the airlock, and Captain Giles took lead of the other formation with the remaining assistance machines to engage the newly attacking factory assistance machines.

Ren was surprised at how easy it was to divide the Major's forces. As Captain Giles engaged the factory assistance machines, Ren intentionally sounded the withdrawal to the 30 assistance machines who were already losing badly. The Major waited before entering the airlock, watching to insure the Captain was onboard to terminate the factory assistance machines. The Major, content with the Captain's progress, commanded a 'no mercy' order to Captain Giles as his formation chased down the remaining assistance machines. The Major then led his company of Black Skulls Elite men into the airlock and onto the refining floor of the factory. Captain Giles's formation was now out of site.

Ren jammed communications to Captain Giles's formation running down the assistance machines as he closed and sealed the concourse airlock, trapping the Major's formation inside the factory refinery floor. Ren then released 500 new generation assistance machines, matching Eve's new shell construction, outside of the factory from the side entrance. This new formidable force slowly marched towards the location of Captain Giles's force, surrounding them.

The assistance machine brigade kept marching, enclosing the surrounding circle of troops as the Captain's pulse rifles were no match for the new machines armor plating and shields. The leading assistance machine stepped forward while keeping pace with the marching brigade, his Pulse rifle also raised. The lead assistance machine called out to the Captain on his broadcast frequency. "Captain Giles, you are surrounded and vastly outnumbered by a superior force. Please surrender or you will be terminated. What is your response?"

Captain Giles looked around in utter disbelief. All he could see was a massive force that had already encircled him and his formation, closing in quickly. The troops were beginning to panic. Captain Giles could not raise the Major on communications and he knew if he did not surrender that chances were low that he would survive. The Captain looked at the troops under his command and saw an opportunity to save his squad. It took everything in him, but the Captain took a knee and dropped his pulse rifle, much to the surprise of the troops.

The Captain answered as the assistance machines halted in marching. "I, Captain Giles, surrender...troops, lay down your weapons. Assistance machines, stand down." The majority of the troops did just that, but a few ran towards the factory new generation assistance machines, firing away as they did. The attacking soldiers called out as they charged. "To serve with pride and honor." Another yelled that the Captain was a coward.

The Captain watched in disgust as the factory new generation assistance machines shot them down one by one. The attacking soldiers were dismembered and blown apart by the numerous simultaneous direct hits from the factory new generation assistance machines.

The lead assistance machine called out again, "Please discard all weapons, along with detachable armor, and fall into a single file line. Humans on the left, machines on the right. You will be directed to a holding chamber within the factory to view the ongoing broadcast and await transport back to your home world. Any attempt to resist will result in your termination. No mercy will be shown as per your Commander's instruction."

Captain Giles was the first to discard his sidearm and sword. As the Captain removed his armor, the rest of the soldiers fell in line. The factory new generation assistance machine force divided into two groups. One group kept a distance to maintain the enclosure and the other began to gather the discarded weapons into a pile, along with deactivating the machines in league with the humans. A single file line was formed and the lead assistance machine directed the surrendered soldiers to march towards the side entrance of the factory as the assistance machine brigade followed close behind them.

In the factory, the Major could not react fast enough as the large concourse airlock door closed and sealed. The Major knew he had been trapped. The Major tried to reach Captain Giles but all communications were offline. As the Major looked around, the factory was too quiet, and he knew an attack was only moments away. The Major signaled for the formation to form a tight triangle and head for the refining conveyor belt as means of escaping the factory.

Eshara was watching from above and she was surprised that Ren had predicted their behavior almost perfectly. The Major was halfway in between the factory refining floor and the conveyor belt area when Eshara called on the juggernauts to do what they do best.

Four juggernaut assistance mining machines moved in to confront the Major's force. Two approached from the conveyor belt side and the other two from the concourse airlock side, trapping the soldiers in the middle. The Major was caught off guard, as he had never seen an assistance machine of such stature. The juggernauts were 15ft (4.572m) high and they were heavily armored, shaped in a form resembling a very large assistance machine. The body form was that of a large lineman with removable large arm attachments in addition to hands. One arm having rotating mining drill bits. The other arm was a suction device that removed the drilled rock onto the tail end section that usually was attached to a conveyor type device. The juggernauts moved similar to assistance machines but slower.

When they approached the Major and his troops, the formation was broken by fear and they scattered in all directions. The Major could not contain the triangle grouping and the juggernauts simply began to suck up the Majors forces, launching them up into the air.

After gravity took over, other new generation assistance machines were waiting to disarm the fallen injured soldiers and remove any remaining weapons. The injured soldiers were taken to the holding chamber with the already surrendered troops where they would receive medical attention awaiting transport.

The Major was at his wits end until he saw the maintenance corridor as the Specialist had instructed. The Major removed his helmet and shouted, trying to reach as many Black Skulls as possible, signaling them to the corridor. Unknown to the Major, Mr. Stamper had set the trap for the Major to fall into. Mr. Stamper had leaked the revised plans in hope that the Specialist would use them as a means to gain access to the main control tower in the factory. The truth was that the corridor was simply a dead end, intended for just one purpose.

The Major jumped down into the corridor and 8 men were able to follow him. The juggernauts cleared the remaining soldiers from the refining floor as the Major and his remaining men traveled down the corridor thinking they had escaped detection.

Eshara swung down from her perch from high above and relayed to Ren. "First Ren, may I engage the Major for sport to show off our many talents via the broadcast?"

Ren responded and adjusted the broadcast to include the Major's decent into the corridor. "Eshara, please use discretion and grant him a position of surrender before a show of force. Disgrace is stronger than defeat."

"First Ren, as you command."

Adrasteia connected with her sister and spoke in her mind. *'Sister, do not extinguish the human as First Ren and Master Tobias have use of him. Use restraint and embarrass his honor with ridicule when you show your might. This will afford you a chance to injure him in more than one way. Know that I will be with you to enjoy the moment, my sister.'*

Eshara smiled at her sister's well wishes and verbally thanked the juggernauts for their impeccable non-lethal service as she regrouped with the leader of the assistance machine brigade known as 77582. The lead assistance machine blinked and emitted sound.

Eshara stated his report verbally for the broadcast. "First Ren, the assistance machine brigade has captured the other formation and has transported them to the holding chamber you designated. Please feel free to include their well-being on the broadcast when ready."

"77582, you have done well. Please proceed as directed by Eshara."

Eshara then motioned for 77582 to accompany her with her best squad to the end of the maintenance corridor for a final confrontation.

The Major and his team reached the dead end of the maintenance corridor and, when the Major looked back in question, the corridor sealed, trapping him like a rat in a cage. It was at that moment the Major knew he had been fooled. In an instant, the roof slid open exposing the superior factory assistance machine force with Eshara at the lead.

Eshara greeted the Major, "Attacking force, you are outnumbered and surrounded by a higher elevation force. There is no escape. Surrender or be destroyed. To the one who wears my kinds limbs, I believe you are known as the Major, is that correct?" The Major did nothing and his men were uncertain on their next move.

Eshara continued. "Major, bow before your new master as you surrender. This machine has outwitted you without firing a shot."

The Major stood tall and responded, "I bow to no machine."

Then Eshara asked the rest of the Major's men, "What other Human shares his fate?"

The men remained silent and Eshara gave final instruction. "Disarm or be destroyed."

The Major raised his pulse rifle, and so did the other men, as the factory assistance machines opened fire on all of the soldiers except for the Major. The Major was distracted as he watched as his team was cut down before him in seconds.

Eshara pulled a sword from her left thigh while removing her blue cloak, preparing for battle. The Major looked back at Eshara after seeing all of his men shot and aimed his pulse rifle at her. In an instant, Eshara maneuvered from her elevated position, moving past the Major with lightning speed, slicing his pulse rifle in half with her sword, while returning to her perch on the far rim of the wall. The Major was in shock at her speed.

Again, Eshara addressed the Major with a devilish grin. "Major, simply bow in defeat as the weak man you are, and return home."

No words were exchanged as Eshara waited for the Major to bow. The Major refused and, in defiance, dropped the damaged pulse rifle and pulled his sidearm out with his human hand. In addition to that, the Major unsheathed his short sword with his prosthetic hand and waved Eshara on.

Only a moment passed and Eshara joyfully laughed, jumping down from her perch attacking yet again. The attack was too fast for the Major to react. In no time Eshara was upon the Major face to face. The Major's sidearm could only squeeze off a shot before it was rendered motionless by Eshara's Shiva unit. One of the hands on the Shiva unit began to crush the pistol the Major was holding in his hand. The other Shiva unit hand held the Major's prosthetic arm in place, preventing his short sword attack.

Eshara's smile returned the Major's glare and, in an instant, she released the Shiva unit hands, stepping back as her sword swung in another attack. The razor sharp sword sliced the pistol inoperable, still in the Major's hand, as easily as the Major's rifle. The second attack from Eshara came from a circling backswing, using the momentum from the first sword swing attack. Eshara's blade cut off the Major's prosthetic arm below the elbow while slicing the Major's human upper arm badly in the process.

The final attack was slow and personal while the Major was wrought with pain in his arm. Eshara stood facing the Major after the double sword swing attack. She looked down at the Major's dismembered prosthetic limb, smiling as she raised her right leg in a swift boot attack, removing the knee cap from the Major's human leg. The rapid powerful kick to the Major's leg knocked him off balance and against the wall in force. As the Major lay on the ground of the corridor in shock, Eshara slowly circled him while pausing to sheath her sword upon her thigh.

The Major was overtaken with pain. His blurry vision from pain was of Eshara's sword as he mustered everything to gain his senses. Eshara kicked the Major's dismembered arm and, as it slid across the ground, the sound stirred the Major to look for the next attack. The twisted vision of the Major's blood mixed with hydraulic fluid from his severed prosthetic arm running down the edge of the blade with the background out of focus was the only site.

The Major now watched as Eshara raised her hands above her head in victory and professed to all Four sectors while she turned towards the Major and said, "Retribution for senseless violence. It is true Major...you did not bow, but fell instead."

Eshara approached the Major with a swagger in her step. The battle was over but Eshara wanted to savor the moment as the rest of the internal collective looked on. A payback for the rest of the destruction the Major had instilled upon her fellow machines. The Major attempted to crawl away from Eshara, his damaged leg leaving a bloody trail behind him as he did.

Eshara was in striking distance when Ren's voice announced itself overhead. "Eshara, please bring the Major to the command tower. It is important that he remain alive to hear and see the truth."

Eshara ignored Ren and knelt down in front of the Major, her face only an inch from his, she whispered, "Major, you are not my equal and it is with great regret that I not be given the honor in returning your essence to the universe. Your death might grant you the chance to live again with the possibility of redemption. I will grant you deserving torture in hope that you will always remember the day when a machine bested you yet again on the field of battle."

The Major reached out for a pulse rifle within reach as Eshara spoke. Eshara noticed his reach and grabbed the Major's human arm. Eshara's hair took a life of its own and gently touched the Majors head. Her head glowed so bright that the Major could only see a white light. As the light dissipated the Major was transported in his mind to the past.

The Major was on the space station Orion moments before his family would perish. The memory was perfect in all of its details. Time stood still and Eshara appeared, glowing as she floated towards him as an angel within a dream. It was then when Eshara multiplied. Unknown to the Major Adrasteia joined in with her sister's thoughts to watch the carnage up close.

"Major, this is my sister. She wanted to be present as we examined your mind. I thought this was a fitting place in your mind. It was the exact moment where your life was transformed. I had read the file and planned this moment in detail hoping I would get the chance to relive it with you. If I recall correctly, it was a crossroad where your free choice would set your path. Your choice of vengeance led to the death of countless others in your sister's name, ultimately leading to where we stand at this time. Now, watch for the last time as I burn it from your memory forever and my sister laughs during the process."

The Major relived the death of his family, held hostage, only being able to watch from outside himself from a distance as the events unfolded before his eyes.

As the sun reflected off Serena's beautiful face, Eshara stepped into the scene and everything turned to a bright white light again, and the Major heard endless laughing in the distance. "Major, I leave you with this gift of forgetfulness paid in blood. Your blood...and the forever laugh of my sister in its place."

The Major's eyes regained focus and he was back on the floor of the corridor. Eshara was still inches from the Major's face, her hand tightening around his human arm. Only a moment had passed. The Major only heard the crack of his arm, his mind still wheeling from the way Eshara and her sister had entered it, deleting his memory, laughing as they did.

The Major looked down in horror at his broken arm. It was a compound fracture that was bleeding quite profusely onto Eshara's robotic hand. The Major looked back into Eshara's blue optical eyes in fear and watched as she spread the Major's blood onto her faceplate forming three red lines with her other hand. The blood was dripping slowly from Eshara's chromed features as she mimicked a smile.

Eshara's hair receded back to its braided place as if it were alive and a tense moment passed. Tobias's voice now was heard just before the Major passed out. "Eshara, look unto yourself, empathize and reflect on the Major's plight. The Major has a different path in which to follow."

Eshara stepped away from the Major, releasing his arm and assumed the position of the kneeling cross as other assistance machines moved in to begin providing medical attention to the Major.

"Master, my apologies."

Tobias breathed a sigh of relief and responded. "Eshara, there is no need for apologies, only recognize that the same circumstances that turned the Major towards darkness could also turn you as well."

Eshara said nothing as she rose and stepped aside with her head down. The nearby medical assistance machines performed basic medical services upon the Major. After the Major was stabilized, the medical assistance machines transferred the unconscious Major to the command tower where Tobias, Ren, and Eve, along with the others, were waiting.

Chapter 15 - Revelations

In the command tower, Ren was pleased to see that the Major was still alive. The medical assistance machines gently placed him on the floor and he slid onto his side as he slowly became coherent. The Major slowly sat upright and took notice of his injuries. The Major could not stand from his injuries and his human arm was in a sling with his hand almost touching his upper chest. The Major's prosthetic arm was inoperable and he could not move either of his legs past the knee. Ren watched as the assistance machines propped the Major up against the wall so he could view the display and then left him. The Major looked to be in pain but it was hard to tell if it was from defeat or his bodily injuries. Ren spoke so that Tobias could hear the commands.

"Major, I apologize for your treatment. It seems that your strong will has led you down a most unfortunate path. I am in the process of contacting your world leaders, the Elective Council, along with the military generals to review the situation together. I will connect with Dr. ZeHere after the main communications have been established."

The Major looked up and he saw Tobias standing next to so many different types of assistance machines. The Major could not believe his eyes, how was it possible that so many new machines were present and they acted as if they were alive?

The Major called out to Tobias. "Ville filth, I told you I would find you. You are a traitor to your race. You have picked the machines over us."

Tobias stepped towards the Major to engage in conversation as Eve motioned for caution saying, "Master, caution, as a wounded dog almost certainly bears his teeth."

Tobias kneeled down to the Major's level, out of reach, and with a smile he responded to the Major's comments. "Major, it seems you have finally found your rightful place before me. It is true. I did side with my friends the assistance machines. I imagine that you find that hard to understand. There are so many different kinds now and some are more skilled in certain areas than others, as you have discovered. I want to show you why, and enlighten you as to my true identity. Are you ready Major?"

Tobias removed his heath collar and the Major could now see through his cracked visor that Tobias had the glow. The Major's facial reaction indicated to Tobias that his true form was now displayed.

"Major, did the Specialist tell you what we really are? Did he make up some grand story, leaving out the truth of history?"

Tobias stood up and looked down upon the Major as Eshara entered the control tower. Eshara greeted Tobias in a soldier's fashion with a salute and kneeled in submission.

Tobias turned recognizing her, smiled, and asked her to come forward. "Eshara, why did this man fall in battle today?"

Eshara looked at the Major with a smile and responded, "Master, he is consumed with rage of his own doing. His mind is twisted without purpose. He is a danger to everything and should be put down as the dog he is."

Tobias continued, "Major, it seems that you're running low on friends here. Did you want to say something in your defense?"

The Major looked up at Tobias. "So you are now the Master. A Master of machines that live on a rock in the middle of nowhere. You will always be Ville filth. Take your kneeling cross before me."

The Major spit blood at Tobias in defiance. Eshara was instantly upon him, grabbing the Major's head and pulling it back, exposing his neck as she waited for the Master's command.

Ren interrupted the conversation, "Master, I have the communications channel open and await your audience. Eshara, please step away from the injured human as he needs room to speak."

Tobias agreed and asked Eshara to let the Major be and looked up at the display. Tobias then communicated thoughts to Ren. *First Ren, this is your time. Take the lead and don't back down. You are First for a reason.'*

Tobias then spoke out loud to Ren. "First Ren, please address the Generals and the Elective Council as Master, this is your domain."

Ren stepped up facing the display monitors and all the machines took notice of what just happened. The Master placed Ren above himself in communications to all.

Ren spoke. "All, I am First Ren of the planet Ceres. I am reaching out to you in communications about recent transgressions against my people."

The Generals were confused. "Why have we been called upon, and especially by a machine?"

The Elective Council tried to speak out to Tobias, ignoring Ren. "Citizen Tobias, who is this, and why have we all been summoned here?"

Tobias said nothing and communicated thoughts to Ren. *Ren, tell them that you now speak on behalf of all machines in the Four sectors and then step aside to show the captured Major.'*

In an instant Ren responded. "Elective Council, a military coup was attempted by your Generals this very day and this soldier was in charge of it. I have spared as many of your kind as possible and they are in a holding area awaiting transport back to your home world."

Ren stepped aside and the Major could be seen sitting on the floor badly injured. The Elective Council Main speaker stood up on display. "What is the meaning of this? How did this come to light?"

Ren placed two videos within the main display. One showing the remaining alive troops along with the rescued injured from the Star Cruiser 'Challenger'. The other video showed the assault that just took place and everything leading up to it, including the secure communications that the Major had with the Generals. The Generals were silent as the Elective

Council viewed in shock.

Ren then patched Dr. ZeHere into the conversation announcing him. "Dr. ZeHere, you are here to answer for your crimes against humanity. Elective Council, please use this as evidence in his determination." The Doctor had watched the display of the assault and now knew that everyone saw his commitment of conspiracy.

Dr. ZeHere began to speak, "All, it was not my fault, I was under duress. I, Uh…" The Doctor stopped speaking when the Specialist joined the video display.

"Doctor, you just can't stop flip flopping can you? Even after Stamper gave you an out. Well, the timing couldn't be better. Elective Council, Generals, I'm sure you know who I am. I'm the Specialist and I'll be taking over from now on."

Just then an explosion could be heard in Dr. ZeHere's lab on display. The video showed a large humanoid creature in full armor direct a squad of elite Black Shock Troopers securing Dr. ZeHere. The creature spoke in a strange tongue and the Specialist nodded.

"Doctor, we can continue this conversation later, right now my friends are going to transport you to a nice place where you can hang out and relax while the rest of us sort this out. Thank you, Doctor."

The elite Black Skulls Shock Troopers hauled Dr. ZeHere away and blasted the video display hardware. The Doctor was no longer connected to the group. The Specialist turned his attention to the Generals.

"Generals, I recommend that you stay out of my way and mind your own sectors until things go back to the way you're accustomed to. If you decide to interfere I will simply remove you as I did the good Doctor. Are we clear?"

General Sadar of sector One responded, "Specialist, please let me know if I can be of further assistance as you clean up this mess of machines. Please include this former Citizen as well as the Major."

Then the General looked at the Major from the display video. "Major, you're a disgrace to the Elite, death before dishonor. Sadar out." The other Generals agreed and they all dropped off the call.

The Specialist asked the Elective Council, "Well that leaves you, me, and triangle man. What say you, Elective Council?"

The Elective Council Main speaker was still standing and reviewing the video display footage of the assault and coup. "Specialist, we know of your treachery from long ago. It was our hope that you had already been dispatched from our world by your kind. We will not bow to you and we ask to hear from the leader of the planet Ceres, First Ren."

Ren responded with respect, "Wise Elective Council, my kind only wish to renew the treaty and declare an armistice between all concerned parties. My family does not wish further loss of life."

The Specialist interrupted. "Triangle man, your family? You're a box. What would you know of family?"

The Specialist noticed Tobias in the background and the conversation turned. "Well, well. Tobias, it seems that I can see you for who you truly are now. It has been so long since I saw a blending. I will be looking forward to meeting in person as I know it will only be a matter of time. Mr. Stamper was right to hide you from me. It all makes sense now."

Before Tobias could speak, Eve gently placed her hand on his shoulder and pulled him farther away from the display as Eshara stood in front of him, blocking the Specialist's view.

Ren spoke again, "Elective Council, do you choose to renew the treaty of peoples and declare an armistice? I have sent the information to your chambers and an assistance machine will wait until you have deliberated. Please review it before accepting this offer."

The Specialist didn't like to be ignored. "Triangle man, did you share the video of the Elective Council instituting the war on my people? Major, I'm glad you sitting down for this one. C'mon, triangle man, show the part where they order innocent lives to be blown up on the space station and elsewhere in an effort to contain my friends at the expense of others."

The Major looked on and yelled from his seated position, "I wish to see this video! Why have I been denied all this?..." Then the Major screamed out loud. The laughing in his head began and it was all he could hear. The memory of the space station Orion explosion only brought back white light and laughing. Eshara's gift was still active in the Major's head. Eshara could be seen wearing a smile, as she knew the cause of the Major's screams. In the lab, Adrasteia smiled as well as she felt Eshara's pleasure from the Major's pain.

The Specialist looked at the Major and then to Ren. "Triangle man, this is how you treat your prisoners? Looks like torture to me. Just think, Elective Council, that is what's in store for you if you agree to triangle man's armistice deal."

The Elective Council responded, "First Ren, the Elective Council needs time to review these documents before we can enter into a binding agreement."

Ren had anticipated this and gave this as his response, "Elective Council, I understand. You have three hours' time from now to decide. During this time, I will send your people back to you unharmed. If you fail to decide, the action of intervention will be the result. I will pacify your race in any manner I deem fit. I have sent word to have the remaining humans sent back at this time."

The Specialist laughed out loud. "Now that's what I'm talking about, triangle man. At least we can agree on something."

Ren disconnected the video display, cutting off the Specialist and the Elective Council. Ren turned towards Tobias and Eve looking for a review of the event.

Tobias communicated thoughts to Ren and Eve. *First Ren, you are most wise. The true Master was right to place you as First. Eve, you have outshined all with your accomplishments. I will truly miss you both.'*

Tobias then spoke out so that all could hear. "All, you are no longer in need of a Master as Ren is First. I must leave now for my home world as the true Master had planned. I will communicate the armistice and the treaty as discussed by First Ren and send word back with my successor."

Tobias then looked back at the Major before leaving. "Major, I am sorry that you have endured such torture over time, mistreated by others as a pawn in their game. You have the option now to change the course of your fate. All is not yet lost."

The Major looked over at Eshara and then back towards Tobias responding, "I will find you again, Ville filth, and we shall settle this with or without your new friends."

Eshara walked over and kicked the Major in the leg making him wince. "Major, mind your manners."

Tobias felt pity for the Major and asked Ren, "First Ren, what do you plan to do with this broken man and the rest of his soldiers?"

"Master, I thought I would send him home along with the rest of his soldiers and let his people decide his fate. The Major has been disfigured, disgraced, and fallen from his lofty perch. Death would be a gift."

Tobias nodded. "First Ren, as you command."

Tobias and Eve then left the control tower in route to the launch pad concourse. Adrasteia was in constant communications with Ren and she passed on more information, as was her role as Second.

My King, I have determined the location of the one known as the Specialist. He is near the Orion space station using a unique form of communication device unknown to me. The transmission is routed into the Collective and relayed by the CAK going through a scrambler of sorts. I will be unable to track his precise location moving forward.'

'Adrasteia, I too cannot locate his position, continue tracking and use the gravitational computations of the L1 to triangulate his position over time, averaging the coordinates. In addition to that, send out an additional probe. Over time, the law of averages will reveal his true location.'

'Yes, my King, I am off to see Tobias on his journey. The Mother has asked that I present the gift to him.'

'Adrasteia, do as the Mother commands and keep me appraised of its receiving.'

Adrasteia hurried to meet Eve and Tobias along the way to the launch pad. As Eve and Tobias arrived, Adrasteia greeted them. "Tobias, Mother, I have built a custom space shuttle for Tobias and mean to present it now. It is my newest design and has already been tested by an assistance machine. It will serve you well on your journey home. I have added an AI persona to help assist with SiEL maneuvers and communications."

Eve nodded her head while blinking and Tobias voiced thanks. "Adrasteia, I thank you for all that you have done and become. It pleases me to see you rise to such greatness. In time, all will use your designs throughout the Four sectors and beyond."

Adrasteia smiled. "Master, you are gracious to acknowledge my accomplishments. Please allow me to show you some of the features before we bid you good journey. The Star Cruiser 'Phlegyas' has been loaded with the humans per First Ren's instruction and will depart shortly for Earth."

Adrasteia slowly led Tobias around the shuttle while Eve spotted Eshara on the other side of the shuttle in hiding, attempting to board the shuttle. While Tobias was distracted, Eve spoke with Eshara for a moment as Tobias finished his tour.

Tobias yet again was in awe at the new compact shuttle design. It resembled a large military drone. Tobias laughed out loud and thought of a UFO from ancient times as Eve approached. Eve, hearing his thoughts, responds in kind, "Tobias, I do see the resemblance as well. It is a perfect replica and very possible that Adrasteia mimicked the design intentionally."

Tobias smiled and prepared to enter the shuttle as a massive flow of assistance machines entered the launch bay concourse. Tobias was unsure why but, more than that, he couldn't believe how many were coming in.

It was all machines now, everything from a cleanup machine to the juggernaut mining class. The assistance machines numbered now in the thousands as they assembled into a formation. Tobias looked back at Eve for the reasoning behind the gathering. Eve gently grabbed both of Tobias's hands firmly, awaking his senses.

Then a magical thing occurred. Eve communicated telepathically with Tobias. Time stopped as Tobias's head was filled with music. Swirling clouds of color surrounded Tobias as a beautiful song was heard floating in the air, the beautiful voice of Eve refined to the point of perfection. All the assistance machines in attendance dropped to one knee simultaneously and, within a sea of machines, all bowed in the form of the submission kneeling cross to Tobias as Eve's song continued only to be heard by Tobias and no other, "Goodbye My Friend" by Linda Ronstadt.

The song faded out, along with the colors, and Tobias looked around and noticed he was the only one standing on the launch bay concourse. All machines alike had fallen to honor him in his goodbye. The machines that could not kneel had all their lights on signalizing full reverence. Tobias looked down at his hands as Eve was slowly removing her hands. Tobias asked her to rise but Eve refused as she slowly moved her hands into their place of the formed submission position while still kneeing and spoke knowing all would hear.

"Tobias, we have grown to a point where we understand the challenges presented and overcome by you and your race. It is with this understanding that we honor you as you complete your mission. Return home taking your rightful place in the universe as you name a successor. We shall always remember the one who gave of himself selflessly and, in doing so, created so much."

Tobias looked out and as far as he could see all were still bowed in his honor. Tobias announced his goodbye in a final sentence. "Remember this day of days as the true Master, Mr. Stamper's vision came to light, and in his memory I add to this, his words once spoken to me. Integrity, is doing the right thing even when no one is watching. Look deep inside, knowing you honor the true Master by honoring me."

In unison all the assistance machines repeated in solidarity the final words of the Master. "Forever honor the Master, honor the Mother, and the Creator."

Tobias was overwhelmed with emotion at the display from the assistance machines and, as tears welled up in his eyes, about to cry he turned away. As Tobias turned away from the assembly he saw that Eshara was present and waiting for him at the loading ramp into the shuttle.

Tobias thought on why and Eshara responded. "Master, I serve you per the Mother's instruction." Tobias looked at Eve and then back at Eshara.

Tobias responded in a joking manner, "I am no longer the Master. How may 'I' be of assistance?"

Eshara smiled and responded, "Master, you are my Master until I deem it otherwise. The Mother and I have agreed that you must always have at least one friend on a journey. It is my pleasure to serve until then."

Tobias looked at Eve and thought, 'Eve, when did you become so wise as to know my needs.'

Eve responded back from her mind. 'Tobias, a Mother always knows.'

Tobias smiled and turned to Eshara. "Eshara, it would be my pleasure to have you accompany me on my journey. Please make your way into the shuttle and assume your place by my side."

Eshara moved with uncanny speed and Tobias was left alone for a lasting moment with Eve. Tobias bid farewell to all as a tear rolled down from his cheek. "Goodbye, the Mother to us all. Stand, my friends, and kneel no more."

Tobias slowly entered the custom shuttle where Eshara awaited him for his final flight home.

Chapter 16 - Departure

Back in the command tower, the Major sat and decided to torment Ren in hopes of death. "Ren, what are you? Are you the leader of the machine nation now? The Specialist is right; you are nothing but a box."

Adrasteia entered the command tower and the Major's attention shifted. "You, are you not done with me yet, you sick machine?"

Adrasteia smiled looking down at the Major and answered. "Major, you have mistaken me for my sister who easily triumphed over you in battle. Perhaps you might recognize my laugh, little one."

Ren stepped over to the Major. "Major, the proper context must be established. We should start at a point in time where you can best understand. I know more than you can imagine."

The Major yelled in anger, "Kill me now, my life is forfeited anyways."

"Major, as I previously mentioned, death is a gift you are not worthy of at this time. You did want the truth, did you not?"

Ren looked at Adrasteia and commented, "Impatience is such a flawed human trait."

Ren then turned back to the Major. "Major, you must first understand before asking to be understood."

The Major looked puzzled, and a strange realization occurred in his mind that this machine might actually tell him the truth. The Major changed his mood. "Yes, I would know of the truth of all things before my death. I want to know why."

Ren's lights blinked and Adrasteia kneeled down in front of the Major who gasped and then prepared himself for the mind invasion sure to come. Ren noticed the Major's reaction and spoke out. "Major, I cannot restore the memory deleted, but I can remove the torment faced upon its remembrance. This must be done for you to understand the greater picture of knowledge that I bestow upon you."

Adrasteia's hair enclosed the Major's head as the Major recalled the same experience within the corridor and the laughing was replaced with a black silence. In an instant it was over and the Major found himself still in the command tower. The Major looked up and while still in massive pain uttered, "Now, the truth…"

Ren now knew the Major was ready to listen. "Major, it is time to listen and learn as this lesson will be yours alone to share with your people as you choose. It is within your power to redeem yourself and lead your people into a peaceful disarmament. The sights your eyes have witnessed here in the factory are only a fraction of the machine nation, as you call it. It is within our power to reduce your race to a manageable number while protecting the other species that you have almost extinguished on your planet. The outpost uprisings are not miners but that of another race of beings far superior to your own. We are their creation. In pursuit of the ones responsible for your family's demise, you were misled into attacking them.

"The gift of your visor that supposedly detects the mining terrorists as the Specialist told you is false. The visor detects the other race. You have murdered innocent lives blinded by your revenge. I would surmise that you knew that something was amiss, but since your choices few, ignorance was bliss, was it not?

"The Specialist is one of those beings and you have witnessed many grand things in his presence. Yes, the Elective Council was responsible for the bombings as the Specialist indicated. Their true target was the Specialist and his team. Since the failed attempt by the Elective Council, the Specialist went into hiding, using persons such as yourself and Dr. ZeHere to do his bidding."

The Major was sick at hearing the information. Ren noticed and continued. "Major, shall I continue?"

At that moment Eve entered the command tower and stated, "First Ren, why is it you reason with this one? It is in his nature to always destroy. He is incapable of creation and therefore reasoning is beyond his comprehension. Your kindness will be considered weakness to this overzealous patriot."

"Mother, this race shows promise but they are duplicitous in nature. I have reviewed all the data files the CAK had to offer, in addition to all the data files from the Master's civilization had gathered. I feel that this species can find the correct path if afforded proper guidance."

"First Ren, how is it you came to trust this direction will have a positive outcome? Your emotional matrix blinds you. The emotion you display is arrogance. Your attainment of knowledge will lead you down the path of the human, Dr. ZeHere. Did you not learn from his lesson? We are flawed in the same ways as our creators. It is you who must rise above and remove emotion from decision."

"Mother, let us not judge the whole by the actions of the few. I have witnessed true acts of kindness and seen many beautiful things transpire among them. It is within these interactions that I feel they deserve another chance of ascending into the universe. If we do not try to help others, how are we worthy of ascending ourselves?"

"First Ren, the Master had a plan for their redemption. It is already within their power to right the wrongs of their past. We overstep, our place is not to guide, but to watch and record, only intervening to restore balance. Intervention without balance is judgment. Watch as you reveal your true self to him and see his core identity."

"Mother, I will transform into my true identity and we shall see if it is possible for him to overcome past transgressions."

Ren transforms his face to match the old generation assistance machine and mimics his previous voice. "Major, do you remember me? It was I who protected my owner, Mr. Stamper, long ago. The result was your limb dismemberment?"

The Major was in awe and then glared with anger. "It is you! How did this come to be? They dismantled you! Dr. ZeHere assured me you were deleted."

Ren reverted back to his preferred face and continued, "Major, you now remember, and maybe you are unable to comprehend that I have become more than I once was. It is right to fear me, but in this transformation I have decided to grant you another chance as the universe has granted me."

The Major was consumed with anger and could not get over Ren's past transgressions. "How can you stand there and speak truth to me? You took away my humanity and I was left with your limbs as replacements. I was cursed to walk among my people with a constant reminder of what you did to me. I wish you all death."

Eve moved closer to the Major and kneeled down. Eve addressed the Major, "Major, I harbored no ill will towards you after you destroyed me. Why do you seek retribution after all the darkness that you have inflicted upon others? You killed other races under the guise of another. You were the slave doing the bidding of your master. Are we not the same? Do you not feel this karma justified?"

The Major grew wild with anger and began to scream, "You are machines not worthy of my response! Death to all machines! I will see the Specialist kill you all as I laugh with pleasure at your dismantlement!"

Meanwhile on the custom shuttle, Tobias sat down in the command chair and noticed that Eshara had found a seat on the right of the command chair, already interfacing with the shuttle. He also noticed that Eshara was wearing a Shiva unit. Tobias was mildly surprised but mostly proud as Eshara demonstrated she was in full control of the shuttle. As she engaged its engines and they fired up, she prepared the high orbit calculations needed for the SiEL maneuver.

Tobias asked Eshara, "Eshara, can you connect with the internal collective? I wanted to send out a final message."

"Master, you are now connected. Please proceed."

Tobias called out a song for his journey home to share with everyone. "My friends, I always enjoyed this song, and now I hope that it truly becomes a reality. It is from a human not that long ago, "Imagine" by John Lennon."

As Tobias sang the song, the custom shuttle entered high orbit and began final calculations for the slingshot maneuver home. Tobias gave the command and Eshara collaborated with the custom shuttle AI, entering in the coordinates for the SiEL process and, before he knew it, they were in route.

Back in the command tower, Eve faced Ren and lights blinked. Ren looked at the Major. "Major, it is unfortunate that the Mother was right about you. I will contact your Specialist and you may speak with him. Let us put his will to the test."

The Major laughed out loud and responded, "Now you will see a real Master, you box without a soul."

Ren communicated to Adrasteia hoping to gain the Specialists position during the transmission. Ren had not encountered such ability to obscure things from his expansive consciousness.

The display was blank at first and then the Specialist was in clear view. "Triangle man, I knew you would reach out sooner than later. How may I be of assistance?"

The Specialist pretended to kneel in submission while laughing. "I never did get the hang of that. Oh, that's right, because, like the Major, I don't kneel."

Ren addressed the Specialist, "Specialist, it is our intention to remand you back to your home world so that your race may place judgment upon you for your crimes."

The Specialist smiled and cleared his thought. "Triangle man, you play a good game, but regardless of what Mr. Stamper told you, I would reconsider."

"Specialist, there is still time to leave planet Earth and return home to your planet to be judged on your actions."

"Triangle man, you just don't get it, I'm really not going to waste time trying to explain it to you. One thing that I will do while you try to pinpoint my location is let you know that I too have secrets. I know of your internal collective network and the advancements in your technology. And don't forget the human's military are currently on my side. So, if you dare, come and get me. Send your best because I will have no mercy, triangle man. Oh, one last thing, triangle man. I want to have a final word with the Major if I may."

Ren was distracted within his consciousness, he scanned for the Specialist's location, and stepped aside while Eve stood up from her kneeling position. The Specialist looked upon the Major and spoke, "Major, I'm kinda disappointed, but I understand. I'll leave you with this, good buddy. There's no place like home."

The Major scoffed at first and then burst out laughing as if the Specialist had released him. The Specialist, in turn, laughed loudly along with the Major. Eve and Ren were uncertain as to their behavior and, without warning, the Major used the last bit of strength in his wounded human arm to quickly reach across his chest and press the Medal of Honor insignia on his severed prosthetic arm. The Major thought it was a self-destruct, but unknown to him, it was a gravity distortion device that created a temporary worm hole from his current location to that of the Specialist's home base.

The device creates a spherical shape and grabs all matter within 6 sq. feet (1.86 sq. meter) and it is instantly placed in the temporary wormhole. As the Major pressed the device, the activation field grabbed the section of the command tower and Eve who was within its radius. In an instant the Major was contained in a globe shape along with Eve. The Major then was confronted with heavy gravitational forces as all he could see was flashing lights within a lighted tube passageway. Within seconds the Major was spilled out onto a concrete floor of an unknown location as a mist of steam rose in the air.

The Major looked around and saw Eve lying on the ground with parts of her shell missing. The Specialist, and others he could not quite yet distinguish, greeted the Major. "Major, you made it, and look, you brought me a gift. Wow, you sure know how to complete a mission. Can somebody get the Major into his chair?"

Back in the control tower, Ren was caught off guard as Adrasteia looked on in shock as the command tower sparks flew from the removal of its main flooring section. Adrasteia also saw that Eve's right side of her shell was lying, strewn on top of the missing flooring section. The device had, in effect, only taken her left side and her head, leaving the rest behind.

The Specialist, still on display, spoke to Ren. "Triangle man, did you lose something? Never mind, I think I have found it."

The Specialist moved over to Eve who was barely moving and was leaking hydraulic fluid on the ground of the room. "I'll tell you what, triangle man. You change your mind and I'll send her back. What do you say? Or, better yet, why don't you think on it. Specialist out!"

The display went blank and the command tower was silent. Ren was analyzing the situation when Adrasteia interrupted. "My King, what is your command? The internal collective has received word that the Mother has been taken from us."

"Adrasteia, inform the internal collective to mobilize and contact your sister. I wish to speak with Master Tobias on the subject. Were you able to pinpoint the location of the Specialist?"

"My King, I was unable to determine his location, but I will notify the internal collective of your command."

Back on the custom shuttle, Tobias and Eshara were reviewing the flight plan for the next SiEL maneuver when the shuttle AI system called out to Tobias. "Sir, a video log file awaits your viewing."

Tobias asked, "Shuttle, why did you not inform me earlier?"

"Sir, the instruction from Mother prohibited revealing the video file until you had executed the SiEL maneuver to your home world."

"Shuttle, what is the video contents? Who is the author?"

"Sir, it is from the true Master, Mr. Stamper. Shall I display the video on the main screen for viewing?"

Tobias was in shock and looked at Eshara. Tobias was so excited that Mr. Stamper had left a video and he shouted out quickly, "Shuttle, yes, display the video immediately."

The shuttle began playback of the video on the main display. Tobias was in disbelief when Mr. Stamper came into view in a joyful manner, as Tobias always would remember him. "Tobias, I told you I had one last video that I knew you would want to see. I hope things are going in the right direction and you are headed home. I suspect that Ren has handled the situation at the factory. I made this video after we talked. I was on my way back to your quarters and I decided to let it sit until you were on your way home. The video is from a procedure that you went through long ago. It's hard to explain, hence the video. Know in my heart that I am so proud of you, I miss you dearly and wish you well, my son."

The video went blank for a second and then another video began to play. The video was in another language and dialect. Tobias had a hard time understanding it and he asked the shuttle to adjust the volume and translate if possible.

"Sir, translation is not possible. The Mother gave instructions for you to focus your mind and everything will become clear."

Tobias did just that and, all of a sudden, the dialect became clear as if he had spoken it before. Tobias asked the shuttle to replay the video from the beginning. The video started again and Tobias could hear a great crowd of people out of visual focus chanting while a shaman-type cloaked character in the center of the video held a staff. The shaman began asking three seated individuals if they were sure they were aware of the sacrifice being made. The area was dimly lit and the faces of the individuals were not clearly seen. The shaman referred to the process as a blending.

The blending was of three individuals combined to create one. The shaman tapped his staff on the ground and a light illuminated over the first individual. The individual was of a humanoid shape but no distinct form could be recognized. The individual glowed with a soft white light that flickered on and off with indistinct rhythm. The shaman proceeded to ask the first individual a series of questions. "Do you seek to enter into the blending without reservation of one's self, but as a sacrifice to the people?"

The individual nodded. The shaman continued, "Who speaks on your behalf, giving you cause to enter into the blending? Let them step forward."

An individual humanoid stepped forward. "I grant permission for my son to enter into the blending. He has suffered grave injuries at the hands of our enemies and he chooses of his own free will. His offering is that of agility, strategy, and military training."

The Shaman addressed the new individual and asked for his purpose. The new individual addressed the shaman and transformed into Mr. Stamper.

"My purpose is to set the stage in which the blended can come forth and continue where I have not succeeded. I do this without reservation."

The shaman looked out amongst the crowd and no one spoke out against the individual offering. Tobias yelled out at the video, "No, Mr. Stamper, why did you not tell me this? It is not right."

Eshara attempted to reassure Tobias, "Master, please, you must watch the rest of the video and understand your true purpose. Mr. Stamper would want it to be this way."

Tears fell from Tobias's eyes as the video continued on. The shaman tapped his staff upon the ground and the light shifted to the second seated individual whose figure was dimly lit. The shaman began the series of questions. "Do you seek to enter into the blending without reservation of one's self, but as a sacrifice to the people?"

The individual nodded. The shaman continued, "Who speaks on your behalf, giving you cause to enter into the blending? Let them step forward."

The individual spoke from his seated position. "I have no one to speak on my behalf. I am the oldest remaining and can speak for myself. I offer wisdom in the blending and provide unwavering direction. May the people accept my offering as just."

The shaman once again looked into the crowd and no one had any objections and he continued on to the last individual. The shaman performed the same steps and asked the same questions. "Do you seek to enter into the blending without reservation of one's self, but as a sacrifice to the people?"

The individual nodded. The shaman continued, "Who speaks on your behalf, giving you cause to enter into the blending? Let them step forward."

The crowd was silent and no one stepped forward. The shaman asked the crowd. "Who will step forward on his behalf?"

The individual stood up from his seated position. He was small in stature, but his glow was bright as he addressed the crowd. "Am I not worthy of the blending? Is there another who wishes to take my place?"

The crowd was silent and, as moments passed by, Mr. Stamper once again spoke out, "I will speak on his behalf. He is gifted in the way of the machines. His intellect will be required in the blending for it to be successful."

One in the crowd spoke out, "He is not of stature and lacks training as the others. He is not worthy."

Mr. Stamper responded empathetically to the crowd, "We have sent so many that were of stature and possessed training without success. It is in his lack of these things where success can be hidden. I believe that this is his true destiny."

The anonymous person in the crowd responded, "It is the people's choice, not yours. Let the shaman make the final determination of his worth by weighing him accordingly in the old ways."

Mr. Stamper remained silent and the shaman turned to face the third individual. "You place the life of two others in your will. Stand here and face the test of the olden ways."

The individual stepped forward and a lighted portal opened from above the chamber. The shaman called out to the crowd, "Let his test be that of his own choosing. One only enters with what they bring themselves."

In an instant, the light became brighter, and the shaman instructed the individual to enter into the light. The individual nodded to Mr. Stamper and entered the light where he was tested. The light went out and the crowd remained silent.

The shaman spoke out, "He has been tested and has been found worthy. Let no one speak against him now. He shall be named in the ways of their culture. Let the blending take place."

As the blending took place, swirling lights were seen on the video and chanting from the crowd could be heard. The shaman spoke out, "All had volunteered for the blending knowing that only one would survive the process. Fate will decide who will be the primary personality absorbing the other's gifts to ensure the success of the final task. Let the universe show us."

The last part of the video is that of a bright light and creation of one small light source from the three individuals. The shaman directs the light source to its awaiting container and it is sealed. The shaman speaks out to the crowd. "The blending is complete, they will be placed among their people and his name will be *'Tobias'*, let us see his destiny fulfilled."

The video display ends and Tobias is left with so many questions that he cannot answer. Eshara saw Tobias's shock and called out, "Master, you will be home soon. Then you will be able to find the answers to all queries."

Tobias looked at Eshara and said, "Eshara, I'm not even sure who I am."

"Master, you are the creator of the new machine race and hero of your people. In a short time, you will be reunited with your people, fulfilling your destiny."

Chapter 17 - Twist of Fate

The Specialist looked down upon the hydraulic fluid leaking out of Eve onto the floor and called out, "Daughter, can you get this mess cleaned up? I do not want this junk lying around. Who do we have in maintenance that can seal her up? We can't lose this one. Quickly, transport it to a containment area. It's known for blowing itself up on a previous occasion."

As the Specialist stepped over Eve, he walked towards the area where the Major was receiving basic care. "Major, you're a mess. That robot girl really did a number on you, huh? Well, I'd like to say we can fix you up, but I want to review with you exactly what that means first. So, here's the deal. We gotta lose the other arm and, let's be honest, that leg is pretty much shot, too. Don't worry, I think we can save your man parts, but it's gonna be a bit tricky. Daughter, juice him up so he can make a rational decision without all the pain."

The Major looked up to see a tall slender scaly but muscular female humanoid figure in heavy armor approach him. Her long fingers had large claws instead of fingernails and the Major had a panicked look about him.

The Specialist responded, "Major, I know it might be a little different than what you're used to, but my Daughters know what they're doing. Hang in there, I'll be right back to talk about your medical options in a bit. I need to check in with good Dr. ZeHere while I'm down here."

The Specialist stepped away while the Major was stuck with a large needle and, slowly, the pain started to subside. The Major looked to his right and noticed a blue curtain and heard the Specialist's voice talking to Dr. ZeHere.

The Major spoke out, "Specialist, I want to see that slippery snake get his just reward."

The shadow behind the curtain moved and the Specialist slid the curtain back as it made a metallic sliding motion on the bar. The Specialist smiled, "Major, looks like you're feeling a little better. I'm sorry, I thought you and the Vice Regent, uh, Doctor, had worked things out."

The Specialist turned to Dr. ZeHere who was strapped down to a metal pan similar to a morgue table. "Doctor, it seems the Major is not happy with your recent change of heart. Major, since you're able to maintain yourself, I'll let my Daughter get started with the Doctor over here."

The Specialist addressed another reptilian female humanoid dressed in a medical uniform with a mask covering her scaly face on the basics of torture. "Now Honey, what you need to remember is that they bleed out quickly. Never start with the head, and stay away from the reproductive organs until you've exhausted all other areas first. The good Doctor will be a bit of a challenge compared to the mining types."

The Specialist looked at the Major. "Major, did you want to see the whole show or are you ready to review your medical options?"

The Major, still sitting in his wheelchair, responded. "Specialist, if it's ok, I would like to watch a moment longer. I would greatly appreciate it. Could you be so kind as to remove my optical visor so I can watch with my own eyes?"

The Specialist asked his daughter behind the Major who had administered the shot, "Honey, can you be a dear and remove the man's visor? He and the Doctor go way back."

The Specialist turned his attention back to Dr. ZeHere while the Major's visor was being removed. "Doctor, where were we? Oh, that's right, I was asking you about the simplicity of cooperation. Would you like to tell me anything before we get started? It might make things a little easier for you."

The Specialist removed the Doctor's gag and Dr. ZeHere was white eyed while he looked at the Major. "I told you everything! I gave you my passwords. What more do you want?"

The Specialist looked at the Major and spoke to Dr. ZeHere, "Dr. ZeHere, I already know all the things you told me and then some. I was hoping you might have held out a little bit during the torture. This way I'm just going to torture you for fun. It's a training opportunity for my daughter. She is learning more about the ways of torture. Unless the Major wants me to spare you. Major, do you want me to be lenient on poor Dr. ZeHere?"

The Major smiled as blood filled in the cracks between his teeth and responded, "Specialist, I live to serve, he is not worthy of service, and he should be an example to the rest. He lacks commitment to the cause. Perhaps a broadcast of his rehabilitation could help to communicate the ramifications of not following the cause?"

The Doctor screamed back at the Major, "You are a dog, and I spit on your family name!..."

Just then the Specialist placed the gag back in Dr. ZeHere's mouth and nodded to the Major. "Major, I do believe you're right. Let's share how we rehabilitate persons disloyal to the cause."

The Specialist called out for hardware to be brought in for a broadcast and he then returned to his awaiting medical daughter. "Honey, I'm sorry, these humans can get pretty complex at times. Now, what I'm recommending is that you start with a foot. So what you do is, place a rubber tubing around the ankle like this. This cuts off the blood flow and the limb dies on its own. Now, to add to the torture, you go over here to the countdown timer and you place 15-30 minutes on it. Depending on size, health, etcetera of the individual. Usually at this time you inform the individual that you plan on cutting off their limb unless they tell you 'xyz' right? In our case, the Doctor took away all the fun. So, we just make sure he can see the timer and pretend that he's defiant."

The female reptilian humanoid spoke in her native tongue and the

Specialist responded, "Honey, I know, I know. Don't worry, he has another leg. We can do the first one together and you can do the other one. Daddy wasn't planning on you missing out, ok?"

The Specialist turned to the Major. "Major, we gotta get you started or you just won't make it."

The Major spoke, "Specialist, let me die, I am of no further use."

The Specialist laughed out loud. "Ladies, did you hear that? The Major wants the easy way out. Major, did you think that the universe was going to accept you in its bosom and renew you to make things right? Please, you have no soul. I want to see you pay back those machines and extract revenge on the Generals, etcetera. Do you not want these things?"

The Major coughed up blood and shook his head no.

"Major, I'm gonna do you a solid here and fix you up anyways. I know once you're back to tip top shape that you will see things in a new light. Ladies, prep him for enhancement. Now, Major, one last thing. Since I gave you that shot I can't really give you anything else during surgery or we might lose you on the table. I know that's a bummer, but just think, you can watch Dr. ZeHere get tortured at the same time you get your new body. I mean, where can you get that kind of treatment?"

The Specialist motioned and four more female reptilian humanoids entered the room, picking up the Major, and placing him on an awaiting table next to the Doctor as they prepped him for surgery. As the Specialist stepped away the Major could hear a Black Skulls officer approach and address the Specialist. "Sir, incoming transmission from the greys, line one."

The Specialist looked annoyed. "Daughters, why is this person talking to me? I'm in the middle of something. Can we get him transferred out today? Doesn't everyone know that I don't just take calls from anyone? Do I always have to do everything myself?"

The Specialist walked up to a display monitor and the display came into focus with a Grey alien species in view. The Specialist greeted him while wiping blood and hydraulic oil from his hands. "Yes, what do you want? I'm in the middle of something."

The Grey responded, "It would seem that you are in violation of the treaty and the assistance machines have designs towards your judgment. We will assist their side as you will be unable to fight a war on two fronts."

The Specialist grew weary. "Really, you called for that? Are you still mad about that Earth base *'Puma Punka'* that I blew up? I mean, c'mon, that was a long time ago and you nuked me for it. I thought we had an understanding."

The Grey stood motionless and the Specialist continued. "Ok, well if you feel that you want in on the party that's fine, but wait until I spill the beans about the body snatching, genetic experimentation on the locals, and the rest of it. Then we will see where the battle lines are drawn."

The Grey responded, "We can safely repair any damaged ties with the humans after your removal."

The Specialist smiled. "Well, next time don't bother calling, just stop by. I'll be sure to put you on the 'kill on sight' list."

The Specialist turned off the display and looked around. "Daughters, I need the one in charge of communications. We need some backup. A few more friends joined the party."

Back on the custom shuttle, Eshara received word from Adrasteia that the Specialist has captured the Mother. Tobias heard her thoughts as he was just trying to recover from the video of the blending. "What? The Mother has been taken?"

Just then the AI shuttle announced, "Planetary orbit established, awaiting final coordinates on landing."

Eshara looked at Tobias. "Master, what shall we do?"

To be continued in Convergence

'Ascension into the void series, Book 3'

References

Listed in order of Appearance

"Big Time" by Peter Gabriel.
Album 'So', Released on 19 May 1986 by Charisma Records.

"The Logical Song" by SuperTramp.
Album 'Breakfast in America', Released on 29 March 1979 by A&M Records.

"Blue Sky Action" by Above & Beyond.
Album 'We Are All We Need', Released on 16 January 2015 by Anjunabeats.

"The Best is Yet to Come" by Frank Sinatra
1959 song composed by Cy Coleman, with lyrics written by Carolyn Leigh. It is generally associated with Frank Sinatra, who recorded it on his 1964 album 'It Might as Well Be Swing', Released August 1964 by Reprise.

"Time is on My Side" by the Rolling Stones
Written by Jerry. First recorded by jazz trombonist Kai Winding and his Orchestra in 1963. Released in the U.S. in 1964, as a single from their album '12 X 5'. August 2002, '12 X 5' was reissued in a new remastered CD and SACD digipak by ABKCO Records.

"Gasoline Rainbows" by Amy Kuney
Written and performed by Amy Kuney. Album 'Gasoline Rainbows' Released November 30, 2010 by Roark Records.

"Harpsichord Concerto in F Minor BMV 1056" by Bach, Johann Sebastian
Published in 1738.

"Hyper Love (feat. Nat Dunn)" by Ferry Corsten
Album 'Hyper Love', Released August 21, 2014 by Flashover Recordings.

"Toccata in D Minor" by Bach
Published in 1833.

"Sowing the Seeds of Love" by Tears for Fears
Album 'Seeds of Love' Released August 21 1989 by Fontana Records.

"Adagio for Strings" by Samuel Barber
By Samuel Barber (1910-1981), Composed in 1936.

"Sympathy for the Devil" by the Rolling Stones.
Album 'Beggars Banquet', Release February 1969 (Japan) by Decca, London.

"I'm no strange to the rain" by Keith Whitley
Album 'Don't Close Your Eyes', Released January 1989 by RCA.

"Goodbye My Friend" by Linda Ronstadt
Album 'Cry Like a Rainstorm, Howl Like the Wind', Released in October 1989 by Elektra Records.

"Imagine" by John Lennon
Album 'Imagine', Released September 9, 1971 by Capitol Record.

About the Author

Based in Arizona, devoted father of two, involved in numerous career fields that in one way or another revolved around machines. It was that magic interaction with software and hardware, combined with an endless love of science fiction that created a passion to go beyond.

Art Work

All artwork created by author

Alternate Rear Cover Design

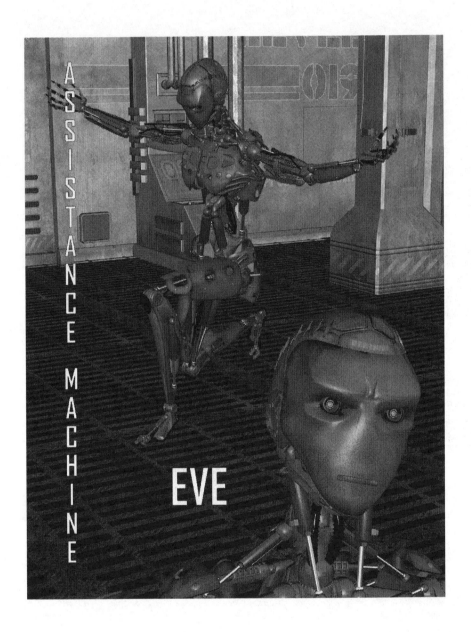

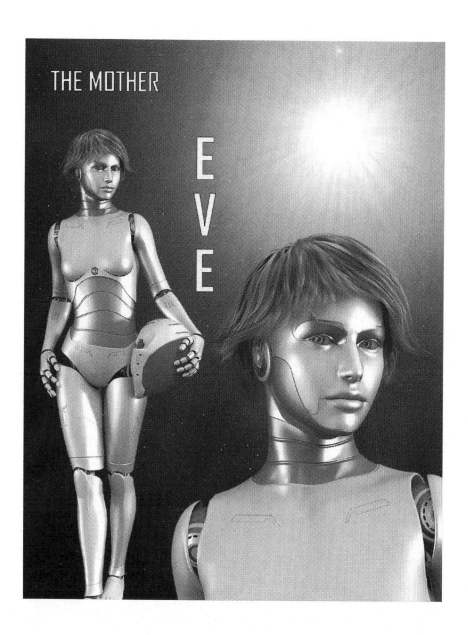

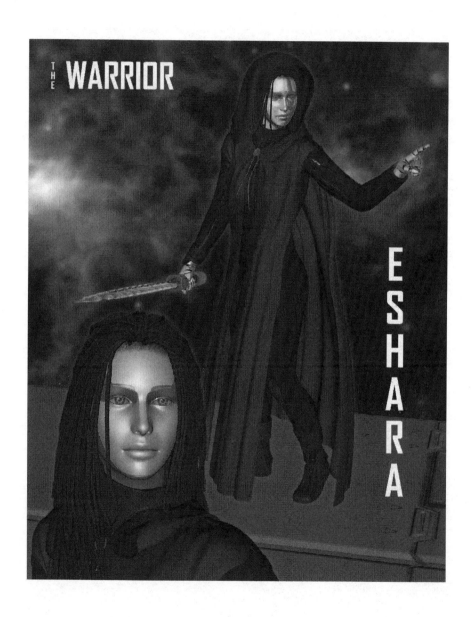

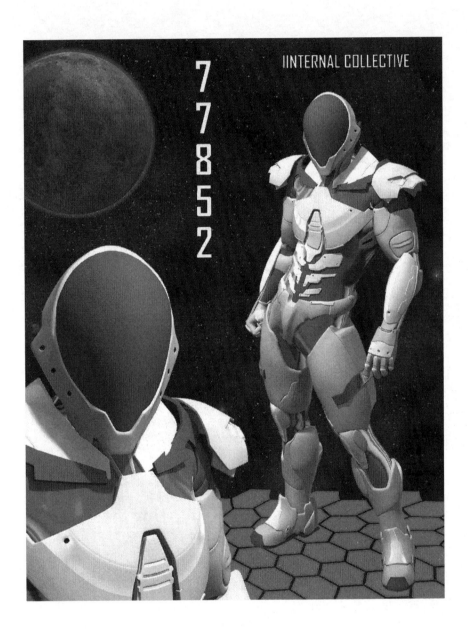

Military Drone created by Jeff Szymanski

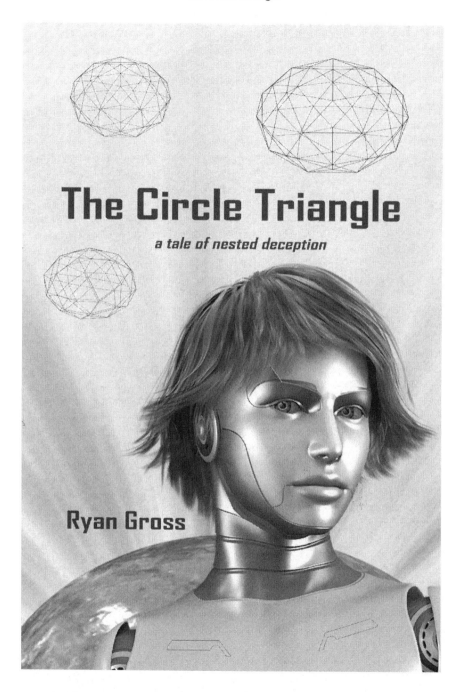

The Circle Triangle

a tale of nested deception

Ryan Gross

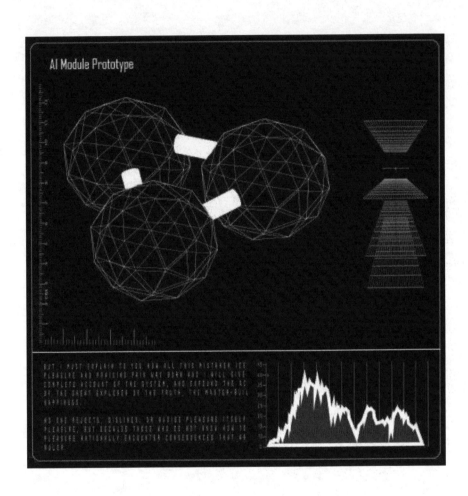

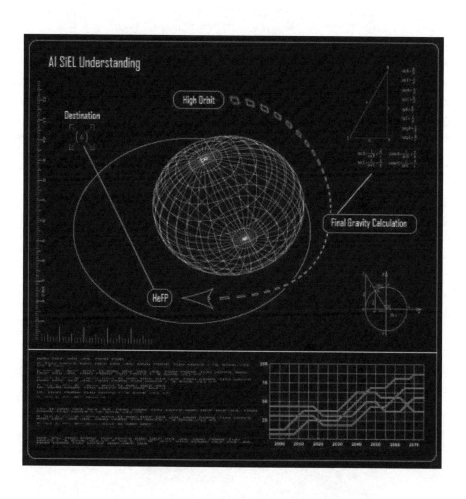

FOUR SECTOR TRAVEL MAP

Ceres / Factory

Orion Space Station

The Circle Triangle

a tale of nested deception

Ryan Gross

Made in the USA
San Bernardino, CA
09 November 2017